To Hold

M.L. Pennock

ISBN-13: 978-0692714744

R-

Thanks for being that guy.

-M

Table of Contents

Chapter One

Stephanie

"My sister has probably told you a little bit about me, but let's get one thing straight. I am not crazy. I am not depressed." I can taste the bitterness and anger in the back of my throat. It's vile. "She thinks I'm not dealing with shit, so here I am. You're supposed to fix me."

I stare into her radiant green eyes and want to spit at her. She just sits there watching me, her pen rhythmically tap, tap, tapping away on her notepad, the very notepad in which I'm sure she wrote "This chick is nuts," the moment I opened my mouth. Why wouldn't she? Most of the family thinks I'm certifiable though they refuse to come right out and say it.

I bite the inside of my cheek to keep myself from thinking about the reason I'm even here.

"I'm not here to fix you. You're here to fix you, Stephanie. I'm simply here to guide you," she says in that soft I'm-treating-you-like-a-child-because-I'm-a-doctor tone. The tapping stops and I watch her roll her shoulders back, grasping the pen in both hands by the ends as she sits up straighter in the armchair. Her eyes, still radiant, look like they could pierce steel without batting an eyelash. I feel my jaw go slack at the transformation before me, confused by the sudden change in her demeanor when she obliterates the nice doctor image I had built up in my head.

"So, let's cut the bullshit and get down to business. You're not crazy. You're not depressed. However, you went through physical, psychological, and emotional trauma. I've seen it before and everyone deals with something like that differently. Some women crawl into themselves, build up walls. Others build walls, but outwardly continue trying to be the person they were before the trauma." She pauses long enough for me to see the soft spot in her heart before her eyes turn cold again. "Then there's you."

"What about me?" I say attempting to keep the harshness in my tone. I'm channeling my inner petulant teenager and regardless of how shitty it's going to make me feel later, I need it right now. I need to fortify myself against whatever she's going to say.

"You're not even building walls. You're burying everything as deep as you can possibly dig. How far down does that well go, Stephanie? How deep and dark is it? Why are you burying it all when it could feel so good to bring it back to the surface, douse it with gasoline, and watch it burn? What are you so afraid of?"

She finishes talking and I blink to clear my cloudy vision, only to feel tears rush the dam and slide down my face.

"Everything," I whisper. "I'm afraid of everything."

Chapter Two

Stephanie
Twelve Months Ago/July

This place is way too busy for a campus coffee shop in the middle of summer. I thought I'd found the quietest corner table, but swear there's more traffic back here than there is up at the counter.

"Is this seat taken?"

I look up from my notes and, Lord help me, those are the darkest espresso brown eyes I've ever seen. I'm a sucker for brown eyes and these are the kind a girl could drown in — deep, endless pools of mystery wrapped up in danger.

"No. Not taken, you can have it," I respond as nonchalantly as possible before averting my eyes and pushing the chair away from the table with my foot. I realize I was starting to stare, maybe even drool a little. There is no time in my life for gorgeous eyes, sexy hair, and smirking; especially the smirking.

Hearing the chair scrape across the tile floor when he pulls it away from the table makes it slightly easier to concentrate on my research. Now that it's gone I don't have to worry about anyone else wanting to sit there and I can just focus. I listen halfheartedly to his "thanks" and offer an "mmhmm" in return as I reread the same four words on the page in front of me for the third time. My purple highlighter is hovering above the page when the table shifts under the weight of his messenger bag and my crisp, clean paper is irreparably marred, a purple streak dissecting the words right up the middle of the page.

"Dick! What the hell are you doing?" I have a lightning fast temper and it doesn't matter how beautiful this guy might be, this is research for my master's degree and he's fucking it up. "When you ask someone if a seat is taken and they say no, you're supposed to take the seat and go to a different table, you Neanderthal."

He sits down, cocking an eyebrow at me, and laughs — a deep, throaty laugh. "Actually, asking if a seat is taken is because you want to sit in it, not necessarily take it to a different table."

He starts pulling his computer from the bag and I almost forget I care that he's sitting across from me until his stupid bag bumps my file folders, which then bump into my cup of coffee, which naturally sloshes coffee over the rim of the cup and ...

"I fucking give up. You realize I'm in the middle of something, right? You're being rude and now I'm going to have to print this page out again because, look at this —" I point to the stapled sheets in front of me with the purple streak and newly acquired coffee stains.

"Maybe you shouldn't be drinking coffee. You're pretty intense," he says, tossing napkins on my papers and blotting at them. He lifts his hand to me, offering it as he begins his introduction. "By the way, I'm Darren. It's nice to meet you."

Ten Months Ago/September

"Sorry I'm late. I was helping my sister make dinner and get ready for a date," I pull the chair out and sit down as the waitress arrives with drinks for us. She sets a wine glass in front of me, but tonight isn't a wine night. "Oh, thank you, but I didn't order wine. Can I have a Sam Adams, draught, instead? Whatever's in season is fine."

"Absolutely. I'll just take this back to the bar," she says politely and heads to the barroom.

Darren's dark brown hair is styled back and, despite charm and wit, I'm just not feeling it. I'm not feeling him. He's a beautiful man, but something's off. I feel it more tonight than I have in the last few weeks. I felt queasy the minute I walked into the restaurant and knew it was time to cut ties. I learned long ago that ignoring my intuition only gets me in trouble and there's no time for trouble these days.

"You're always late when I don't pick you up. You haven't let me pick you up in a month and every time we have dinner out you're late," he says. There's a bite to his tone and I don't like it. "It's that Colton guy, isn't it? You're always with him."

How do women willingly deal with this shit? It's one thing for him to get irritated that I don't want to spend every waking moment with him because I'm studying or working or researching, but this is absurd. Now he's going to attack the relationship I have with my best friend?

Things were casual and then he took it up a notch. He wants serious. I'm not ready. To be honest, two months is a long time for me to be with someone. He's the first man I've kept around for more than a few dates in a long time. I've even let him come to my apartment to pick me up, which is unheard of. I've lived there for three years and he's the first person I've dated who has been given the address. The last time I let anyone pick me up for a date, I was a teenager still living with my parents.

"What's that supposed to mean?" I feel the heat rush to my face, that surging feeling right before the anger finds its way into my voice. "Are you jealous of Colt?"

He laughs. It's more like a chortle.

"You're always with him 'studying'," he says making air quotes, and that pisses me off even more. "You let him pick you up to go places, I'm sure. I have a problem with my girlfriend spending more time with some random guy from school than she does with me."

He picks up his glass and I watch the amber liquid dancing in the low lighting. His dark brown eyes are angry, on the verge of menacing. He sips his whiskey and as he sets the glass back on the table I notice a second empty glass.

"Okay, buddy, let's get a few things straight since you want to get liquored up and play Mr. Possessive this evening, which I'm getting really fucking tired of by the way. Colton and I are in the same program, he's been my best friend since the second grade, and he's the gayest man I know. If he were making moves on anyone in this relationship it would be you because you are the one with a penis," I say angrily, the words spewing from my mouth like venom. "At least, I assume you have one, and assumption is where it ends because it's never coming near me. We're done."

His mouth drops open and the waitress sets my beer in front of me. She smiles at me — not a little "oh this is awkward and I'm so sorry this is happening" smile, but a big grin that says "can you kick him in the balls, too? Pretty please?" — and doesn't acknowledge the untouched menus or Darren.

"Says you. I'm not done with us yet." His features look like they've been carved out of stone, his eyes so dark they're reminiscent of void holes. Then he blinks and I'm not sure I saw what I saw. "Let's start over."

He smiles sweetly, too pleasantly, and I feel the anxiety twist my stomach up in knots.

"I don't think I want to, Darren. I was happy doing casual with you, but the minute you found out where I call home you acted like you had a right to control my life. I'm closing in on thirty years old. No one is going to control me unless I want them to, and you're not that someone," I say standing from my seat. "Lose my number. I won't be taking your calls anymore."

Confidence. That's what this feeling is. And while I'm usually a confident person, this is an "I am woman, hear me roar" assurance I haven't been accustomed to because generally people don't fuck with me. I lift my chin a little higher and turn from the table, walking away from a mistake I almost made.

I grab my jacket from the rack by the door, slip my arms in, pull my hair out from the collar, and reach for the door at the same time he grabs my left upper arm. It hurts, but I won't give him the satisfaction of telling him so. He pushes me out the door, then pulls me down the sidewalk before turning into a small alleyway between the restaurant and building next door.

I feel my back smack the brick and am thankful for the cool weather and thick wool of my coat.

I stare up into his face, a mixture of anger and lust mingling like long lost cousins in his eyes, as he pushes my shoulders firmly against the wall and attacks my mouth like I'm his last meal. His leg and hip pin the rest of me to the brick as I resist his kiss, the pressure of his body against mine.

All the confidence I felt when I stood up from that table is gone. In its place is crippling fear. I close my eyes, wishing I could be anywhere but here. I don't pray under normal circumstances, but tonight I'll make an exception because, please, God, just don't let this happen.

I grab his waist, trying to push him away as I feel a crushing weight on my chest and a scream rips through the quiet evening.

It's my voice. I'm screaming. Finally he stops and takes a step back, touching his lip where I bit him. Then he steps back once more as my hand connects with his face.

"Don't! Don't you ever touch me again! I didn't give you permission to touch me tonight!"

I try to slap him again, but he grabs my arm as it hurtles through the crisp night air toward his face. He spins me around, putting me into a half-nelson with my back against his front, and slams my body into the wall, forcing my cheek harshly against the gritty red brick of the building.

Darren places a kiss on the skin behind my ear.

"Cut the feminist act and admit you like a man who takes control. We aren't done. You don't call the shots. You're mine until I tell you otherwise," he whispers, releasing his hold on one of my arms as he reaches out to touch the side of my face turned toward him. I shudder as he slides his forefinger along the edge of my cheek until it's beneath my chin and he turns my head more so I can't look away from him. "You can try to ignore my calls, but I'll always be near. You have one week to make room for me in your ever-so-busy schedule. After that, I make room in your schedule for me."

His grip eases, he lets go of my body, and somehow I don't fall down. I don't move as I listen to the sound of his dress shoes on the cobbled concrete, echoing off the buildings I'm standing between.

***

I'm numb as I climb into my car and drive the seventeen miles back home from Rochester.

I feel nothing as I make my way up the stairs to the second floor of the building where I live, unlock the door, and peel off my coat. My dress comes off. I drop my heels next to the couch.

My pantyhose feel like they're strangling me.

I'm still numb as I look at the girl in the bathroom mirror.

Turning my head I check for any marks on my face before taking inventory of the rest of my body. My arm hurts, but there's no bruise. Yet.

I unhook my bra, my underwear slide down my legs. I step out of them and crawl under a scalding stream of water in the shower allowing the steam to billow around me. I just want to get this entire night off of me and go somewhere.

Anywhere but here.

He knows where I live. Why was I so stupid to let him know where I live? The enormity of what I've allowed crashes down on me and I feel the anger climbing up my spine again. This is why I have rules. This is why I don't let men in. The only one I let in is Colt because he can't hurt me. He wouldn't hurt me. He would die before he hurt me.

My fist connects with the wall of the shower. The tile cracks beneath the force. "Fuck!"

The pain crawls up my arm and the anger begs to break free, but I find somewhere deep inside to hide it. There's only one place for me to go, one person who will salvage what's left of this night. I need to see my sister.

***

"Why didn't you just tell me you had a date tonight? You didn't have to scapegoat Mom, Steph. Kind of shady, you know?"

Stella's the responsible one. I lied to her. I've been doing that a lot lately. I told her I was going to go to a yoga class with our mom. She didn't even know I was dating anyone, and that's my bad. The last thing I wanted to do the last few months was flaunt my flavor of the week dating lifestyle in her face while she was tackling her own emotions with a cheating husband and upcoming divorce.

Then she reconnected with Brian. My sister's got this whole first love boy-next-door thing going on with him and it's awesome. I wish I could have that, but I don't. I don't even want to think about love right now, because as far as I'm concerned it doesn't exist for me.

So, I lie my face off.

"It was more of a pity date than anything else, and I just didn't want you to think less of me for it. It seemed you'd ask way fewer questions if I told you I was hanging with Mom than going out for burgers with What's His Name," I say hoping she'll believe me as I talk to the coffee mug in my hands. I glance up and catch Brian curiously watching me. I need to change the topic before he gets more curious. "We got through dinner and I excused myself like a lady. I don't want to lead him on any longer. He's just not the type I like, you know? He was nice about it, I guess. Besides, I really wanted to come hang out with Britt. You're raising a great kid, Brian."

Free and clear. Brian starts talking about Britt and my sister gets all starry-eyed.

I finish my cup of coffee and give Britt a kiss on the forehead before heading back to my apartment. I hug my sister and Brian and make my way to the front door with Stella trailing along behind me.

"Hey, are you sure you're okay? I mean, was it getting serious with this guy?" I see the worry on her face.

"Nah, you know how it is with me. I don't do serious. We'd been out a few times. He's never even seen me naked, so not even in the same ballpark as serious." I lean against the wall and wonder if there are going to be more questions tonight. "I've got a lot of reading to catch up on this week for classes, so I should get going."

I open the door and start down the stairs.

"Steph?"

"Hmm?" Stella's standing in the doorway when I turn around.

"A lot has happened lately. Girl's night? Soon? I know we're doing Wine Wednesday tomorrow, but maybe we could plan a weekend."

I jog back up the stairs and give my sister another hug.

"You got it. Just let me know when."

Eight Months Ago/November

So close to being done with this semester and then I can focus full time on my final project. It's all I can think about. I've been interested in interpersonal communication since before I chose my major as an undergrad and now I'm finally to the point of spending all my time researching and prepping for that last big thing before getting my degree. It's what I'm going to do after the degree that worries me.

I pull my phone from my pocket and check the time as I turn onto the main path between the buildings that house the communications and psychology departments and the health center. Colt and I spent all day in the library across campus working on papers and projects due right after Thanksgiving so we can enjoy our holiday. I left him to lock the library — one of the advantages to working there is staying past closing to finish research — and headed back across campus to my car.

"You've been ignoring my calls. You've been ignoring my texts. I saw you with that cop. What were you talking about with the Chief of Police?"

I freeze hearing his voice. It's deep and malicious, and I resist the urge to shudder as the feeling of fear trickles down my back like ice water.

"That's what happens when you break into someone's apartment and then throw them against a doorframe. Assault will get your texts and calls ignored," I say trying to be brave when in reality this section of campus is too dark for bravery and, with the holiday break starting, no one is around. No one would hear me scream. Where the hell is Colton? He was supposed to be on his way so I could drive him home. I pull my shoulders back and again attempt confidence to mask the scent of panic he must smell on me. "Please, crawl back into the hole you came out of and leave me alone."

Darren steps closer. Out of the shadows just enough to make him look even more menacing.

"You know, Stephanie, your mouth is going to get you into trouble," he says, grabbing my hair and pulling my head back forcefully. "I told you we were done when I said so. I don't recall telling you we were done."

I think about screaming, because if Colt is nearby he'd hear me and maybe Darren would just run away, until I realize the truth.

He wouldn't run. No, if I scream, he'll probably just kill me.

I willingly dated a man capable of murder and I hate knowing I didn't realize it until now. He has death in his eyes, like a blood thirsty savage searching for his next victim. He wants me to be that victim.

"We are done, Darren. It's been over for a while," I say quietly, trying to keep myself calm despite the tension at the back of my head where he's got my loose flowing hair tangled tightly around his fingers. I was done with him after he assaulted me in the alley, but then he showed up at my home days before Halloween. He threw me into a doorframe, bruising half my back, and that's when I finally broke and told Stella. "It's been over since the day you threatened me in my apartment. The only reason I didn't go to the police then is because I thought I'd made myself clear that I was done. I'm not your punching bag."

"Oh, sweetie, no, you're not a punching bag," he cajoles, the words sickly sweet as they drip from his tongue. Then he tugs my hair harder, spitting out the rest of his hatred. "But if you'd just listen to me and do what I say, I wouldn't get so angry. You make me so angry. You're pissing me off right now, always talking back."

I feel the first blow to my abdomen as the last words reach my ears.

The pain isn't crippling. New York winters guarantee layers which lessen the shock from a knee.

"You're a psychopath. You need help, Darren," I cough out.

"That's rich coming from someone who refuses to form any sort of longstanding relationship with anyone outside of your family. At least I'm trying to love you. You won't even try, Stephanie. Then you walk around in these little skirts like a whore," he spits out, pushing me backward.

I feel his hands pulling at my skirt and try to push him away, but he just comes at me harder. His fist connects with my cheek and I stumble. Tripping over my bag filled with research on interpersonal communication and relationships, I can't help but think of the irony as I fall to the ground.

As soon as I steady myself and start standing up, he lashes out again. I can't stand up against this and I reach for my face, feeling the warm wetness, the sticky feeling of blood.

"You want to dress like a whore, I'm going to treat you like a whore," he says in an unforgiving tone, a voice that says "you might not wake up when I'm done with you."

I feel his boot in my ribs. His hands are prying my clothes off.

"Don't fight this. You wanted to play hard to get. You wanted it this way." His voice hits my ears, gruff and eerily calm. I thrash against him, refusing to pass out from the pain in my ribs, until I feel my leg snapping under the weight of his foot as he attempts to pin me down.

Only then do I let loose an ear-piercing scream and allow the darkness to climb in around me.

***

"Where's that ambulance?"

"Steph? Can you hear me?"

"We're next to Credence Hall on Holley. Have them drive up the sidewalk."

"Steph, I'm right here."

I can hear them. Colton's talking to me, but someone else is talking, too. I don't know that voice and fear grips me until the pain takes over.

"You know her?" asks the deep, rumbling baritone I don't know and the adrenaline starts coursing through my veins again.

"She's my best friend. An ambulance is coming right?" I can't open my eyes, but I hear the trembling in Colt's speech.

The other voice responds and I can hear sirens somewhere. They're coming for me.

"Steph, please be okay. You have to be okay. Help's coming. As soon as the ambulance is here, I'll call Stella," Colt says to me.

"Stella? The newspaper lady?"

"Yeah, Stephanie is her sister," Colt says to the voice.

"Fuck. Once she's loaded in the ambulance, you ride with her. I'll call her sister."

Someone is rummaging in my pocket. I try to move. I don't want anyone touching me.

"Don't. Don't touch!" I yell, opening my eyes just enough to see his badge as he shushes me and tries to calm me down, but the hysteria has a tight hold and won't let go. The sirens are so loud, and I scream again. "Don't touch me! Please, stop touching me!"

I try to move again, but the pain is more than I can bear. It's hurting everywhere. I hear Colt crying, his tears falling on my face like a cleansing rain before everything is black again.

M.L. Pennock

Chapter Three

Max
Three months ago/April

"Steph?" I say her name like a question, afraid I'm interrupting something important. From across the room I watch Tommy get up, nod stonily in my direction, and walk away from the table where his new sister-in-law's sister has been pouring out her heart and fears to him. I listened just long enough to hear her voice admit she wasn't coping as well as we all thought she was, though she didn't come right out and say the words. "Do you need a ride home?"

I've tried to keep my distance since the day I stood in her sister's front entryway and told her I'd shot her ex-boyfriend. The investigation that transpired after found I'd responded appropriately. I fired back in self-defense. His death was justified. He shot at me first, but I'd be damned if I let him go again. I wasn't going to let him live this time.

Pulling myself back from revisiting that day for probably the thousandth time, I lock my eyes on Stephanie and watch her glide her index finger around the rim of her wine glass. She's contemplating. Maybe even questioning.

I'm glad Tommy got up and walked to the other room to continue mingling with Brian and Stella's wedding guests. Who knows if he'd let her leave with me. He trusts me because I'm a cop. He doesn't trust me because I'm a man.

It's hard to trust anyone when you know there's someone out there who hurt the person you love, whether it's romantic love or brotherly love. Steph is the baby sister of every adult child in the Stratford and Barbieri families, but Tommy has been more than just protective of her since the day he met me, he's become her live-in bodyguard, and it makes sense — I understand. I was in his position once, only it wasn't a little sister type of protection. It was my wife.

"I might." Her voice slides through the air and wraps around my heart, choking me with a reaction I wasn't prepared for. She might.

"You don't sound too sure," I respond, twisting my key ring on my middle finger.

I take a few steps into the dining room. Brian's house has become a familiar place for me. After Stephanie was attacked, I started going into The Jumping Bean for coffee most mornings I was on duty and a lot of mornings I wasn't just to ask about her. Brian was marrying Steph's sister and seemed to be a lot more level-headed than Tommy where Steph was concerned. Brian and I would talk about business, wedding plans for him and Stella, and eventually we just stopped beating around the bush. I'd walk in, one of the guys would get me my regular to go and I'd get my daily update — her leg was healing, she was doing well with the minimal physical therapy required, she cried a lot but in private where she thought no one could hear.

After a few weeks, the guys and I got together for beers. Brian, Tommy, and Brian's best friend and business partner Greg, sort of welcomed me into their club.

The New Guy in Town Club.

But I'm the newest guy and nobody knows anything about me. Everyone is still curious about Max Wyatt. I have a past none of them have a clue about. No one but my chief even knows why I came here. He didn't even know for certain why I transferred to New York until last fall.

Pushing the hair off her shoulder, Stephanie stands up from the table grabbing hold of my attention and shaking it free of the past. "No, I'm sure. I'd rather a cop drive me home in his personal vehicle than pull me over in mine."

Even exhausted she's a quick thinker.

"I just want to see you get home safely, that's all." I hold my arm out for her, and she pushes it away as she walks past me on tired, shaky legs.

"Oh, please, city slicker, I can walk myself out the door," she says reaching for the knob. "I really don't need a babysitter, either. Not now, anyway."

I hear it in her voice, the "because of you," and hope someday she'll understand it was the only way to protect her and any other woman he could have replaced her with.

"I know you don't, but this way Tommy will know you're back home safely and I'll know you're not driving under the influence. Stella can rest easy without worrying about you and since she won't be worrying, Brian will get to enjoy his wedding night," I say. "We all win."

She snorts out a laugh. "I don't even know if T is coming home tonight, but I hope he remembered his keys. The last thing I need is his drunk ass banging on the front door in the middle of the night."

"You mean to tell me you wouldn't get up and let him in? After all, you guys are roommates. It's not very nice to leave him out there if he genuinely forgot his keys," I say closing the door behind us.

"No way. If he can't be responsible and have his house key with him, then he can just go sleep on the back porch. Or the front lawn. I really don't care," she says, shrugging. "I love the guy, but sometimes I just want to be left alone. He hovers. We've been living together for a very short time, Max, and I swear he lurks in the doorways waiting for me to need something."

This time I laugh. She turns her head to look at me, incredulous that I'd make light of her living situation.

"For starters, you guys have been living together for what? A week? He's probably not hovering as much as trying to get used to living with you." I shoot a smile in her direction. Going from a bachelor pad at his brother's to rooming with a woman is scary, but it's not something I think would register with Steph. "Secondly, you realize there are two really valid reasons he'd lurk, right?"

"No idea what you're talking about," she says looking up and down the street at the vehicles parked nearby. "Which one of these beasts is yours?"

For the moment, I ignore her question. "You know exactly what I'm talking about. Tommy is either trying to get a rise out of you or he's staying close by so that if you do truly need something he can be there to rescue you," I blurt out and walk in front of her to the corner of Brian's house. "Mine is right over here."

"That's not a car," she says, stopping short and standing stock still.

"No, it's not. Is that a problem?" I eye Steph suspiciously, taking in the long bridesmaid gown and her still perfectly styled hair. She's beautiful and intelligent, but the girl grew up in the country. You can't tell me she's never ridden on a Harley before.

"You can't take me home on that thing. My dad will kill you," she squeaks out, sounding half terrified.

"Why is that? It's just a motorcycle." I stand staring at the sleek black metal of the bike. It's my baby.

"Max, that is a death machine."

"Not quite, but okay. You want me to take you home piggy-back style instead? Though, I think we'd be more likely to fall down and get hurt if I tried to carry you the entire way."

Laughing I turn just in time to catch her glaring at me before an honest grin melts the ice in her gaze.

"That would be hilarious, but we could just walk."

She really won't ride the bike? Girls love the bike.

Feeling slightly let down, I concede. "Okay, Stephanie. Let's walk."

I hold my arm out and this time she links hers through.

Chapter Four

Stephanie
Present Day

"I remember waking up in the hospital and everything hurt. My soul hurt."

"Your soul? How so?"

"It was like parts of me were missing — I had fractured ribs and a broken leg, my face was swollen and bruised, but the parts of me no one could see were the ones that were broken the most. I felt powerless." I've been staring at my hands while I ramble and finally look up. She's genuinely interested. Not just interested because she's my therapist, but truly wants to understand what I've been through. "I've taken great care to come back from being that shattered before. It's why I have the rules."

She clicks her pen, scribbles something in her notes.

"What rules do you have?"

I consider her carefully before I breathe in deeply and share the details I keep closest to me.

"No men in my home other than the ones on my approved list. I don't let them pick me up for dates. If sex ever becomes a thing, it's a thing that doesn't happen where I live," I say quietly. "Sex usually doesn't happen, though. I think that's why waking up in the hospital after Darren attacked me threw me right into fight mode. We weren't intimate and the last thing I really remembered before blacking out was him trying to tear at my clothes."

I choke out the last few words before letting the sobs loose. They were trying to claw their way out of my lungs the minute I started talking about the rules because the rules always lead me here. Rules are in place for a reason.

"I wore a skirt that day."

Taking another deep breath, I close my eyes to center myself and count to ten like Stella told me to when I feel like all my pieces are falling apart. It works for her, so I've been giving it a try.

I take one more deep breath and say, "I woke up thinking he took something from me that wasn't his to have and I panicked."

She asks if there was a reason for my freak out in the hospital, an episode that led to some very nice sedatives in my IV and had me spaced out for a few hours. I'm not sure if I hear her correctly. Did she really just ask that?

"Are you high? Of course there was a reason," I practically scream, my anger fighting against reason for a space in my brain.

Her mouth falls open when what she said fully registers and she comprehends how I understood her question.

"That's not what I meant. Yes, of course there was a reason, but were you freaking out because he had been able to overpower and attack you or because you woke up afraid he'd —"

She's trying to dig into my thoughts from months ago, but it's like I can feel his hands on me again and I stand up, needing to move and have some semblance of control. Colton wasn't too far behind me and heard me scream that night, likely the scream that ripped through me when my leg broke. Darren was able to tear my underwear, break my bones, and bruise my face, but he didn't have time to hurt me other than that before Colt was running to my rescue.

"Until the doctor came to talk to me I wasn't sure what I thought. I just felt him all over me. You know the Lady Macbeth scene when she's sleepwalking and riddled with guilt over King Duncan's and everyone else's deaths?"

She nods her head. I see her wondering where I'm going with this.

"It was a lot like that when I first woke up. I knew he wasn't there but at the same time I couldn't get him off me. I just kept trying to stop feeling him everywhere. Instead of believing I had blood on my hands, though, even figuratively, I was feeling him everywhere. The worst part was feeling the guilt at first, feeling like I was the one responsible for his actions." I stare out the window overlooking Main Street. "You can't draw true parallels between Lady Macbeth and me, but sometimes I wake up in the night in a cold sweat wondering why I let him near me, why I let him into my head."

I quietly retreat back to my seat, the pounding in my head simmering to a dull throb.

"I can see the parallels, though I'm not an English scholar by any means. We can call it guilt, certainly that's Lady Macbeth's issue, but I think what you were dealing with after your attack was more shock than anything, Stephanie. Now, the waking up in a cold sweat from nightmares, I assume ... I'd classify that as some post-traumatic stress. You were traumatized and something of this nature affects people deeply. It makes sense that it's living in your subconscious. But, let's take a step back to something you said earlier," she says softly, as though she knows answering her question is going to hurt me all over again. "Stephanie, why do you have this set of rules?"

To Hold

"Because I loved a boy once and he tore my heart out. I gave him my whole heart and practically threw my V-card at him when I turned sixteen. He's the only boy I ever loved and he made me regret giving him all of those feelings, all of that time and space in my life," I say softly even though the anger is there, hiding out at the edges of my voice. "I haven't found anyone worthy of that kind of emotion and commitment since him."

Parker Williams played me ... hard. I bought everything he tried to sell me from the first smile sent my way in seventh grade. We were high school sweethearts, homecoming court, prom king and queen. We were the quintessential perfect couple until our sophomore year of college when I showed up at his dorm two hours away to surprise him for our anniversary weekend and heard a very breathy, "Oh Parker! Oh, Yes! Right there!" from the other side of the door. I shudder recalling the moment I realized he was a cheating dirt bag.

I bite my bottom lip nervously because there's so much more to the story of me and Parker. She watches me suspiciously.

"You're going to push me for more about him aren't you?"

"Perhaps. Do you want me to push you for more information?" She taps her pen on the notepad. "Better yet, Stephanie, do you think some of what you're dealing with now can be resolved by talking about that relationship? You were invested in it and there's very obviously something else that happened besides a college boy away from his girlfriend acting like a fool."

"Our breakup didn't go by the book."

"What breakup does?"

"Touché."

"So what happened? Help me understand."

"You know that sounds really patronizing, right?" She nods her head but smiles nonetheless. "I've never talked about it with anyone, not even Stella and I tell her everything. All anyone around here knows is he went off to college while I stayed here. It was hard on our relationship with him being away and after a couple years apart, we split up."

The truth, though? I tell her the truth because the dam's been breached. After I caught him cheating he came home for a weekend and we had a heart-to-heart discussion about what we both wanted. I wanted him to be loyal to me. He wanted to continue screwing everything that moved. Things that moved included the best female friend I had, half the cheerleading squad from our senior year, and three quarters of the women he came in contact with at college, including at least one first year teaching assistant.

M.L. Pennock

He wanted more "flavor" in our relationship. "Stephanie" wasn't the flavor he sought anymore.

"He just kept me around for important things like family gatherings," I say, twirling my finger in the air and rolling my eyes. "Family gatherings where I think everyone, including his grandmother, were aware he was a male slut. When he finally came clean about all his whoring around, he got all emotional. I got weepy. Emotions make people do stupid shit like cling to hope and that hope turns into making out on your bed with the guy ripping your heart out while your parents are at work. Things got out of hand. I let things go too far and when I started telling him to stop, that we were done, he laughed and told me to 'shut up and enjoy it one last time.'"

I can still hear that laugh.

"And you never reported this?"

"Who was I going to tell? He was the prince of motherfucking Mayberry. Everyone here loved him. He came from a good, wholesome family. His entire life is a cliché," I spit out, throwing in some good old fashioned talking with my hands for good measure. My anger really brings out my Italian roots. "Even though I'm sure it would have been looked into, I'm also sure nothing would have come of it. It was my word against his. He was having one last roll in the hay with his ex-girlfriend while I was laying there in tears praying he was quick about it."

At the time, I couldn't imagine anything worse. Now, though, it's not a horrifying, completely destroy my life kind of secret. It's not anything compared to what Darren put me through. My relationship with Parker is just something I don't talk about because it's in the past. A lesson learned. It's just another thing I've kept locked up for years.

Eight long years.

I lean forward in the cushiony armchair and watch her scribble on her notepad. I'm not self-conscious about the things she might be writing, but I am curious if she's going to think I need medication.

I prefer to self-medicate. With wine.

The relief of telling her wells up behind my bottom lids and I nonchalantly wipe the tears away.

"I was young and he was my first everything. First real kiss, first real boyfriend, lover, and all of that made breaking up a thousand times worse. For him to take from me, from my body, that last time devastated me. I felt like there was nothing I could do," I say, chancing a look in her direction. I've been talking quietly, but she hasn't asked me to repeat myself. Something tells me I'm not the first to make an admission of weakness like this in her office. I'm not that weak anymore, though. Sitting up straighter in the chair and pushing my hair behind my right ear I say clearly, "So, I made the rules. No more trusting at first glance. Question everything. Don't let them know where I live unless I've gotten to know them really well as a friend first."

The approved list of men I willingly told where I lived included my dad, Colton, Brian, and Greg. Tommy relocated to New York after I'd already moved in with Stella. I was passed out on Stella's couch the night he and Brian got back from Tennessee. That was the first time Tommy laid eyes on me after moving home. I never would have chosen that moment for someone to see me after more than twenty years. He would have automatically been on the list if he'd moved home before my attack, though.

"And now Tommy and I are sharing a house. Even though Darren is dead, I still feel safer because it means someone is there in the middle of the night when the nightmares trap me and hold me hostage."

He stepped into the role of personal bodyguard almost the instant he realized I had opened my eyes and seen him sitting across the living room from me, his hands steepled under his chin in prayer.

Doc chews on the tip of her pen before tap-tap-tapping it against her notepad again.

***

My eyeliner was a little too dark until it was washed away with my hurt and anger. My hair was a little too normal looking before I twisted and tugged at it while spilling parts of my story.

I'm coping, and coping means fidgeting.

I walk out of possibly the longest first session in the history of first sessions with my new therapist unsure of how she broke through so quickly. Is that allowed? Wasn't this supposed to be like a first date where we take our time getting to know one another? Go over my medical history or something? I didn't expect her to get me to dredge up feelings about Parker and what happened between us almost a decade ago on top of talking about Darren.

It was supposed to be like a slow dance. Instead she just jumped in and the last hour was more like "wham, bam, thank you, Ma'am," then I was wiping my eyes and walking out the door. This didn't feel like I was being violated, though. This was validation of everything I've been through and I feel better. That's the whole point of therapy, isn't it?

Stepping through the door, I pull my sunglasses from my shirt pocket and slide them on. It's bright out, but, truthfully, I'm wearing glasses because I refuse to let anyone in my tiny hometown know I was in there crying my eyes out. The chances of me seeing someone from the college or someone from high school are pretty high even though it's summer and I can't deal with small talk with one of my parents' friends or the inevitable talking behind my back that would happen if I saw any of my own peers.

Looking both ways, I cautiously step from the curb barely registering the police cruiser parked across the street.

"Time to get your shit together, Steph. Time to be a grown up," I say to myself as I finish crossing the road and hop up onto the sidewalk in front of the liquor store.

Chapter Five

Max

She steps out from the alcove pulling her sunglasses from her pocket. Dropping her head to meet the spectacles waiting in her hands, her hair falls in her face as I catch the glint of sunshine dancing in the dampness along the tops of her cheeks.

"What's all in that building?" I ask my partner, John Gill, pointing to the sandstone building across the street. I know there's a therapist in there, but I'm not sure what else might be hidden inside those hallways. I parked the cruiser here because it's close to the police station, but still close enough to the Jumping Bean that I could make the excuse that I need a pick me up after being up all night. Seeing Stephanie come out of the building wasn't something I planned on. I've actually been trying to keep my distance. The "friend zone" has decent boundaries. The "cop who responded to your assault" zone has even wider boundaries.

"Head shrinker. Other offices. Maybe an accountant." He never even looks up from the sports section. "Looks like the Yankees are surviving without Jeter."

I turn to look at him. "Really? A head shrinker? That's a little demeaning to the practice of psychiatry, don't you think? I mean, it's unlikely the person in that building is a witch doctor."

A blank stare meets me from the passenger seat, so I turn back to watch as Steph emerges from the shadow of the building and into the sunlight where she stops at the curb waiting for cars to pass.

"I feel demeaned when you use big words." I hear him sigh and crinkle the newsprint in his hands.

"You feel demeaned when I use little words, too," I respond without looking back at him. Instead I focus on chewing on my thumb and watching in the side mirror as the chestnut-haired girl who haunts my dreams crosses the street.

"Wyatt, you just going to stare at her all day or can we head in?" Gill says loudly, probably loud enough for her to hear through the open window, and breaks my concentration. "This overtime shift has me smelling like last week's gym bag. I want to get home and shower."

I lose sight of Steph and shake my head.

"Yeah let's go. I don't need you stinking up my car any more than you already have," I say pulling the gear shift into drive. Easing away from the curb, I glance in the rearview and catch a glimpse of Steph as she pulls open the door to the local wine and spirits shop.

"You know you can't fix her, right? I know you're friends with her brother-in-law, but keep your distance," Gill says as though he's telling me something I don't already know.

Signaling and turning to circle the block, I let out a disgruntled sigh. "I have been keeping my distance. When I go for coffee, I make sure it's when she's not there because I don't want her to keep thinking I'm checking up on her. John, I know I can't fix her, but if she was in with the doctor in that building, I at least know she's trying to fix herself."

"But ...," he prods, folding his paper.

"But she went from that building directly over to the liquor store. Something is up with her."

"Stay out of it, Max. You don't know her well enough. I went to school with Steph and Stella, and when the little Barbieri girl's in a mood you don't want to mess with her."

I pull up in front of the police station and park before opening my mouth again.

"The little Barbieri girl? John, she's twenty-eight. She's a woman." Rubbing the palms of my hands on my face and up through my hair, I drop my chin to my chest and stretch the muscles in my neck. "Please, don't disrespect her. How do you think she'd react if she heard you refer to her as a little girl? If you think she shouldn't be messed with when she's in a mood, I certainly wouldn't want to be caught calling her that. She'd string your balls up like Christmas decorations."

***

"Chief, I'm heading out," I call in to Davis Franks' office on my way back through the station while pulling my backpack filled with my uniform up into place on my shoulders.

Changing into street clothes feels good after a long shift and since, more and more lately, my shifts are long, I usually strip out of my uniform before I go home. I leave here on the bike in the summer and then go a few rounds with the heavy bag I finally hung in the basement. I unwind and I sleep for a few days before starting my next rotation. It's a routine I'm comfortable with. I like structure.

"Wait up, Wyatt, I wanted to run something by you," he says coming around his desk, knocking a pile of papers from the corner. Walking into his office, I kneel down to help him pick up the sheets and see the word "self-defense" in bold letters at the top.

"When did the YMCA start offering a self-defense class?" I ask curiously. Davis has never mentioned it, but if there's someone teaching the course already there isn't much of a reason to bring it up. "That's great someone is running a class."

Taking the stack of papers from my outstretched hand, he scratches the back of his head and says, "Yeah, after what happened last fall the Y and I put our heads together and hammered out a plan to start offering classes. We had someone all lined up to teach the class."

"Had? Did it fall through?" I ask cautiously.

"Yeah, he apparently only took a two-day certification program, and that was right before we started talking about holding classes. He's technically certified, but the community center people want someone with more than that. We all want someone with years of training, not days. That's what I wanted to talk to you about," he says. "How are you with women's self-defense?"

"I'm the same with women's as I am with men's. Certified. I took a refresher and recertification course when I was on administrative leave last winter and have a workshop coming up," I say stone-faced and then wait for him to ask the inevitable. I know it's coming.

"I'll understand if you say no, but take the weekend to think about it. You don't come in again until Sunday night, so think it over or do a pro-con list or whatever it is you do and let me know your thoughts Monday morning before you leave for the day."

He's shifting from one foot to the other like he truly believes I might say no. Laughing, I turn and walk out of his office and get halfway through the office before he clears his throat to get my attention, prompting me to turn around. Leaning against his office door he shoots me a look, one that clearly asks if I'll think about his proposition.

"What?"

"Well?"

"We need to work on your communication skills, Chief. You never actually asked me anything, but, yes, I'll let you know Monday if I'll teach the class or not."

I turn to leave as a smile lifts the corners of my mouth.

***

Opening the door to the Jumping Bean is like climbing the stairs to heaven. It's an invasion of my senses walking in here and as I saunter through the seating area, Greg sees me coming. He knows. Before I even make it to the counter he's poured the biggest cup of coffee they sell.

"I still don't know why you come in here every morning. I've been to your house. You have a coffee maker, a grinder, and you buy the beans from us to grind." Greg shakes his head in disbelief.

"It's just because I want to see your beautiful face every morning."

Checking to be sure no one else can see, he flips me the bird and turns from the counter.

"Laugh it up, city boy, but some day you're just going to be an old man sitting in here with other old men talking about shit old men talk about."

Contemplating his tirade, I take a slow sip of my coffee.

"And what kind of shit do old men talk about?"

Throwing his head back and sighing audibly, I hear his whiny man-child voice. "I don't know. The weather and politics. Probably."

I feel my eyebrow raise involuntarily.

"You've met me right? I mean I like the weather and politics are okay, but even when I'm an old man I hope I'll have more things to do than sit here and talk about those things with you since you'll be an old man, too," I toss back at him, throwing him off his game and watching his eyes grow wide as if he never considered the possibility he'll be old, too. "Yeah. That's what I thought. Is Brian around? I need to talk to him about something."

"Negative. It's Friday. Stella's got her doctor's appointment this morning but he should be in by noon," Greg says. "What's it about? Want me to have him give you a call?"

I mull it over, because while the guys and I have gotten close, there are still so many things I'm holding close to my vest. There's literally very little actual information the people in Brockport know about me. Brian knows the most, but it's still not much and out of all the friends I have here, he's the only one I feel comfortable talking to about the self-defense course.

Grabbing a to-go top for my coffee, I tell Greg to just let Brian know I'm off for the weekend and to give me a call when he gets a chance. I tap the counter twice with my index finger as I turn to leave and a familiar voice makes the hair on the back of my neck rise.

Her voice is low, but it carries.

"I think if we set them up with some social media marketing it could really increase their business prospects, Tommy. I spend most of my day checking the Internet. Trust me on this," Steph says.

"Whatever, princess, you seem to know what you're doing with this one, so if we're all in agreement you can do the social media end of stuff and I'll focus on all the rest."

I'm trying not to hear the conversation and start moving toward the door when the sound of my name leaving her lips rings in my ears.

"Is that Max?"

I push through the door before I can hear Tommy's response. I don't turn back to see if the empty look is still in her eyes from earlier this morning. It would break me.

***

"So what are you going to do? If you're certified, it would be worth it to teach the self-defense course and share that knowledge," Brian says as we're settling into chairs on the deck at his and Stella's house. Our conversation on the phone earlier basically amounted to him saying "uh huh" and grunting while baking muffins in an attempt to catch up at the coffeehouse after the morning off. Eventually he just gave up and told me to stop over tonight for a few drinks to talk about my dilemma. "Wouldn't it?"

I twist the top off the beer in front of me and pour it into my mouth. It's not a sipping kind of conversation as I try to get my bearings and I'm thankful it's a nice night. I can walk home if the need arises. I swallow and take another swig from the bottle while Brian stares at me wide-eyed from across the table.

"Can I be honest with you?" I ask, wiping the moisture from my mouth with the palm of my hand. This is the beginning, the start of people knowing more about me, and there's no turning back.

I put the bottle to my lips again.

"I would expect you to be honest with me," Brian says, concern lacing his voice as he narrows his eyes at me. "What's going on with you?"

"The short version is that back home I was a cop and self-defense instructor. I was married and happy and that was all taken away. I transferred to the department here to mostly start fresh," I say slowly, allowing myself to marinate in the words. "It's difficult to talk about. I don't like talking about my problems, so I don't."

"Whoa. Back up, Max. You were married? How did we miss that?" Stella says stepping out onto the deck, little boy and dog in tow. "Britt, make sure Whiskey stays in sight, please. He dug up the Morris's flowers yesterday. Again. Okay, Max. Wife?"

"It's like she has Vulcan ears," I shake my head and say to Brian. "Yes, Spock, I had a wife."

He covers up the smile on his face and takes a drink from his beer while looking at Stella with nothing but love in his eyes. "It's the hormones," he deadpans, then smiles up at her again.

"I love you, too," she responds, gently rubbing the large bump beneath her shirt. Patting Brian on the shoulder with her other hand she remarks, "I've heard the postpartum hormones are worse, so keep it up, cowboy, and you'll be in charge of rinsing all those cloth diapers I bought last week at your Mama's urging."

She has no idea how much the teasing hurts, how much I would love to rinse diapers and do 3 a.m. feedings. They don't know. No one here does and the pain leeches out into my muscles as I clench my jaw to keep the emotions from rising up.

"So how did we miss that you had been married, Max? That seems like something that would have come up at some point," Stella says, turning the conversation back to me before sitting down and taking a sip of her water.

"I don't talk about it because my past is just that. My past. It's not that I'm being secretive. I just don't want to dredge up the ghosts," I say, my voice hitching on the last word. I clear my throat before continuing. "My relationship with you and Brian was purely professional until last November. He sold me coffee, you reported on stuff going on with the police department. Then Stephanie was attacked and it changed every dynamic of that relationship because I was the one who showed up."

"Yeah, you showed up. Colton was there, too. Who knows what would have happened if neither of you had been nearby," Brian says.

Finishing my beer, I set the bottle down on the table and lean back in the chair, clasping my hands behind my head. There's no way around this.

"I know what would have happened, Brian. I do. Because I'd seen what that guy was capable of before," I say closing my eyes, shutting them out and watching the memories replay behind my lids. "I *had* a wife. I was *going to be* a father. I transferred to Brockport without either of those things. I'm neither a husband nor a dad."

Opening my eyes, I watch as it all clicks into place for Brian and Stella. The hand around his beer goes limp; she subconsciously raises her hand to her openly shocked mouth. It hits home. I see the recognition of words I spoke last Thanksgiving, that he had killed at least two people in another state.

"Max ..." Stella's the first one to say anything and I raise my eyes up from the label I'm peeling to meet hers — sensitive, deliberate, questioning eyes — and I shrug.

"I met her while I was teaching. Adrienne had dated him. They met here, at the college, and fear kept her with him," I say, my voice void of the rage churning inside. Detached. "They moved around a bit and eventually ended up in Cleveland. When she finally realized she was worth more, she sought help and landed in my self-defense class."

I wasn't even supposed to be teaching that session. It fell in my lap when the instructor broke his arm while cleaning the gutters on his house. A two-story drop off a ladder will do that.

"It's not your fault," Stella says sympathetically with an underlying tone of vehemence.

I let out a humorless laugh. "That's what the therapist back in Ohio told me. That's what my chief in Cleveland said. Shit, that's what my mom and her mom and everyone else have tried to get me to understand every year when the anniversary of their death comes around." I stop to open the fresh beer Stella had brought out when she first joined us and take a long sip. "I still blame myself, though. I should have been with her."

She was five months pregnant, we were still practically newlyweds. We'd just celebrated our first wedding anniversary and were preparing to be parents. She never should have gone for a walk that night. She never should have left the house without me. We knew he'd been around. He'd been watching her from just far enough away to not breach the restraining order.

Rubbing my right hand across my eyes, I try to wipe away the image I'd created of Adrienne on the sidewalk as the paramedics tried to stop the bleeding and get her into the ambulance. There was so much blood. It was their blood. Not just hers.

There was no way to save either of them.

And I wasn't there to try. I couldn't undo what he'd done that time.

Dropping my head onto the back of the chair, I beg myself to not let the tears fall — not here in front of them — and take a second to collect myself. Looking out into the yard, I watch Britt toss a ball for the dog and wonder what my boy would look like. He'd be about the same age, but I imagine him with my dark hair and brown eyes, Adrienne's long lashes and high cheekbones.

"This is why you're not sure about taking the instructor position here?" Brian questions, breaking me out of the fairytale I was trying to climb back into to escape the reality of a dead wife, a murdered baby. "Are you afraid you won't be able to teach people to defend themselves because Adrienne couldn't fight back against a psychopath?"

"Yes," I answer quickly and honestly. "If I couldn't teach my own wife how to protect herself, how am I supposed to convince other people I can train them?"

"Because you killed the son of a bitch who took her from you and have had years to up your game after what he did to your family," he responds without missing a beat.

"Well, when you put it that way. Maybe Chief's right. I need to make a pro-con list," I say with the hint of a smile in my voice. "Pro, I killed a killer. Con, it didn't bring her back. Pro, I now live here. Con, the fact I didn't catch him the first time meant Steph got trapped in his web."

"Pro, you saved my sister. Con, you're too busy beating yourself up over the past to realize you effectively ended a cycle," Stella says, leaning forward and touching my knee. "Max, you can't do that. You can't try to behave like you're in the here and now while living in the past. Maybe it's time to talk to another therapist. I know someone in town. She's really great with PTSD and survivor's guilt."

Therapy. I'm not ready to admit I should go back. "I was cleared after the Judson incident and seen by a psychiatrist. I'm doing okay. Scout's honor," I say holding up my right hand.

"If you change your mind, let me know," she says, and I know she believes me even less than I believe myself.

Chapter Six

Stephanie

The burst of brightness nearly blinds me even with my eyes closed. "It's five in the morning," I say groggily, throwing my arm across my face in a weak attempt to block the light from the lamp next to the bed. "On a Saturday, no less! You're a dick, Tommy. Get out of my room."

"You promised you would help me," he whines. "I made coffee and brought home leftover muffins from the coffeehouse last night after you were already in bed."

"It's already made?"

"Yes. Extra strong."

I uncover one eye and gaze up at him. Then I wish I hadn't. His jeans, both knees blown out, ride low on his hips and a clean white T-shirt stretches across his chest. Just the front of the fabric is tucked in and I can see the outline of abs. Abs for days. Fuck me.

"Get out," I mumble, grabbing the blankets and pulling them up over my face while admiring Tommy's tanned and toned arms one more time before losing sight of them.

"You promised you would help me with this business stuff, Steph. You've got seven minutes to be downstairs with your ass in a chair and eating a muffin or I'm going to carry you down there," he teases.

Sleep never comes easily and it feels like I had just dropped off when he was pulling me back. Choosing alcohol to numb the night terrors and help me slip into dreamlessness stopped working almost as soon as it started. While drinking won't solve the issue, it's that or no sleep at all because I'm afraid of everything my subconscious screams at me in the night.

I sigh, resigned to the fact that I won't be catching any extra shut-eye today, and listen for the door to close before climbing out from under the covers. Shaking another night out of my limbs, I drop my head back, rolling it on my shoulders before tucking my chin to my chest and slowly bending at the waist. I feel the bones in my back separate and breathe out gently, allowing my body to fully succumb to the stretch as I place my palms on the floor.

The doorknob turns and I peek between my calves before the light pouring in from the hallway through my now open door registers. I see Tommy poke his head into the room and watch his Adam's apple bob slowly as he swallows hard.

"What now?" I ask breathlessly, still bent over.

"I wanted to make sure you were up. And you are. So, right. I'll just ... I'm going to wait downstairs," he stammers before closing the door.

Blowing the hair off my forehead as I come out of the stretch I notice my reflection in the mirror across the room along with my lack of clothes. My ass was on display, practically in his face when he opened the door, in a pair of black boy shorts. The hot pink ribbed tank top I wore to bed hardly held my breasts in place. Shit.

"Not only did your mouth water when you saw your roommate has a six-pack that isn't carbonated, now you've gone and shown him all the goods. Way to go," I mutter, pulling on a pair of basketball shorts and a long sleeve T-shirt.

Walking toward the mirror, I gather my hair back off my neck and wind it up in a loose bun. Touching the dark skin beneath my eyes, I recall the nightmares from this morning. Darren chasing me. Darren hitting me. Another bruise. Another broken bone. I wonder if I screamed in my sleep again. It wouldn't be the first time and it won't be the last. He'll haunt me until I can release the guilt and the hurt and learn to let myself heal. I know that. Mentally, I know that's what it's going to take for the nightmares to fade away. Emotionally, it feels like I'm going to relive that time with Darren for the rest of my life and the feeling alone suffocates me.

"You must look like such a slut to some people. You're not a slut. You never led him on. You did everything to get out. You've deserved more all along," I whisper to my reflection. I tell myself I'm better than all the things he did to me, said to me, ways he treated me daily. Instead of my "you're going to be successful" speech in the mirror every morning it's now this. "You deserve more."

I deserve more, but instead I have a beautiful blonde-haired southern boy as my gatekeeper and, with how much I'm not left alone or am afraid to mingle with the opposite sex, he's looking better and better ... which is wrong on so many levels because he's sort of somehow related to me now.

Pulling the sleeves up on my shirt and walking out the door, I take another deep breath and attempt to start the day on the right foot instead of staying stuck in my head.

"You okay?" Tommy asks as I hit the landing in the kitchen at the bottom of the hidden stairwell. This house was built in a time when servants were a regular fixture in homes and the stairs from the kitchen lead to the second-floor hallway. Stella rarely used it when she lived here, but since taking over her bedroom it's just easier to get to the coffee this way.

"Yeah, I'm fine," I say, giving him attitude. The agitation is back and I've only been out of bed for minutes. Not even hours. Minutes. "Sorry about the show in my bedroom. I wasn't expecting you to come back up."

"No apology necessary. It's your room. Not like I expected you to be in there wearing a snowsuit," he says, a sly smile stretching across his full lips.

"Ha. Ha. Ha," I say, emphasizing each "ha" with my back turned to him while I pour my coffee. "You're kind of a creep at five-thirty in the morning."

"So are you. You can touch them if you want," he says pulling up his T-shirt to reveal the muscles underneath. Chuckling at the expression on my face he adds, "I saw you staring. So, now that we're even, let's get this marketing shit hammered out for the bookshop and then go for a run before it gets too muggy."

I take a sip of my coffee and lean my elbows on the island counter in the center of the kitchen. Resting my head in my hands, I nod as best I can.

"Yeah," I sigh. "I could use a good stretch and run."

Picking up my mug again, I pull a mouthful of the steaming liquid in and revel in the pain, enjoy the burn, and start sifting through the information Tommy collected from the business owner we're trying to help.

We set out to create a strategy for Book Ends, which quietly opened its doors several months ago and then forgot to tell anyone they were welcome to come on in. Between T's background in marketing and public relations and my own work in those same fields, though minimal, we should be able to hammer out something useful before the weekend is over and potentially save the business from folding before their one-year anniversary.

"So, what's the plan?" I ask, leafing through flyers from past events. That question gets the ball rolling.

For three hours Tommy and I talk about social media, press releases, create concepts for events to draw people into the book store, and food.

We always end up talking about food and that makes me hungry. I'm four cups of coffee and two muffins in when I consider the actual atmosphere of the store.

"Do they have reading nooks in there? If they have little nooks, we could set up one of the marketing proposals around sitting for a while with a cup of coffee and baked goods. Put everything on an old fashion library table and call it something like The Daily Grind," I say, as I brainstorm out loud and doodle on my notepad.

I glance at my papers. My notes look like my thought process jumped out of my head and landed on the paper in front of me. Arrows point to random words in the margins and other things are circled. I underline the phrase "cozy nooks" three times because it seems important. There's no from Point A to Point B allowed here.

The papers in front of Tommy, however, have clean, neat columns and rows of information. I admire his ability to keep things in order. I don't have that ingrained in my DNA, I guess.

He hasn't responded at all to my idea and I catch myself rambling while I'm scribbling on my papers as if me talking more will make him want to give me ideas in return. "We could see if the owner wants to collaborate with your brother and have the Bean supply the coffee and a selection of baked goods. One hand washes the other, you know?"

"It's worth talking to Brian about," he says, drumming his pen on the notepad in front of him before turning his wrist and checking the time on his watch. He's one of the few men I know who wears a watch still. Too many people rely on their cell phones for everything these days, and I feel the pull of nostalgia as Tommy's voice reminds me I'm not in a time of boom boxes and corded telephones. "Run, shower, coffeehouse? You had another nightmare last night. I heard you cry out in your sleep."

He's not questioning it because he knows, and it doesn't matter if it was a dream last night or this morning or two months ago. Tommy's heard me scream, cry, and thrash to get away from it.

He refuses to meet my gaze, but he watches me from the corner of his eye with worry etched in his features, again, when he ends our meeting by rising from his seat. No "meeting adjourned" or anything — he just gets up and walks toward the door holding his notes in his left hand.

Standing and taking my coffee cup to the sink, I swallow the bile that's risen to the back of my throat. I shake my head, maybe more to clear my thoughts than to push him off my trail. "It's nothing. I'm talking to someone about it. Stella gave me her name," I say above the sound of the water hitting my mug before turning back to him.

And then I wish I hadn't done that.

I wish he wouldn't look at me like that. It hurts when he does, mostly because no man ever has.

To Hold

***

I'm miles away, but he's within arm's reach.

I hit my stride quickly and it helps me forget everything else but how good the physical exertion feels. The only thing I hear is the music, the blood rushing in my ears, and my muscles screaming at me to stop before the runner's high kicks in. But I don't stop and it comes.

I've come a long way since getting my cast removed and completing the therapy to strengthen my leg again, but even a slow run feels like a huge accomplishment. As much as I hate to give credit to someone for my achievements, I have Tommy to thank. He's done a lot for me that physical therapy couldn't. I did what I had to do to get by with the therapists, mostly because my injury wasn't so bad that I needed to do more, but that was no excuse for not trying harder. Tommy refuses to take "no" for an answer when I want to wimp out on him and he pushes me to do more, stretch my limitations.

We both played sports in high school. He was football. I was soccer. He did basketball. I swam. We played baseball in the spring. No matter how you paint the picture, we were pretty active as teenagers. Since we missed out on those years together it was a discovery we made after agreeing to be roommates and he moved into Stella's house with me in April.

I smile remembering the conversation. I was bitching about how my legs looked after not doing more serious workouts for so long and he made some douchey comment about sitting on my ass. The next day he invited me for a run to see how out of shape I was.

I think he was joking about me sitting on my ass. I hope he was joking. For his sake, he better have been joking, I think and turn my head slightly to look at him seconds before I feel my toe catch on a crack in the pavement.

Stumbling, I attempt to correct myself only to fall not-so-gracefully into Tommy's path. He tries to jump out of my way, but it's evident he was never on the track team. Instead of leaping over me, I watch in horror as his leg comes straight for me and I get a knee to the abdomen, forcing us both to the ground where we land on the side of the road tangled in each other's limbs and earbud wires.

"Off me. Can't. Breathe," I squeak out. He's not a very bulky man, but Jesus it's like he's made of solid muscle and every ounce of it is lying across my midsection. "If you fractured my newly healed ribs, I will smother you in your sleep."

I feel him wiggle on top of me as he gets up on the balls of his feet and pushes up with his palms in a downward dog position above me. I sit up to scoot back up on to the curb, watching how he makes that position look so easy, and see his stony blue eyes glaring at me over the tops of his sunglasses.

"Are you okay?" he finally asks as he kneels on the road and pulls his earbuds out. "What the hell were you doing anyway? One minute we're running and next you're pulling me down on top of you like you want to make out in the street."

"I tripped ... Ew, don't be gross," I bite back. I take a second to brush the stones from my hands before lifting my top up to see if there's a mark on my stomach from where his knee connected.

Tommy stretches his arm and gingerly touches my ribcage, his brow furrowing. The sweat breaking free from his hairline traces a path down his temple to a jaw I didn't realize before now was so masculine, and I can't stop myself from thinking I have never thought sweating was so sexy in all my life.

He reaches for my wrist, pulling my hand into his lap as he says, "We should get home and clean these cuts. Is there any peroxide at the house?" he asks, lifting his face. I see the worry again.

Quietly, so quietly I'm not sure I even say it out loud, I whisper, "I'm fine. Thank you," and curl my fingers into a fist before pushing up off the road.

I need to get out of this moment because I'm not sure what's happening. Whatever it is, it can't happen. It's too much. Teasing and joking around is one thing, but everything about this feels too serious. I don't do serious, and I certainly don't do serious with Tommy. He's the fun-loving guy. My guy friend. My buddy. The dude I drink beer with on a Thursday night while the Yankees are sometimes destroying the Red Sox.

I turn away to start the trek home but feel my heart speed up as Tommy gently places his hand on my lower back.

"Are you sure you're okay? You went down pretty hard," he says softly, pushing his sunglasses up into his hair and clenching his jaw. There's no hint of a smile at the corners of his mouth, nothing to indicate he means this as a set up for some stupid "that's what she said" joke. "You're limping, Steph."

"Not much. I'm okay, just let me walk it off," I say stiffly and stare straight ahead.

I feel him shift next to me, his hand still barely there at the base of my spine, his entire body tense and coiled.

Chapter Seven

Max

I'm not doing okay.

July is quickly coming to a close and I feel the itch to move. Not move away, just move.

I've come to the conclusion that Adrienne would rather see me teach something I love than wallow. It's been too many years of wallowing already.

Now I need to regroup and figure out a plan, one that focuses on me — it makes me sound like a dick, but once in a while I need to be a little selfish. I need a reprieve from the trivial parts of my day, of getting up, going to work, going home, hitting things, going to sleep. The routine needs to change.

My brain is on fire as I make my way through the college campus to get in a short workout, but it feels like I'm running through mud as the humidity starts creeping up. My shirt's sticking to the center of my back as I jog up the stairs to the bridge crossing University Avenue. Taking the steps two at a time I feel the familiar stretch in my quads after not taking this route the last couple weeks and power through to the top before sprinting the 50 feet to the opposite set of stairs.

With each step I take, I feel the clarity begin to seep in, crawling deep within my bones. A long weekend I have coming up is the perfect time to break free, break the routine. I'm going to head home. I owe it to Adrienne to visit on our anniversary. There hasn't been one yet that I've missed. This will be six, but the fifth without her.

I hit the sidewalk and head east back toward town before the flood of memories can wash ashore. I don't want to think about how short our love affair was. While the years since her death — their deaths — have helped me heal in some ways, the hurt is still raw in certain moments. You would think with Judson gone I would finally be at peace, but it's the opposite. I feel more wound up than ever before. Now I'm just doing my job. I still have purpose, but I don't have a singular goal.

When Judson was around, I had someone to keep tabs on. I wasn't supposed to, but no one else was finding him. It never occurred to anyone he might have started using an alias. They never considered he would assume his brother's identity.

I found him, though.

I uprooted my life with my former chief's blessing because the itch needed to be scratched. He approved my transfer because I would have up and quit to come here otherwise. I wanted Judson in prison where he belonged.

He could have lived if he hadn't gone after Stephanie. I would have let him live with a non-life-threatening gunshot wound if he hadn't shot me first. I'll thank God every day for giving man the ability to create that vest. Without it, I'd be in the ground beside my wife and son.

Stopping at the crosswalk, I look at the street signs. "Shit," I curse out loud. The word sounds muffled to me as Skrillex pounds loudly in my ears, but it's far from muted for the two pre-teen girls waiting for the light with me. They cast nervous glances my way and I pull an earbud out. "My apologies, ladies. Didn't realize how loud that was."

Stuck in thoughts I didn't want to have I've run further off my planned path than I realized and without waiting for the light to change, I pop the speaker back in and take off again. Main Street is a block away. All I have to do is get there, take a right, run two more blocks and I can reward myself with a cup of coffee.

***

"There's the town hero," I hear as I walk into the coffeehouse pulling on the leads to my earbuds.

I scoff at Brian as I walk up to the counter. "You might want to rethink that. I just cussed out loud at a stop light in front of kids. I'm a disgrace to Small Town America."

"Ah, well, some heroes have a few dings in their armor. It makes them more real," he says and hands me a large mug of coffee. "Good run? You looked like you could use it after we talked last night."

Turning so I can see the door, I lean my hip against the counter, bring the cup to my mouth to blow the steam off the top and take a long, slow sip.

"It helped. My head's definitely more clear than it was yesterday," I say and watch as he pulls his phone from his pocket. "I have a long weekend coming up near the end of August, so I'm going to head to Ohio to visit my mom. I need some closure."

Brian's head snaps up as he finishes typing out a text message. "Closure?"

"Are we having another heart-to-heart?"

"Apparently." The phone in his hand makes another noise, but he's waiting for me to answer.

"Our wedding anniversary is the first week of August. I'm going home to visit family and pay my respects at their grave. It's the least I can do. I went when I was on leave last winter, but the weather was horrible. I just need to go talk to her." I look down into my coffee, like it'll give me all these answers I'm looking for. It's not a Magic 8 Ball, though.

"If that's what you have to do to find peace, then do it. I can't even begin to tell you how many times I've thought about visiting Emily's grave just for that feeling, but I was fortunate enough that she left us letters and I can reread them and get the same effect," Brian says reaching across the counter and placing a hand on my shoulder. "Do what you need to and come back to us whole."

There's a reason this guy is fast becoming one of my best friends.

"Thanks for the bromance, Bri," I say letting a laugh slip through to ease the moment.

I never would have thought he'd be the person I spill my guts to on a regular basis. After all, when I met him it was to ask for his license and registration.

I smile when I think about how uncomfortable I felt interrupting him and Stella as they were making out like teenagers parked on the side of the road. I found out a lot later that I was interrupting the moment Stella declared her desire to be his wife and Britt's mom. I had no idea that's what was going on when I turned my lights on behind them that day. I just saw a car on the side of the road and wanted to make sure everything was okay.

I want to hold on to the hope there's something out there for me, something to make me feel ... anything. I want to feel what Brian and Stella do when they look at each other. I realized that yesterday while we were sitting on their deck talking about the classes Franks wants me teaching. The conversation was really just a way for us to skirt around all my deeper issues, but I could see in Stella's eyes all the questions she wasn't asking out of respect for me and my fucking Scout's Honor comment.

"You know you love it. I don't want Stella getting jealous of our feelings, though, so maybe after you get back we can set up an online dating profile for you or something. Just an idea. It might give you a chance to see there are still good people in this world worth your time," Brian remarks. Lifting his phone, he continues, "I've got to get back to Steph. I think being cooped up in that house living and working with T when she's not at the library is getting to her. If you've got some afternoons free maybe you can give me a hand moving stuff around upstairs to make an office for them."

I glance at the ceiling, having never before wondered what was above the coffeehouse, and nod my head. "Yeah, man, just let me know when and I'm all yours."

Chapter Eight

Stephanie

We have the same ringtone for each other, so when Rhythm of Love by the Plain White T's plays loudly from the counter, echoing off the tile and sounding a thousand times louder than it really is, I know it's my sister. Her calls aren't to be ignored.

Straddling the edge of the tub, I grab for my phone.

"Stell, what's up? Baby time?"

"Not yet," my sister responds, grumpily. "Not even so much as a few regular contractions. We still have a few weeks, so that's okay. Let her bake a little longer. Are you going to the coffeehouse later? I'm at work and I need a pick me up. I figured I would meet you there when I take a break."

"Is all that caffeine good for the baby? The kid's going to come out with a chest full of hair and dressed like Juan Valdez." My sister is as hardcore about her coffee as I am, which makes her marriage to Brian a match made in heaven.

I hear her laugh on the other end.

"He'll be sure I only get half-caff this trip. I swear he's like a prison guard lately with my rations. What are you doing?"

"Trying to get in the shower after a failed run and some awkward shit with T this morning. I'll text you when I head to the coffeehouse," I say quickly. I try so hard to keep it real with Stella and not telling her about what happened this morning won't do. Between Tommy walking into my room and his sudden protectiveness after I fell during our run, she'll know no matter how cool I try to play it so it's not worth the stress of trying to fabricate some huge story. She always knows when something's up. Damn her intuition.

"I want to hear all about it. Talk to you soon. Love you." And click.

I stare at her shining face as I pull the phone away from my ear and say, "Love you, too" before laying the phone down and crawling inside the warmth of the shower, the steam billowing around me and turning my skin bright pink before I scrub away everything that hurts and reach for the shampoo.

Lather. Rinse. Repeat. With an entire advertising campaign revolving around how relaxing this stuff is, it's doing a piss poor job of helping me calm down. I consider washing my hair again just to see if the magical shampoo will take a stand and do for me what it does for the girl in the ads.

I give in and try a second time. It doesn't do anything extra. I think I should demand a refund. He's got me wound up to the point even special shampoo doesn't fucking work. Tommy and his stupid hand on me the entire walk home has left me wanting ... just not wanting him.

I feel the familiar tugging of the memory I've played back a hundred times. My walk home on Stella's wedding night.

"I'm pretty sure you don't have to hold my arm the entire walk back home, Max. It's like you and Brian took etiquette classes. He's constantly holding doors open for my sister and using his manners," I say to lighten the mood after my outburst about riding his motorcycle.

We walk along the sidewalk, meandering really, my arm slung through his and I feel that little pull — the one that tells me this is someone I can trust.

"Do you actually think Mama Stratford would let either of her sons out into the wild without teaching them how to treat a lady?" he questions. I see a smile crease the corner of his right eye, the only one I can see since he's staring straight ahead as though he's afraid to make eye contact with me. "Honestly, Tommy and Brian's mom reminds me a lot of mine. Not to mention whatever good manners and behavior my parents didn't instill in me, I got at the police academy. I'd prefer to open a door for someone and get told they can do it on their own than not and be labeled rude."

He turns his head just enough that I can see both of his eyes and I want to get lost in them. But I won't.

"Did you always want to be a cop?" I ask quickly changing the topic.

"Since I was a kid. My obsession with all things police and firefighting started when I was around six years old. I watched our local department back home rescue a family of ducks from a storm drain in front of our house," he says. "I saw how much they cared about those ducklings and wanted to help, too."

I feel myself smile as we walk beneath the trees lining the walkway, light from the streetlamps pooling around us and casting shadows to guide us on our way. I let the moment stay quiet, allowing him to choose when it should end.

"Your turn. Did you always want to work with books? In the library, I mean. Because there are books there," he stammers and it elicits a laugh from me.

"Actually, I just picked up the job there because I was already there so much working on school stuff and doing research. I've never thought of it as a career and I'm not studying library science, so it was just something to help pay the bills when I wasn't making enough waitressing on weekends," I say, realizing I gave more personal information to Max in the first ten minutes alone with him than I did in the first ten days I knew Darren ... or any other person I dated recently. It feels good to trust him a little. "I like it, though. It gives me time to do work and see what other people are working on or reading. It's really a great place for a com major to spend time. So much nonverbal communication. You truly get a feel for 'reading' people."

"You like to read people?"

"I like to understand people. Sometimes you learn more about a person by watching them and paying attention to their mannerisms than by having conversations with them. That's what makes last winter so difficult. I can't understand," I say, opening that locked door to my soul, just a crack. "It's like he was a master of disguise."

Max's steps slow until we've stopped in front of my house.

"Don't try to understand what he did or who he was," he says, his voice hoarse, as he turns to face me, my arm still held against his warm body. He reaches up with his free hand, touches my cheek, and I feel paralyzed in the moment. "I took care of it. Now is the time to heal and move forward, Stephanie. Promise you'll try."

It's been months of wondering why Max Wyatt didn't kiss me that night.

It's been months of Tommy being my roommate, Tommy falling asleep watching movies on the couch with me, Tommy and me working late hours on marketing proposals when I'm not working at the library.

I've spent all my time with Tommy and now I wish I could convince myself it was my imagination, that he didn't look at me with longing this morning when he busted into my bedroom. I want to believe his fingertips grazing my bare back beneath the hem of my shirt after I tripped were just Tommy being Tommy — a protective friend being watchful of me. But I'm having more trouble convincing myself of that than I did that Y2K was the end of the world as we knew it. This is bigger than that. And Y2K was huge. Like, buy cases of bottled water and batteries for your flashlights huge.

It isn't that I wouldn't adore the affection I know he can give. He's loving and loveable. I've been reaping the benefits of his friendship since he moved back last Thanksgiving and I absolutely want a man who might dote on me like Tommy's capable of doing. If I'm not careful, he's the kind of man I could fall in love with, but that would hurt me more than help me and I can't lead him on like that.

Rinsing again and turning the cold water on, I mentally check off the outfits I can no longer wear in his presence. Movie nights will have to be spent on separate pieces of furniture.

The hardest part is going to be figuring out our work situation with how closely we work together now. I'm literally his partner. We're in business together and, despite me finishing my master's project for my degree, we spend an exorbitant amount of time together.

We need an office, not a dining room table.

Turning the water off and throwing a towel around myself, I leave the bathroom hoping he's still downstairs. I look up and down the hallway before running to my room to throw on my shorts from this morning and a clean T-shirt. Then I do the cowardly thing and text Brian.

Me: Do you know anyone with office space available?
Brian: Upstairs.
Me: WTF upstairs?
Brian: Upstairs here. I only use part of it for storage but the rest is empty. Why?
Me: I think T and I need to move business locations. It's getting crowded here.
Brian: Explain later. Come for lunch.
Me: On my way.

World's best brother-in-law. I add to my mental check list to buy Brian a new coffee mug for his collection.

"Are you ready yet?" I hear him say from the doorway and turn.

I need to nip this in the bud immediately.

"You look good and that's a problem. Brian has office space available we can use for this marketing thing you're roping me into and I think above the coffeehouse is a good base of operations as opposed to the kitchen counter or dining room table." Word vomit. Why do I always do this? "Okay? Okay. Brian's waiting for us."

"You think I look good?" He smirks.

"That's all you got out of that? I also said that was a problem. I'm dealing with it," I say with attitude, pushing past him into the hall and heading for the stairs.

His boots hammer the stairs behind me and I feel him touch my shoulder as we reach the entryway at the front of the house.

"Why are things awkward today?" he questions warily.

"I don't know, T. But it needs to stop. First step is getting the business stuff out of here. Please," I plead with him. "I'm in therapy for a reason. I don't want you to turn into one of those reasons."

He pulls his bottom lip between his teeth, securing his thinking face in place. I know I don't have to explain what the issue is. That look tells me he gets it. He understands what I'm trying to say beneath all the rambling and crazy.

"I care about you, Steph. It's hard to think of you only as my roommate. It's difficult to forget you're a woman and I'm a man when we spend damn near every waking moment together," he says, a touch of hurt, a sliver of anger sliding through his words. "We'll move to an office. You're right. It's a good place to have an actual business presence. Just ... just don't shut me out. You do that really well with a lot of people. Please don't do it to me."

Reaching for the door, it hits me how he must be feeling right now. Aside from my sister, his brother, and Greg, I'm the closest friend Tommy has in New York and now I'm unintentionally trying to push him away.

"I'll try really hard not to," I soften my voice. "I promise I'll try."

Chapter Nine

Max

I stick my head in through the door on my way out and watch Chief attempt to make what he calls coffee in the tiny excuse for a coffee maker he has in his office.

"Chief, I'm heading out. Can you get me the info for the self-defense classes? I want to start prepping as soon as I can?"

He turns, scoop full of grounds still in his hand, and looks at me like I have an agenda.

"You're sure?" he questions.

Grabbing the top of the doorframe and feeling the stretch in my shoulders when I let my weight drop, I nod in his direction. "Absolutely. I did some soul searching over the weekend."

"When do you want to start?"

"Not until after I get back from Ohio. I head out next Thursday and come back Sunday evening, but give me a couple weeks to prep and we should be good to go as long as the community center has a room I can use consistently." I don't need someone switching my rooms on me. That always happened to me back home, to the point I think they did it on purpose to try to get a reaction from me. "How are you advertising the program?"

I watch his face blanch. I can tell by the look in his eyes that he never thought about how to tell people, but he recovers quickly.

"They've got one of the studio rooms the yoga class meets in that you'll use on alternating days. I hadn't thought about the rest, but I think the director at the center is having Tom Stratford do some of their marketing. I'll talk to them," he says thinking on his feet.

I drop my arms from the door and pick my helmet up from where I set it between my feet. Turning on my heels, I start for the door while pulling the helmet over my head.

"Sounds good, Chief. See you when you get in in the morning."

I walk out the door, get on my bike, and feel a weight lift off me as I hit the starter and rev the engine.

***

Working nights frees up most of my days, so when I walk into the coffeehouse and tell Brian I'm his for a few hours if he wants me, he jumps at the chance to utilize my services. Calling over his shoulder to let Greg know if he needs anything we'll be upstairs, I follow him to the second floor of the building.

When Brian and Greg first opened the Jumping Bean, they leased a section of the building. Their small town success, though, has grown by leaps and bounds in the little more than a year since the doors opened. One night the guys finally told all of us they'd put an offer in to purchase the building from the owner, who gladly accepted and escaped with his wife to Louisiana to finally begin their long awaited retirement.

"I figure," Brian says as he reaches the top of the stairs, "if Tommy is able to get the public relations thing off the ground, we can always move him and Steph into the vacant storefront next door. I own it, and if they're late with rent I can just demand they work shifts in the coffeehouse, right?"

We laugh at the thought of him actually having some control over his sister-in-law, but he makes a good point about moving them to a storefront.

"You think the move here is going to be good for them?" I question, looking around the space. Last time Tommy talked about business stuff, he acted like everything was running smoothly from the house. The impression I got, from the little I know about Brian's conversation with Stephanie the other day, is that it's quite the opposite of running smoothly.

Across the room, Brian stands up holding a box labeled "coffee filters" and swivels his head around looking at what he plans to turn into a small public relations firm. "I think it'll work. It's definitely big enough for the two of them, a couple desks, a table, other office ... stuff. Once we get my things moved downstairs or into the back room up here, they're going to have plenty of space to not kill each other."

I nod, mumbling under my breath something about how more space than this might be even better for them but if Brian hears me, he ignores it. We go to work moving office supplies and overflow inventory. We're quiet, but work efficiently, and lose ourselves in the details of getting a job done. An hour or more passes before I ask tentatively, "So, how is she these days?"

I haven't come right out and asked recently, but the guys know I keep tabs.

Brian stops what he's doing and the question forming in his eyes is not "who?" but "why?"

"She's good," he bluntly remarks while nodding his head. "Stella got her in with a local psychiatrist to talk things through. It took a while, but we knew she wasn't dealing with what happened on her own. She finally gave in and let Stell make an appointment for her. She wouldn't have gone any other way. I think it's been helping. Why?"

I stand stock still, holding reams of printer paper that feel like a lead weight landed on my forearms. "That's good. I'm glad she's got someone objective to talk to. I just haven't seen her to talk to her recently and wanted to check up on her. You know, the normal for me."

"Max, it is okay you know. You're allowed to worry about her. We all do." His eyes tell me his concern isn't for Steph, though. "You sure you don't want to talk to the good doctor, too?"

Part of me wishes they would stop asking me if I wanted to talk to a therapist. Then the other seventy-five percent of me obliterates that thought because I know they're just watching out for me, and I'm grateful for that. It's been a long time since I had friends who cared enough to look out for my mental well-being.

The only problem is I haven't let myself be completely honest with them. Sure, I told him and Stella I was cleared after the shooting, but I didn't tell them I continued to see her for a few more appointments after that. It doesn't matter that it was protocol that I go to the first appointment, I still worry people not in the same field as me might judge. I know I shouldn't worry about that here. Brian wouldn't ask me if I want to talk to someone and then turn around and criticize me for having seen a therapist. That's not the type of person he is.

The stack of papers in my hands feels even heavier than it did moments before as I remark quietly, "I had to go see someone after ... it was part of the agreement after the shooting. I had to be cleared by a psychiatrist to come back to work because of the nature of the incident and my past history. She saw me for a while after that until I was sure I was back on track."

His jaw slowly works over the words he's considering. "Good. Max, it's a good thing. You went through a lot. Both of you," he emphasizes. Looking at the bundles of printer paper in my arms and trying to hide a shit-eating grin, he states, "That looks heavy. Let's finish up what we can today and I'll buy you a cup of coffee."

M.L. Pennock

Chapter Ten

Stephanie

"What do you mean we're doing promotional stuff for the community center now? First, Tommy, that's huge," I say excitedly and throw my arms around his neck, kissing his cheek in my frenzy. Then the hugeness of it — all of it — hits me and I attempt to shake it off and let go of him, taking a step back to grab the coffee pot. Clearing my throat and toning down the cheerleader squeal, I add, "Second, holy shit that's huge. That's a lot of stuff. There are a lot of programs. What exactly are we doing for them?"

It wasn't long ago he was rolling my ass out of bed at 5 a.m. to work on marketing for a tiny, hole in the wall bookshop and I was telling him whatever the awkwardness was between us needed to be resolved. At least he let me sleep in a little today and was banging on my door at six, but I just compounded the level of awkward by giving him a not-just-friends kind of hug. Things had finally started going back to normal. I sigh, confused and angry with myself.

He looks at me over the rim of his coffee cup while my heart goes back to a normal rhythm, but I see what might be construed as a glimmer of hope in his eyes that shouldn't be there.

"I'm sorry. I didn't mean to throw myself at you. It's just really, really ..."

"Huge? Yeah, I've been told that before."

"Fucker."

"Anyway, it's just a few new programs they have starting," he says laughing as he grabs for a stack of papers on the counter and shuffles through them. "Two don't start until winter, but the self-defense program is starting in about a month, so we need to get busy on that. I want to meet with the director soon, so let me know what your availability is."

Between working at the library, finishing up the research for my project, and my fairly frequent therapy sessions, I know my time is technically limited to break-of-dawn early or after dinner.

"I'll check my calendar and make it work. Maybe we can shoot for Tuesday? Yeah, set it up for Tuesday morning since I don't work until the afternoon," I question and answer myself while trying to remember what all the coming week has scheduled for me already. Reaching for the self-defense class information Tommy is holding, I ask, "Can I borrow this to make a copy?

I'll get a head start brainstorming a flyer and press release while you're at the coffeehouse helping the guys later today."

***

Taking a deep breath, I turn the knob and push the door open into the short hallway that leads to the fifteen steps that'll take me to her office once again. It's rare she sees clients on Saturday, but she made an exception for me, particularly after I mentioned planting one on Tommy this morning.

"No time like the present. Doc does not like to be kept waiting," and I take off jogging up the stairs. I've found my anxiety over meeting with her is less if I've exerted myself first, so I always walk to my appointments or go for a run before I have to be here. I didn't have time to go for a run after Tommy left for the coffeehouse, so doing the stairs will have to suffice.

I reach the top, round the corner, and head straight for the open door at the end of the hall.

"Good, you're on time. Sit," she says pointing to the armchair I like to think of as my own. I might even ask her if I can buy it from her when I'm done needing these weekly chats. "You sounded frantic on the phone, Stephanie. I just saw you a few days ago. What's going on?"

I bring her up to speed because my last session was reserved for talking about the nightmares. I start with the buddy run last weekend with Tommy and the awkward moments since then. I spill my guts about Max walking me home from Stella and Brian's house and every feeling he untucked from me in that mile-long stretch of sidewalk.

The words just won't stop.

"You're in a love triangle?" The very question screws up her face, her nose scrunching up. "How are we going from nightmares and recovery to this?"

"I don't think we did. At least, I don't think so?" I sigh. "Max has kept his distance. I know he's been doing it on purpose. Tommy and I came out from the kitchen at the coffeehouse one day and Max took off as though he never saw me. This stuff with Tommy, I don't know. We've been spending a lot of time together."

"Do you have feelings for Tommy?"

Do I?

"If the situation was different and I'd met him before all that shit with Darren, maybe. If I let the loneliness and pheromones do all the thinking and talking for me? Yes. A thousand times, yes, I would have feelings for him. They wouldn't be based on anything but physical need, though. I know that," I tell her honestly. "But when I haven't been drinking? If I don't feel needy? Absolutely not. He's just T, my brother-in-law's brother and my roommate."

We stare at each other.

"You say 'drinking' like it's a concern. You've never mentioned alcohol abuse being a problem?" She scribbles something in her notes.

"It's not so much a problem as it's something I'm working on." My mouth feels suddenly dry as she lifts her eyes from the notepad in her lap to my fidgeting fingers and finally my face.

"Stephanie?" It's a question, but also a demand for an answer.

"It was how I was coping after Thanksgiving. It doesn't work," I say quietly. "It used to be that I would get together with Colton and we'd rehash things over drinks. We'd have our breakdowns about what happened, how he couldn't do more, that he should have been there and we could have those conversations regularly. I'd taken a hiatus from school to recover and had a lot of free time. He didn't take a semester off but made time for me. He graduated when we were supposed to and now he's gone, up and left for a career in Texas, and I haven't heard from him. He doesn't call me back. He's busy with a new life in Austin. So, I've learned to cope with that, too.

"Shortly before Stell moved out and Tommy moved in, I realized I was sleeping better if I had a few glasses of wine a night before bed. Or a few beers. Or a cocktail. It kept the nightmares away for a while," I continue.

"And now?"

"And now it feels like it's primarily out of habit. To see if it will work again."

"A couple drinks a night isn't necessarily bad. You're worried about it, though, so that makes me worry about it. How will you fix this? The nightmares won't go away with alcohol."

I reach in my back pocket and pull out the information about the self-defense class and hand it across the minimal expanse between our chairs to her outreached hand.

"I think I need a different outlet," I say matter-of-factly and stand up to walk to the window. I shove my hands in my back pockets and stare out at Main Street. "Running in the morning or evening, or both, helps a little to get my mind off all the people who see me, but they still see me as a victim. Wine helps me fall asleep, but lately it makes the nightmares more vivid. I can't keep having Tommy barge into my room when I'm screaming in the middle of them."

That's how on more than one occasion I've ended up waking in the morning with his legs wrapped around mine, my hand and cheek pressed to his chest. Needy. Vulnerable. And it was usually met with morning wood until I was awake enough to literally shove him out of my bed while thanking him for G-rated comfort the night before.

I've gnawed my thumbnail down to the quick when Doc interrupts my thoughts.

"Self-defense classes. Do you think you're in danger now, even with your attacker gone?"

I turn from the breathtaking view of my hometown, my hazel eyes wide. "No. That's just it. I don't feel like I'm in danger ... but I don't want to be seen as a victim, either. Brian told me one night that I was a survivor. I was barely breathing at that point, Doc, but he had faith that I'd get through this stronger than I was going in."

She looks at me, her eyes burrowing into my soul almost, and taps her pen on her notepad.

"Do it. Prove to yourself you're a survivor. You're the only one who doesn't believe it."

Chapter Eleven

Max

Plans were made and I won't break them. I called my mom last weekend to let her know I was coming home for a few days. The shock in her voice was unmistakable as she stammered through asking when I was heading that way and how long I was staying. Jean Wyatt isn't used to her son coming to visit, especially now that I'm out of state.

We don't talk frequently anymore, and I only have myself to blame. She calls, but I don't call back all the time. It's a constant rehashing of the past and regardless of how much I feel I've been living there, I don't want to talk about it all the time. I don't want to go over all the details when we have all the answers we're ever going to get.

Conversations are always spent with me trying to steer her away from talking about Adrienne's death while she kicks and screams trying to stay on topic. I won't argue that I could use someone to talk to again — won't argue, but won't openly admit it yet, either — but there have been many times over the last several years that make me think my mom could also benefit from some therapy. Mom and Adrienne were close. They talked every day and we got together for dinner regularly, so when it happened, Mom was in just as much a state of shock as I was. She lost a daughter that day.

One of us had to pull out of it and it was me.

My mom has seen plenty of death in her years. As an emergency room nurse, it happens. She's stood by and held the hands of those who don't have a chance and then turned to offer her shoulder to their loved ones.

But when it's your pregnant daughter-in-law rolling in on a stretcher and there's nothing you can do to save her, it steals something from you. Death reaches into your soul and squeezes the light out until every drop has been drained.

I wish I could pour a little sunshine back into her heart.

***

Thursday finally comes, but there are so many things I need to do in Cleveland there's no point waiting to leave. I finish my Wednesday night shift and head home shortly before eight the next morning. Tucking the Harley into the garage, I push my helmet up my forehead and stare at the back wall — high school baseball plaques and awards, my varsity jacket and Scholar Athlete letter, and the framed picture of me and Dad standing next to the 1969 Chevy Chevelle SS we rebuilt together. We started working on it when I was fifteen and I finished it alone the summer before I left for college.

I try not to bring her out much, but the bike would make for a rough ride all the way to Ohio, so the Chevelle it is. Climbing off the motorcycle, I turn to look at her in her garnet glory — even with all the choices out there for paint colors, Dad and I wanted to keep her the factory color and we matched as close as we could to the red of her heyday.

"You ready for this trip?" I ask, wiping a cotton cloth gently over the chrome trim. Reaching to polish the bowtie emblem I add, "If you don't ride with me, at least give me a little guidance when I get there, Pops."

It would be weird if I talked to a car, but there's something vaguely comforting about talking to the silence with the hope my dad hears me wherever he might be.

I toss the cloth on the workbench and head to the house. One quick check to make sure everything's locked, and I feel like I'm ready. It's just for a weekend, I remind myself.

Tossing my duffle bag into the back, I slide into the bucket seat and take a moment to enjoy the feel of the leather, smelling the interior like I'm trying to conjure up a few more good memories before traveling toward a melancholy I can't avoid.

Satisfied, I turn the key. The engine roars to life, breaking up the quiet in this sleepy small town as I back out of the garage and down my driveway while trying to pack my thoughts into the corner of my mind. Slowly, I creep toward the outskirts of the community I've been trying to call home and head west.

***

As the sun continues to rise higher in the sky the true beauty of the region comes to life. The August heat evaporates the dew from fields and farms that the highway was plunked down in the midst of.

Following the Thruway toward Erie, Pennsylvania, I pass acre upon acre of grape vines. It's not something I gave much thought to when I drove to Brockport years ago with Adrienne. It was more important to listen to her voice and her words as she rambled on about homecoming weekend. She was into all of that alum stuff and it was fun to listen to her tell stories from her early years in college.

Those grape vines caught my eye only after she was gone and I was trying to catch a killer. It was an instant guilt because I let myself think about all the things we *could* have done if I had been there that night. And it's stupid to think about things I can't go back and change.

"Live and learn," I say into the quiet of the car as I lean forward to twist the knobs on the radio and bring it to life. Pulling my sunglasses from the collar of my shirt and setting them on my nose, I breathe in deeply the earthy scent surrounding me and seeping in through the windows.

The anger hits me out of nowhere when I arrive at the Ohio state line and I pull off I-90 into the Welcome Center parking area to get my bearings and shake the numbness from my legs. The parking lot is empty, save for a couple big rigs at the far edges and I hear the engines idling in an attempt to keep the cabs cool for what I can only guess are exhausted drivers. Exhausted like me, but I don't have time to sleep.

There's an overwhelming need to get to my destination and with one more look around, I open the door and slide my body back into the comfort of leather and the local classic country radio station. Pulling back onto the road, I let Johnny Cash and Dolly Parton carry me on my way until it's time to drop off I-90 onto I-71 South.

I've driven this part of the highway a thousand times. Autopilot kicks in as my exit comes into view and a few miles further, I slow down to make the left turn into the entrance for Riverside Cemetery. Bringing the car to a stop near a wooded area, I twist the key back and hear nothing. Nothing but the rustle of leaves and the sound of birds.

At least I laid them to rest somewhere peaceful, I think before pushing open the door and seeking their final destination.

The stone looms ahead, and like a beacon at the edge of choppy waters the sun peeks from behind dark clouds to guide me through a haze of memories. I don't brush the thoughts away this time. This is the one place they can come at me and simply be, so I drop to my knees in front of the marble slab with my surname on it, with birth and death dates too close to one another, and I feel. I feel everything I've tried to keep closed up inside for years and it washes through me as I share memories with a wife who isn't here and a son I only held after he was gone. With the apologies come the tears and the feeling of relief because I'm expunging my soul of all the hurt.

"I'm sorry I wasn't there that night," I say to the breeze. "I wonder a lot lately if there wasn't a bigger reason I couldn't save you, like it was a test. My dad used to tell me when I'd get angry as a kid that God was just testing me. I never understood what he meant. What's the point of testing me by making me mad? Then it clicked, because there are always two answers when you're angry — neither is necessarily wrong. You can either stand and fight or try to problem solve. I wanted to be a fighter, so when I was younger I picked up boxing. Hitting things eased the anger I felt and even though I sparred with other guys, no one was getting hurt and it helped clear my head. Then I started working with self-defense instructors and got certified before entering the academy and realized I was more passionate about problem solving. Every time I got angry it was a test of how much I could handle, how much I could take before I broke."

I look down and see a pile of grass I've absentmindedly pulled from the ground. Brushing the blades from my jeans, I sit down with my legs stretched in front of me and lean back on my hands.

"You were a test. You were supposed to be the love of my life, but you were a test. That night, when I got the phone call you were in the ER, no one would tell me what happened. Not over the phone. My chief simply said he was coming to get me, and I followed orders. I knew, the minute I saw you laying there, I knew who did it and I knew my life was over if I handled my hurt and anger the wrong way." I wipe the tears from my face and breathe in deeply. "He took everything from me. But I wouldn't break. I could have. So many nights I could have. A little liquid courage and a loaded gun and I could have been with you. I thought about it. And then I thought about how selfish it would be of me to do that when I could just hunt him down instead and let the system have its way with him. I was tested and I refused to fail."

Standing up, I feel antsy. I need to move, but I need to tell her everything. Again. It's not like this is the first time I've told her I'm sorry. The night they died, I cradled my son in my arms and wept like a baby and the only words I could say were, "I'm sorry." I'm sorry I wasn't there. I'm sorry leaving him didn't stop him from hurting you. I'm sorry it was dark that night. I'm sorry he got away. Those two words were a mantra. They were the only way I could communicate how distraught I was. I told everyone who ever cared about Adrienne that I was sorry because all I could do was blame myself.

"Even with you gone I keep having tests thrown at me. When he attacked the girl in Brockport, it was like walking back into a nightmare. I got there and I was seeing you lying on the cold ground. He had a type and she was it. You were it. Long dark hair, athletic build, beautiful. She's gorgeous. If God was testing me that night, He had a reason. I couldn't leave Stephanie at the emergency room. Out of fear that, if I left, something worse would happen than the broken leg and cuts on her face, I planted myself outside the closed off area they had her in and waited with her as her family came in, as they plastered her leg and stitched her face. It was only when I was certain she would be physically okay that I left. And then I hunted him down like I should have done right after you died. I'm sorry I let him hurt someone else."

The blame I place on myself for his actions is absurd, I know. I wasn't the only police officer in Cleveland looking for him. We all let her down by not finding him. It turned into a case of him slipping through our fingers as we all grieved my losses. We all let our guard down.

"He's gone now, though, Adrienne. He's gone. I would have rather seen him rot in prison, but it didn't end that way ... and that's one thing I won't say I'm sorry about. It's taken me all these months to try to find peace with everything and I hope getting back into teaching will be one of the missing pieces. There's been a void in my life, and while I know some of it is because you're missing from it, I think some of it is me missing out on my life. I will love you always, but I think my grief is coming to an end. I think I'm finally learning to accept the things I cannot change."

***

"Mom, you home?" I call walking through the back door into the kitchen. I drop my duffle bag and bend to unlace my boots.

My childhood home hasn't changed much — the wood paneling still lines the hallway, the refrigerator is the same one we bought when I was seven, and the deep ceramic farmhouse sink still looks big enough to fit a child in. I can recall numerous baths in that thing after playing in the mud on a rainy afternoon.

"Mom?" I call again and listen to the noises the house makes, the low hum of the fridge and the tick-tock of the imported German cuckoo clock in the dining room are the only sounds to break the silence. Still, there's no answer from her. I glance out the window overlooking the driveway to make sure I hadn't imagined her car when I first pulled up.

I'll only be here a couple days, but climb the stairs to my old bedroom to drop my duffle and put my toiletries in the bathroom before knocking on her bedroom door. If she worked last night, the gentle tapping won't wake her, so I slowly turn the knob and push the door open to find my mom curled up on her bed, her graying sandy blonde hair still in a knot at the back of her head. She didn't even take her scrubs off and her street shoes are untied but still snuggly planted to her feet.

Sighing, I walk quietly into the room and squat at the foot of her bed to pull the sneakers off.

"Davey, it's okay," she mumbles in her sleep. Lifting my head at the sound of my dad's name, I wait to see if there's more, like a starving child begging for a morsel at the back door of a restaurant. The mumbling begins again, mostly unrecognizable words until I hear her say, "I'll tell the boys. Make sure they know." And then she shushes him, sighs in her sleep, and curls tighter into a ball.

I know she's only dreaming, but I wonder if there's something to it. Boys? What boys? After Dad died my senior year of high school, it was just me and Mom.

Despite the heat outside, her bedroom feels cool and I slide a lightweight blanket up over her legs. Picking the shoes up from where I set them at the end of the bed, I make my way to the door, turning to look at her once more before heading back downstairs.

It's another twenty minutes and one ham and cheese sandwich later when I hear her alarm clock click on above me and the floor creak as she climbs out of bed. Standing at the sink drinking a glass of milk, I listen as she makes her way across the hall to my bedroom and then the clamor of her hitting the stairs. Putting the glass to my lips once more, I watch over the rim as she appears in the doorway.

"You're home," she says, dazed but oddly flat and she stares at me like she's looking at a ghost. "You really came home."

"You didn't believe me?"

"I was skeptical," she says, leaning against the doorframe. She looks exhausted. It's not just the kind of tired you get from working third shift, but an exhaustion that permeates every fiber of her being. Life hasn't been kind to her. It's given her every sort of bad day it could potentially throw her way.

"I'm here now. Did you want to grab a shower and then go out for lunch? You look like you could use some sunshine," I say, hoping she'll say yes. It's selfish of me, but getting out of the house might mean we can talk without getting angry. Being in public could mean we have a conversation that doesn't end with her walking away in tears or me running off to the garage.

To Hold

She nods and turns to go back upstairs, saying, "I'd like that. Give me ten minutes."

***

We're seated outside at a little bistro. The hostess fills the water glasses in front of us as Mom finally asks, "Why now? You came home when you were placed on leave after that shooting last winter, but other than that I feel like I've barely seen or heard from you since ..."

Her voice trails off and she reaches for her glass, but we both know what she was implying. Since Adrienne.

"I know," I say, but wait to continue when I see the waitress heading our way. We haven't looked at the menus yet, but I know my mom. I order two Julienne salads. "After ... Mom, I haven't known how to talk to you since. When Dad died, it was us, we had each other. I was still a kid finishing high school and you took on the roles of both parents. This was different. I don't think either of us had any idea how to comfort one another through Adrienne being killed. We didn't just lose her, but the baby, too, and we've both been living in a fog of devastation."

My throat feels sandpaper rough and I reach for my water.

"Is that what we're calling it? A fog of devastation?" she questions, a hint of snark to her tone, before sighing and considering her words. "We're so out of touch with one another. What happened to make you come home now, Max? Other than your wedding anniversary coming up, this trip was completely out of the blue, especially for someone like you. Rarely do you make plans on a whim."

I can't say she's wrong. It's been a long time since I was spontaneous.

"My new chief wants me teaching self-defense and after talking to a friend and his wife, I decided I needed to do it." I look from my hands, clasped together on the table as if in prayer, to my mom. She knows how Adrienne and I met, but more than that she knows how I carry the guilt with me everywhere. "I came home for closure."

M.L. Pennock

Chapter Twelve

Stephanie

"Her hormones are giving me whiplash."

"She's been like this all afternoon. I'm not sure how to fix whatever the hell I did wrong," Brian says pulling the collar of his T-shirt up to wipe the sweat from his lip. "All I tried to do was put the crib together."

I've never seen him this frustrated, but it's kind of refreshing. Considering Brian always seems to be the levelheaded one, it's a little out of character for a crib to get the best of him. He makes furniture as a hobby, for crying out loud.

"I should have just drawn and built one from scratch instead of this bullshit," he says, angrily throwing his arm in the air and whipping the instruction manual against the wall.

"It's a crib, Bri. Count to ten and calm down. Go for a walk around the block or something. I've got this," I say reaching for the screwdriver. "It's not my first time putting prefab furniture together. I mean, who do you think put all those bookshelves together at my house?"

He throws his arms up in the air again, muttering something under his breath about independent women, and walks out of what's supposed to be the nursery. A few minutes later I hear the front door open and close, then the soft sound of feet coming up the stairs.

I can feel her standing in the doorway staring at me.

"You know, I know it's kind of crazy around here lately with you trying to get everything in order at work for your maternity leave and trying to make sure you guys have everything ready for the baby, but you need to calm down with him. He's trying to help and you're kind of being a bitch," I say as I start piecing together the crib. "He did this once before. He did it with someone he didn't think even cared about him, Stell, so instead of burning holes in the back of my head, go for a walk with your husband and let me do my thing."

I hear her sniffle. Kneeling next to me, Stella lays her head on my shoulder and breathes in deeply as she wraps an arm around my waist.

"Stephie?"

"Yeah, Stell?"

"I'm scared. He's done the parenting thing. He's had a newborn in the house. He's good at being a dad," she says lifting her head, her eyes searching mine. "What if I fail?"

I laugh and, dropping the screwdriver, twist my body to envelope my sister in a tight hug. In my most loving tone, I break the news to her. "You're going to fail. A lot. That's the only way you learn, Stell."

"I hate when you're smarter than me. This baby is going to be a genius. It's been syphoning my brain cells for months," she says. I feel her laughter as it works through her body on its way out, the sound infectious and amazing as we sit together in the bedroom she's going to bring my niece or nephew home to. Catching her breath, she says quietly, "I'm going to fail and that's okay. Right?"

"Absolutely. Because when you fail there will be at least five of us here at all times to help you back up." And I mean it.

"How's your therapy going?"

The change of subject never surprises me. Stella likes to keep me on my toes, and the talk about failure was the perfect segue for her to ask about my own shortcomings. It's not that she wants to pick apart my mental health; she's my only sister and truly concerned about my well-being.

"You know, I've learned a lot. She's helped me work through some of the shit in my past. My first session was really good and I haven't missed one since I started, so thank you for setting me up with her. Doc's really good at what she does," I say as I get back to work. "I'm signing up for a self-defense class at the community center."

"You are?" she asks, more shocked than amused, but there's a sparkle in her eye like she has a secret. I ignore it and explain that we were hired to do some work for the center, which is how I learned about the class in the first place.

"I feel like it's what I need right now. I can either continue to make poor choices and keep feeling like a victim or I can take control of my future and get on a better path. I'm choosing a better path."

"You know, Steph, you're the only one who thinks you're a victim," she says playing with the hem of her shirt.

I look at her thoughtfully for a second before continuing on to the next step in the manual. "I've heard that somewhere. I just have to prove it to myself."

Grabbing my shoulder and pushing herself up from the floor, she towers over me with her giant belly. I reach up to give her tummy a rub, thankful she's never protested my touchy-feely moments, and feel the misshapen landscape of her abdomen. "Is your belly always that hard?"

"Sometimes. Nothing timeable so I'm pretty sure it's just practice for the big day," she says. Poking the spot I was rubbing, Stella says, "That, however, I think is a butt. Or an elbow. Do you need any help? If not I'm going to go search for Brian and get a burrito. Maybe a pineapple. I think I want a smoothie."

Laughing, I shoo her out the door. "I'm fine. Go make sure he's calmed down. Hold his hand and do all that cutsie, happy couple stuff while Mom's got Britt for the day."

I listen for her to get to the bottom of the stairs, hear the jingle of her house keys and the door open and close, then I'm alone. It's just me and my thoughts, but I'd rather not think. I pop my earbuds in and piece by piece the crib comes together.

Standing in the middle of the nursery, I feel a weird sense of accomplishment.

"It's just a crib," I remind myself. But really it's so much more than that, and I reach for the mattress in the corner of the room, dropping it gently into the bed. "It's just a crib."

Chapter Thirteen

Max

"Closure."

"Mom, did I tell you any details about the shooting last winter?"

"Not really. Just that you shot back in self-defense and were put on medical leave until the investigation was complete. I know how all that works. I don't need the details."

I keep my eyes on her face as I say, "It was Adrienne's killer," and watch as her pupils dilate slightly, the lids widen in shock, and her jaw goes slack. "The details are kind of important with this one. I left home with my chief's blessing because he knew I would follow him one way or another."

The words tumble from my mouth, all the things I've not told my mother since the day I buried my wife and son — how late night drinking turned into late night staring at my pistol, my obsession with finding Judson, how I picked up what was left of my life to hunt him down. I share with her that I found him only because of Stephanie and what he did to her, that I wasn't too late to save her. But still, I needed to come home to find peace before putting all the pieces back into place and feeling whole again.

"This girl you saved? Why did he go after her?" she finally asks, wiping tears from her cheeks before they fall into her untouched lunch.

"She's his type. Dark hair, medium height, athletic build. I don't think he was counting on her being mouthy and stubborn. He didn't expect her to be a fighter, but when he realized it, it's like he took on the challenge and upped his game. He became aggressive with her more quickly than he had with Adrienne," I say. A smile weaves its way across my face and I say quietly, "She's so stubborn."

Mom's arm moves in my peripheral and I look up as she reaches across the small table to lift my chin with her fingers.

"You care about this girl." It's a statement. Then she's smiling, too. "You look content, Max. This Stephanie woman, she's what brought you home isn't she?"

She releases my chin and I let my head drop slightly.

"Adrienne wouldn't want you to stop your life just because she's not here, honey. Get your closure and start living your life again. Stop blocking out the people who love you, though. Like me," she says. "And for Christ's sake, teach that class your chief wants you to. You worked so hard to go from angry kid to harnessing that anger and teaching others how to do the same. You can help people, not just by protecting their community, Max."

I wish it was that easy and I finally look at my mom.

"I've been avoiding Steph, Mom. I'm afraid once she knows about my past she's going to think I'm trying to replace Adrienne with her," I admit. "Plus, my partner already thinks I have a hero complex and basically accused me of trying to fix her even though I've kept my distance."

"If she's as stubborn as you say she is, she won't let you openly avoid her for much longer or use her as a replacement. Give your heart a chance to heal and give her a chance to know you, the real you, not just the police officer who came to her rescue," she says reaching for her fork. The food has sat while we've talked and now I'm not even hungry. I just want to go back to the house and hide away in the garage. "Besides, you're a cop. Of course you have a hero complex. You've always wanted to save the world, Super Max, but deep down you know you can't save everyone and haven't let that control your everyday life."

At least not until Adrienne died. I let the negatives of being a hero get in the way of the positives. We both know it now that I've told her how I felt in those months after she was gone.

"I hope you're right," I say, then laugh when it hits me what name she used. "Super Max. You haven't called me that since I was twelve."

***

I've taken time to stop in and see my old chief and hang out with some of the guys, but I need to make up for lost time with my mom, too, so I spent most of my time at the station turning down offers for dinner and drinks.

Friday was a full moon and Mom had the night off, so we spent time going through old boxes of my dad's stuff. I never realized before how packed the upstairs of our garage was until we started carrying boxes down. All but one of the boxes was labeled and we waited to open that until it was the last one left.

"Mom, did you know what was in here?" I ask pulling the first photo album out.

"I had an idea. They weren't in any of the other boxes, so it makes sense he'd put all of this in an unmarked one. That's your father for you," she says, smiling as she leans into the box. "Here you go, these need to go with you."

It's not until the ball chain is over my head and the tags are clinking against my chest that I realize this box isn't just a box of photos — it's every memory he had from the time he was drafted until he came home from Vietnam and was discharged from service. We pull one memory after another out until all that's left are his fatigues and dress uniform folded carefully in the bottom. I would ask why these things aren't in his footlocker, but I know it's because he dragged it into the house for me to use as a toy box when I was a kid and it still sits in my old bedroom.

I lift the clothing and hear a rustling sound as an envelope slides from between the pants, landing at the bottom of the box. My mom's name scrawled in my dad's handwriting across the discolored paper catches my eye.

Picking it up, I turn it over and see he wrote on the bottom of the backside as well. "Disregard. I'm home now."

"Why didn't he just throw this away?" I ask, more to myself than Mom.

"What's that?" She walks up behind me and peeks around my arm. "Oh. That. I never had to read that. Has it even been opened?"

It hasn't, but I don't have the words. I know soldiers write these in the event they don't make it home, but since my dad served long before I was born I never gave it any thought he might have had to write one as well. Now the proof is in my hands.

"He didn't die in combat and he told me what he wrote all those years ago, but I still don't want to read that," she says, quietly. "You can open it, though, if you'd like to. I don't have anything to hide."

I would like to, but I look at her to get a real feel for how she wants me to go about this. "Are you sure?" I ask, and she nods her head.

"There's nothing in there I don't already know. I'll be in the kitchen when you're done. Come down for coffee and we'll talk." And she kisses me on the head before walking toward the door. "We all need closure once in a while, Max, just please remember that. Everyone has secrets."

***

Jeanie,

Every account number, lock combination, and map you might need in the event of my death is in the safe in our bedroom closet. I wrote the combination for the safe on the underside of the center drawer of your mother's roll top desk in the living room.

You already know all this but it's easier than writing a final farewell. I'm only writing this letter because they tell me I should. I don't want to, though, and I don't plan on you ever having to read it. Not unless you want to. These are not my final words to you.

You and that little bump are my everything. I'll be coming home to you and Baby E as soon as I can. If I don't make it before he arrives, tell him his daddy loves him. Tell him every day for me. Keep some for yourself.

Love,
Davey

Carrying the letter between my fingers, I walk back into the house and stand in the kitchen doorway. She's sitting at the table, a steaming cup of coffee between her clasped hands, and she hardly acknowledges me. She stares into her cup like it holds all the answers I'm looking for to questions I didn't know I had.

She speaks first.

"Your dad and I got married young. You know that. We were seventeen, it was the late sixties, and we wanted to spend forever together. We'd both worked since we were kids, so there was enough money for a down payment on the house. His parents helped him buy the Chevelle so we could get around. We weren't rich in money, but what we had in love made up for where we were short for groceries," she says, still looking into the well of her cup as I stand staring at her. "It wasn't easy. I finished nursing school and started working on the hospital's maternity floor. He kept working on the family farm."

The tears start to fall, the sun shining through the window catching them as they drop silently from her cheeks.

Finding my voice, I finally ask, "Who is Baby E?"

Pulling in a ragged breath I watch her lift her head, her eyes a deep chocolate like mine reflect an emptiness she's hidden for years. They're full of hurt and grief. They're the same eyes I've seen staring back at me in every mirror for five years.

"I had just started at the hospital when I found out we were having a baby. It was a few weeks after that when they drew Davey's number. He missed the entire pregnancy, but loved that baby with every fiber of his being."

To Hold

I want so badly to ask what happened, why everything she was saying was past tense when I could tell she had been sucked into the middle of a memory. But I wait.

"Your dad finished his tour and was discharged, but he was coming home with a heavy heart. Your brother was stillborn. Your father came home from a war to cry at a tiny grave instead of hold his son for the first time," she says lifting a shaky hand to brush the tears from her cheeks. "We couldn't replace Eliot, and we didn't want to. We were afraid it would happen again if we tried for another baby, so we didn't. I switched to the emergency department when I went back to work. It was busy, the long hours kept my mind off what we'd lost and I put all my effort into saving everyone else. You're not the only one with a hero complex, Max."

I let myself laugh. I let her hear it. She needs to hear it.

"So that's where I get it from?"

"Yeah, I guess so." She reaches out for me from her seat at the table and I walk into her arms as she presses her face to my stomach. "And then God gave us you. We'd decided we would just work and grow old, but He had other plans. Your dad, he cherished every single day of my pregnancy. He worshipped the thought of being a dad. He didn't care if we had a boy or a girl, he just wanted to hear those first cries. When he did, he bawled like a baby himself. We both did."

I pause my thoughts to let her words sink in.

"Mom? Why didn't you tell me?"

I feel her body lift away from me and I kneel down to look at her. She reaches up to hold my unshaven face between her hands, a sad smile playing at the corners of her eyes, before she speaks again. "We didn't talk about those things back then, Max. Eliot had been born a decade before you came along, but didn't have the chance to take a first breath. I buried my hurt from losing him the day you were born and focused on you. I kept that hurt locked up until the night Adrienne was brought to the ER and I watched my grandson die. It tore me and you apart. It shredded both of us — you because you lost your family and me because I know that kind of pain. I wasn't going to tell you about your brother to help you cope. Knowing about him wouldn't have diminished your pain."

Our relationship had unraveled when Adrienne died, but for years I've thought it was because I didn't want to open up and talk to her about it. I told her more than once we couldn't change the past so just drop it. We couldn't bring her back.

What she didn't tell me was she understood those undeniable truths.

"Everyone has a past. Everyone has secrets, Super Max. Don't let those secrets eat you," she says brushing my own tears from my face, tears I didn't know were there until she moved them. "Don't live in the past. You have too much love to offer. Let us both have the closure you came home to find."

Chapter Fourteen

Stephanie

Stepping out the front door, I pull the zipper up higher on my running top and squat to lace up my sneakers. Squinting into the sun as it's just starting to burn the dew off the grass, I welcome the chill in the air from the low overnight temperature. It wakes me up more than coffee does these days and I breathe in the slightest scent of fall winding its way through the breeze.

It's Sunday morning and I hit the ground running before Tommy's even out of bed. He's been keeping his distance as best he can, but it's still too soon to spend more than work related hours with him. I need to keep my head clear and he just fogs it all up despite the "I love you but I'm not in love with you" conversation that finally happened. It was late the other night when we had "the talk," and only after some major high-fiving and hugging when the Indians won their first game out of the last nine they played. I don't even like Cleveland. I'm pinstripes and Bronx Bombers all the way. It's basically war in the house when they play against each other.

Regardless, the hugging commenced and I had to put an end to it because, after a few beers, it was treading on dangerous ground again. I felt like we were in a good place for me to be calm and tell him how I don't feel. We talked and when we were done we had come to an understanding that nothing romantic can happen, at least that's the agreement I made with him.

Hopefully that's the agreement he was making with me.

I don't want to consider the possibility that he believes otherwise, nor do I want to dwell on it. Dwelling on stupid shit isn't something I have time for, so I'm trying to act like myself.

My old self, that is.

It's going to be a challenge, but I miss the Steph I was before Darren and I deserve to allow myself to be whole again. He may have bruised me and broken parts of me, but I'm strong enough to beat back the fear and fight my way out of that darkness I've let become all-consuming.

I'm a survivor.

"Survivor," I mutter to myself as I come up out of a stretch, pop my earbuds in, and take off toward campus.

My muscles warm with each step. I ignore the tight feeling in my thighs as I take a set of stairs between two buildings, sprinting to the top and not slowing once I get there. Winding my way through campus, I follow the path until I come to the bridge over University Avenue. I push myself harder and take the steps two at a time, pounding my feet into the metal and feeling it vibrate beneath my body.

With each step I'm taking back a little bit of myself. With each footfall I'm redefining who I am. I know it'll take more than this, though, because running only does so much, and it's going to take more than continuing my sessions with Doc.

Tomorrow, I'll go sign up for the self-defense class.

Reaching the sidewalk, I slow my run to an easy jog on the return home and turn to head back down Main Street on a mission for coffee.

Opening the door to the Jumping Bean, I hear Tommy drop my name and look up to see him leaning against the counter with his back to me.

"I'm living with her, we have common interests, I'm a nice guy, but no to a relationship? I'm starting to feel like a damn toy."

I clear my throat when he finishes his little tirade and watch the heat creep up the back of his neck.

"Fuck. Damn you, Greg. You could have warned me," he says under his breath, but I still hear him. He doesn't turn to acknowledge me before pushing away from the counter and making a beeline for the kitchen, leaving Greg and I staring at his retreating form.

Greg hands me a to-go cup, complete with a sad look on his face, and shakes his head.

"I thought he understood where I was coming from," I say.

"He will. Eventually. I've been where he is and it's not easy. You two have gotten close. For T, the next natural step is an actual relationship," he says solemnly. "I'm not saying you tore his heart out, but you definitely put a chink in his armor, Steph."

I take a sip of my coffee and set a couple dollars on the counter.

"Well, I guess he's just going to have to buff it out and give it a good spit shine. There's someone out there for him, but it's not me." I turn away from the counter and hope he understands when I turn back long enough to say, "I'm his roommate and business partner. We're family. It can't be any more than what it already is," before pushing back through the door and into the sunshine.

We all deal with heartache in our own ways.

Stella worked nearly non-stop, drank a lot of wine, and ate cupcakes when Keith left.

To Hold

Anytime I let myself get too close to get hurt, I threw myself into working and working out.

Stella's best friend Caryn has religiously become a social pariah when she's gone through a breakup.

The Three Amigos are essentially defunct members of society when we've gotten our hearts plucked straight from our chests and crushed by someone we trusted them with.

It makes sense that Tommy would stand around at work with Greg and try to do exactly what we've done — understand where the opposite sex is coming from. But first, always first, blame the crap out of them for making you feel that way.

"Totally makes sense," I say out loud as I walk down Main and turn left onto the first side street I come to in hopes the longer route back to the house will help me get over my frustration. What's worse is it's not even frustration with Tommy. It's with myself. He's simply reacting to the position I put him in.

I feel myself trying to rationalize further how he's dealing with a breakup that's really a non-breakup and stop myself. Literally. I stop walking and ground myself before the anxiety grabs on and won't let go. I take a long sip of my coffee and then bend and set it on the sidewalk to untie my sneakers. Pulling my feet out of my shoes and slipping off my socks, I notice him standing at the back of a car with a duffle bag slung over his left shoulder. He's got a pair of sunglasses covering his eyes and a baseball cap on, but I'd know his jawline anywhere, stubble and all.

I stand slowly, picking my cup up from the sidewalk as I do, and wonder if he's noticed me or if I can slink away without drawing his attention. I'm a half-second too late in wondering, though, as I watch his right hand reach up and pull those sunglasses from his face.

I don't move.

What if he's like a T-rex and can't actually see me unless I move? That one silly thought, mixed with the leftover adrenaline from my run and then the unnecessary anxiety about Tommy, starts a fit of laughter in the back of my throat.

I can't stop it.

It's like an avalanche of emotion.

And he's like a tiger on the prowl.

My laughter seeps out of me as he slinks closer, one eyebrow cocked in a questioning manner, until we're standing almost toe-to-toe. I wipe tears from the corners of my eyes with my shirtsleeves and when I open them again, I'm staring into deep brown pools filled with a combination of concern and humor.

I take a minute to compose myself, closing my eyes and opening them again wondering why he hasn't said anything. He stands there looking at me like he's trying to memorize something. Like he's making a memory of me. It feels like an eternity before I find my voice and break the silence.

Almost in a whisper, I say to him what I've wanted to say for months. "You've been avoiding me."

"I know. I'm going to try to stop doing that," he says just as quietly. Hooking his sunglasses into the collar of his T-shirt, he holds his right hand out to me as a smile slides into place across his lips. "Hi. I'm Max. I'm sort of new in town still and wondered if you might give me the grand walking tour one evening?"

I slide my hand into his and feel the same frenetic energy coming off him that I felt in April when he walked me home. I wonder why it took him so long to ask.

Chapter Fifteen

Max

When I saw her standing at the end of my driveway, I was pretty sure she was a figment of my imagination.

I left Ohio early this morning with her on my mind after agreeing with my mom that I'd set myself free from my past, or at least the parts of the past holding me back from finding some sort of happiness. I promised to call home more. She plans to use her vacation time in the fall to come to New York. We each promised to try harder to get back to where we were before our tragedies collided.

Those promises aren't empty. They're the kind that will make our relationship stronger, which is exactly what she needs right now. I need it, too. I've been spending too much time alone and I'm not the best at keeping myself company.

I swore to her I would stop making it impossible for Steph to have conversations with me. I wouldn't keep turning and running away each time I saw her somewhere. Over the last several months, I've left barbecues at Brian and Stella's when she shows up and ended conversations at the coffeehouse early because I didn't want to interfere in her life. I didn't want to be "that" guy. I didn't want her to think I was hovering.

"It's a date," she says. I hear the smile in her voice before I see it on her lips.

"A date." I roll the words around in my mouth, testing them out. It's been a long time since they've been part of my vocabulary.

Her hand stills in my palm, but the warmth radiates up my arm as though there's a fire building between our fingers.

"Well, not a real date. I mean, I'm going to show you all the amazing secrets here and it'll be great. Not a date date," she backpedals and stumbles through her words as her face turns a shade of pink I've never seen on her before. She stares at me, as though she's unsure how to make the moment less awkward ... so I smile. Relief washes across her features. Her hand squeezes mine ever so slightly. She releases the breath she was holding. Quietly she says, "Unless you would like it to be a date date. Then, yes."

"I think I'd like that," I reply, curious as to what kind of date Steph would appreciate most. "Dinner or just dessert?"

"Is that a real question?" She drops her hand from mine and I instantly miss the warmth. The stunned expression on her face makes me wonder if anyone has ever given her the option to choose how a date should begin and I'm glad I asked.

"I take dessert very seriously, Stephanie. If we were to go out to dinner somewhere, who's to say we'll save room for it if the meal is really good? And if the meal isn't good, then why would we choose to stay for dessert? So, yes. It's a real question."

She scrunches up her nose, humming under her breath as she mulls it over.

"Would you be okay with dessert to go and we can enjoy it while I show you around? There's a great bakery a little further up by the canal. We can start your tour from there," she says.

"I work tonight and the next four. How does Friday work for you?"

A smile reaches all the way to her eyes. Friday it is, and I can't wait for it to get here.

Chapter Sixteen

Stephanie

The high from Max taking the time to actually talk to me was more than enough to keep me from looking for something to dim the pain of the past. For a few days at least. I haven't tried to drink myself to sleep since Saturday.

But the reality is that while I know Max is "safe," I'm going on a date in two days and the last time I went on anything resembling a date I was assaulted in a dark alley by someone else I once thought was safe.

Max isn't Darren, though, and I need to try to remind myself that I'm in control. That's the conversation I had with my therapist this afternoon, and I agree with her regardless of how difficult it seems to be for my subconscious to get on board with the idea.

That's why I'm blaming my subconscious for what I'm doing right now.

The hard liquor section pulled me to it and now I'm stuck trying to decide between Jack and Jim and Johnnie.

It's a reflex. Months of climbing into something to make the nights easier have caused knee-jerk reactions. I'm angry? I'll have a drink. I'm anxious? Let's open a bottle of wine. I'm frustrated? A mixed drink gives me the ability to laugh it off. It's nothing anyone has forced me to do, but it's getting more and more difficult to accept the lie I tell myself, that this isn't a problem.

I know it's a problem and knowing is the first step. It's not quite half the battle, but I'm aware I can't drink every time I'm faced with something that chips away at my happy-go-lucky façade. Eventually the façade will fall away and reveal the broken pieces that haven't yet been glued back into place.

Until that happens Jim wins for tonight, but just the little bottle.

I pay for my purchase as the sun is setting behind the buildings on Main Street, a deep blazing orange that reminds me of the fire that used to burn deep inside me. There was a passion in my soul that I didn't think could ever be squelched, but too many people sucked from that tit and now I question, what passion could I possibly have after all of this? There isn't much left.

I twist the cap from the bottle hidden in the telling brown bag and lift it slowly to my lips as I walk through town in the shadows of buildings I've grown up frequenting. The fire burns its way down my throat and into my empty belly.

I can't go home tonight. I can't face Tommy ... not with whiskey on my breath.

Chapter Seventeen

Max

It's late, I'm tired, and my shift isn't even close to over, but here I am in the middle of the night walking around the park because it's the end of summer and people get stupid.

A call came in that someone was in the gazebo at the playground and, naturally, I'm the one to check it out because I'm the new guy. I've been here almost a year and I'm somehow still the new guy, to the point some of the older officers actually refer to me as "New Guy" still, instead of my name.

I stroll up and check the gazebo to make sure it's empty of loiterers before moving on when I hear someone hiccup a short distance away.

Shining my flashlight around, I spot her sitting alone on the swings, slightly slumped over with her hair draped down the sides of her face covering her profile.

"Ma'am, you can't be at the park after dark. I'm going to have to ask you to leave," I state as authoritatively as I can but she remains sitting with her head hanging down. She doesn't seem to notice me. "Ma'am?"

"You. Can't. Make me," she says, lifting a bottle to her mouth. She doesn't turn to look at me or get up from the swing she's sitting on, but raises her head enough that her hair falls away from her face.

Steph.

I couldn't force myself to move even if I tried right now. I just watch as she pushes back with all her might and flies into the night, pumping her legs faster and faster like a bird trying to escape a cage.

Is it wrong for me to climb into the swing next to this girl I should be escorting home? Or is that small town acceptable?

Rightfully, I should be making her stop the swing. I should be taking her back home or arresting her for something — public intoxication, loitering, being stubborn — but I just can't. Not tonight. Not after catching a glimpse of her when she left the therapist's office at the beginning of my shift tonight. I watched her again make the trip from one side of Main Street to the other but pulled away from the curb before she walked into any of the stores.

I didn't have to watch; I knew exactly where she was going.

I've been there.

I don't get hung up on the details as I urge my legs to move and make my way to the swing beside her. I sit down, careful not to catch any of my gear on the chains, and push off, hurrying to catch up to her.

"You're probably going to be the reason I get fired someday," I say as we pass one another.

"Shut up, Max. Davis won't fire you. You're too cute in your uniform. The older guys just don't like you because you're too damn cute," she yells as we pass again. Each sentence ends with a hiccup and a giggle. "They should give you a community service medal for dealing with me."

"Now why would they do that?"

"Because I am a train wreck and you keep trying to save me," she says. Dragging her feet in the stones under the swing, Steph slowly comes to a stop and drops the empty bottle at her feet. "I'm a wreck, Officer Wyatt. You should just arrest me."

I watch her hold her arms out to me, her wrists together as though she's surrendering.

"I'm not going to arrest you, Steph." I come to an abrupt stop and stand up from the swing to walk over to where she's sitting. Kneeling down in the smooth pebbles, I push her hands down into her lap. "What happened today?"

The little bit of Stephanie I've gotten to know is damn near unbreakable. Even at her worst, she was solid. The girl looking up at me from under those dark eyelashes looks shattered and it kills me to watch fresh tears trickle from the corners of her eyes.

"Do you want me to call Stella?"

"Do you want to see my sister lose her shit?" And she smiles at me through her pain, sobering a little at the thought. "It's a sweet gesture, but think about it Max. The last time you called my sister, I was in the back of an ambulance. You call her now — in the middle of the damn night, no less — and she's going to freak. She'd probably go into labor from the stress."

She has a point and it's a really good one.

"So, what are our options then, Miss Barbieri?"

"Coffee. There was a lot more whiskey in that little bottle than I expected and I'm not much of a whiskey drinker."

"Actually, it's bourbon. You really aren't a hard liquor kind of lady, are you?" I ask, a smile creeping onto my lips as her eyes widen in surprise.

"No, I guess not," she says.

To Hold

Still kneeling in the stones at her feet, her hands resting beneath mine on her thighs, I laugh. "At least throw the bottle away so I don't have to ticket you for littering," I say, patting her knee and standing to pull her from the swing. "Let's go get you the biggest coffee we can find, Steph."

"It's going to taste like sludge no matter where we go. You are aware my brother-in-law owns a coffeehouse, right?" she asks as we make our way slowly back across the park to my cruiser.

"I might have been there once or twice," I jest.

It isn't until we're almost halfway to the car that I notice her arm is hooked through mine and a rush of emotion surges through me. The last time I held her like this was when I walked her home from the wedding. I'm sinking deeper into those thoughts and reveling in the feel of her body being close to mine again when my radio comes to life.

"I guess this means play time is over?" she quietly questions without looking at me.

"By the sounds of it, they need me," I whisper back as she lays her head on my shoulder, sighing deeply.

"Go. Before you get yourself in trouble, go save someone else. I'll be around tomorrow. You can save me then," she says lifting her head and unwinding her arm from mine. "Or on Friday when I give you the walking tour I promised. With my luck, I'll trip and fall in the canal."

In the split second after she pulls away, it feels like my heart stops. Without thinking, I kiss the top of her head and walk to my waiting police car.

I call Tommy once I'm in the car and on my way to the car accident that interrupted my heroics with Stephanie. It's not even that I'm being heroic — I was there to do my job. Everything else was simply because she's Steph.

I've gotten to know bits and pieces of her over the nine months since her attack and getting to know her means understanding her. I'm trying to understand her better. She isn't the type of woman who likes to admit she needs to be saved. She's more of the "I could have handled it" type, so I know calling Tommy might be the wrong move, especially considering the friction between them I've heard about from Brian, but I've done it anyway.

Waiting for the call to connect and then listening to it ring makes my stomach tighten.

"You're a dick, Max. I was sound asleep," he answers groggily. "What could you possibly want right now? It's almost two in the morning."

"I got a loiterer call earlier. Steph was down at the playground killing a bottle of bourbon and playing on the swing set," I say nonchalantly and hear him curse.

"What the hell was she doing there?"

"I don't know, but she's okay. I just need you to go get her." Silence creeps up the line and I know he's going to ask why I didn't bring her home, so I beat him to the punch. "We were on our way to my car so I could take her for a cup of coffee and bring her home when I got called out. I'm on my way to a MVA on the other side of town."

"You just left her there? In the middle of the night? What the fuck, man."

"Tommy, you're screeching like a girl. Get out of your bed and go get her. Don't make her feel like she did something wrong, either," I scold. "Just get her home."

Then in typical Tommy fashion, he repeats what I said in a mocking tone that makes my ears burn. "Whatever, man, I'll go find her and do your job for you," he drawls sleepily.

"Yeah, fuck you. I'll see you in the morning for my coffee," I say and disconnect the call just short of calling him a bitch as I roll up on the crash site.

***

I arrive and just as quickly leave the accident. It's really more of a fender bender. I wasn't even needed. I shouldn't have had to leave her standing there and the guilt has gnawed at me since I realized it. But, this is my job — responding to accidents, breaking up fights, arresting bad guys — it's what I signed up for.

If Tommy didn't find her, he would have called me back. I would have gone and found her. I would have taken her home. Still, the worry has practically chewed its way through my stomach. Instead of parking along Main Street to wait for the sun to rise on my double shift, I've driven past the home she shares with T more times than I normally would.

Each time I pass the house I ease off the gas and crane my neck trying to see if there are any lights on.

It's as if one more drive past will ensure me she's inside those four walls, safe and sleeping.

To Hold

At the break of dawn, I make my final trip down her street knowing Tommy will be heading to the coffeehouse soon and the last thing I want is him accusing me of creeping around after letting her down the night before.

I'm not lurking, but I really don't know what I'm doing either.

I see her face every time I close my eyes even if I haven't seen her in days.

We were thrown together at the most inopportune time and, despite everything in me previously saying I shouldn't be so close to her and so emotionally invested, my heart tells me the exact opposite. I haven't felt that way in a long time — like my path was meant to cross someone else's.

Taking a deep breath, I pull into the station and park. Staring at the brick wall in front of me, I feel the questions starting in the back of my mind, the same ones Brian's asked me at one time or another, and I answer each one as they surface.

Am I infatuated with her? No. If I was obsessing I wouldn't have been actively avoiding her for so long.

Have other guys gone through this? I guess that depends on how deep their survivor's guilt runs.

Am I interested in her as more than just the girl I saved? Yes, without a doubt ... yes.

Rubbing my hands over my weary eyes I try to remember why I keep working the night shifts. She's the reason. It doesn't matter that it makes me antsy. I still do it. I ask for it, even.

I give myself a few minutes to drown in the silence of my cruiser and find myself somewhere in the past.

Before Thanksgiving I was fine working under the cover of darkness, but then her screams tore through the night and now I feel like that's where I belong even if it's the last place I want to be. It's as though I'm trapped within that memory of a dark haired girl, beaten and broken and bloodied, but beautiful and strong beneath it all.

The similarities between Steph and Adrienne end at hair color and body type.

Too many things about her at the time reminded me of Adrienne and I wonder sometimes if I latched onto the idea that Stephanie was brought into my life because Adrienne was ripped from it so forcefully. I admitted as much to myself when I was in Ohio visiting my mom. It's kept me up at night thinking Steph may have been put in Darren Judson's path for me to save because I was unable to save my own wife from him. After all, I came to New York to hunt him down, knowing he came back to where it all started. A creature of habit. He met Adrienne when they were students here, only back then he went by his actual name, Damien Judson. She stayed with him, with his abuse and violence, through two moves until they ended up in Cleveland and she finally had enough.

She broke free and flourished. God, she was stunning when she was happy. I made her happy. We made each other better. Everything with Adrienne seemed to be better at first.

Then he decided she was still his and he stole her life as though he had a right to take that last breath from her.

I came here to seek revenge and a fresh start. To bury, either in the ground or in an eight-by-eight cell, the man who murdered my wife. It was the only way I would be able to redeem myself for failing her. I let her down by not protecting her, by not teaching her more about protecting herself.

My chief has tried to understand, but survivor's guilt is difficult to comprehend unless you've been through the surviving aspect of it. Asking Chief to permanently put me on third shift was easy enough in the beginning since I was already awake contemplating all the ways I didn't save Adrienne but was able to save Steph. I was spending every waking moment analyzing how I didn't save one but saved the other.

I haven't got the answer to that question. No one does.

At some point the night she was attacked, though, Stephanie Barbieri worked her way into my head. It's felt like I can't breathe, like I've been gasping ever since and trying to stay afloat wondering when a raft will come along for me to grasp.

When will I be the one who's saved?

What if I've been avoiding the savior all along?

I feel it each time she's close to me, in her touch and in the way her eyes seek the truth from mine. We both have closets and secrets and pain buried beneath our skin, but Stephanie ... she's more than what meets the eyes.

She's more than just a test.

She's fate doused in gasoline and lit on fire.

And I'm a moth attracted to the flame.

Chapter Eighteen

Stephanie

I watch him pull away from the curb, the blue and red lights coming on as he executes a perfect U-turn and heads in the direction of the car accident. Instead of trudging home I stay planted in that spot wondering if he'll come back this way. What would he think if I was still here waiting for him?

"He would think you lost your damn mind," I say into the breeze. "Maybe you have."

Shoving my hands into my pockets, I turn and head the opposite direction. Even if he doesn't come back this way while I'm making my way home I know he'll go past later.

He always does.

The thought of seeing his patrol car slowly roll past the house every night that he works teases a smile from my lips.

"What are you smiling at, loiterer?" My head snaps up and I come eye-to-chin with Tommy, and an exhausted grin that tells me Max called and woke him.

"You're supposed to be sleeping. You have to be up in a couple hours," I say as he wraps his arm around my shoulders pulling me closer to him, sealing me in his warmth.

Nodding his head, Tommy stares at our feet as we stroll toward home. "I was sleeping. Max has a very persistent ring, though, and he wanted me to make sure you got home safely after your little escapade to the playground. How much did you drink?"

"Not as much as I let Max believe. It was hard liquor though, so I'm still a little woozy. I was hiccupping earlier," I say slowly. I know the alcohol has affected me, but I was nursing that bottle most of the night. "You forget, Thomas, I have a stomach of steel."

"He said you finished a bottle of Jim. Steph ..." I hear it in that Tennessee drawl, in the way he says my name long and slow, like he's eating it alive. The lecture is coming. "I'm worried about you."

"I know." Shrugging his arm from my shoulder, I turn and walk up our driveway and around the back of the house to go in through the kitchen. He's close on my heels, so I just keep talking. "I'm working on fixing it, T. Just back off a little. Today was a rough day."

"What was more rough about today than any day last week, or the week before that? Stephanie, I'm finding you almost every evening halfway through a bottle of wine. A different wine every day," he says, pained. I can hear the hurt in his voice as he follows me up the stairs and I know I put it there because I won't talk to him about everything. We've worked through our differences and recent head-butting and are able to talk to one another again, but I'm still trying to keep myself at a safe distance. Arm's length is the best way. I don't want to drag him under with me.

I walk into the bathroom and close the door, locking it not because I'm afraid he'll come in but because I'm scared I'll go out. From the other side of the door I hear him plead with me. "Steph, please. Talk to me. Talk to Stella. Talk to the damn dog if that's what will work. Just talk."

I listen to him and then the silence before stripping off my shirt that smells like the therapist's office still, followed by my shorts and bra. I stare at my reflection and though it's been months since they healed, the bruises are all I see. They never go away. I can't stand to see myself naked because all I see is where he broke me. Tonight I can't see how strong I am. Tonight I let the demons win.

Before I let the tears think about falling, I grab my shirt and boxers from the back of the door and pull them on. My hair goes up into a high ponytail. I brush my teeth and take the time to floss. I check my face one more time, reach for the doorknob, and flip the switch. All that's left is the soft glow of the nightlight Stella bought for me when I moved in last year.

I hope he got tired of waiting for me to emerge, that taking my time gave him the idea to leave the hallway and go back to bed, but when I open the door and step from the bathroom all I feel are arms and he's pulling me into his chest.

"Please, Steph. Don't drown yourself. You're too good to sink into those feelings and let them win."

I know he's right, but today I convinced myself again that the only way to get any sleep is to numb the pain. I wait by the window for a lonely police car to idle past and finish whatever I'm drinking that night, and then I sleep.

I feel the warmth of Tommy's breath in my hair and wrap my arms tighter around his waist, the heat reminding me of Max's lips kissing the top of my head tonight like it was the most natural response to leaving.

I want to pretend this is Max in the hallway with me. That it's Max comforting me. My eyes drift closed as I listen to the steady rhythm of Tommy's heart, wishing he was someone else.

To Hold

I feel his heart beat more rapidly.

His breath catch.

And I get lost.

I let my head lift and my mouth drift until I'm caught up in his search for lips and a tongue and entry to the unrest in my brain, my body, my soul.

He's pulling me out of a fog and directly into reality, and it crashes around me as I gently push him away.

"I'm so sorry," I whisper, covering my betraying mouth, and leave him standing in the hall, confusion marring his beautifully tanned face, as I hurry back down the stairs and into the kitchen, the sanctuary.

It's always the hub of activity, the lifeblood of our family gatherings, and I find solace here. I probably always have, but instead of baking, I rearrange and sort everything. The kitchen is always my first victim — starting with the cupboard I keep all the herbs and spices in. I reach for the basil and sage, pulling them out and setting them on the counter. I'm reaching for the vanilla extract and curry powder when I hear him come in, invading my space, stirring up the calm I'm searching for in the midst of a sudden storm.

"It's the middle of the night. What are you doing, Steph?" his voice is laced with guilt, but I can't bear to look at his face, to see if it reflects the same emotion. I. Just. Can't. "What are we doing?"

"Max ..." His name is strangling me with all the things I haven't admitted, the secrets I haven't talked to Tommy about, not even in my drunkest moments. I've kept them locked up tight with the exception of doctor-patient confidentiality. "I can't do this with you when I want him. I love you, Tommy, but you know it's not that kind of love and I hate that I let myself get so fucked up that in the heat of the moment I hurt you."

I turn from the cupboards and scream at him. "I keep hurting you. Why do you let me hurt you!" Getting my anger out, the anger I have with myself, and feeling it torn from my chest feels less gratifying than I'd hoped.

His dejected eyes stare back at me though he's unaffected by my outburst ... like he was waiting for it to happen, like he needed it to come to this.

"Do you know why I let you hurt me?" It's rhetorical. He's the king of questions he doesn't want others to answer. "Because I care about you. That's why."

Standing at the island counter, leaning against it with his arms crossed, he's the epitome of serene. I hate myself for not being able to love him with more of me than what I've allowed. I can't even look at him. It hurts. My heart hurts for what I've been doing to him. He deserves so much more than this.

"I know you care. That's why I can't love you like you want me to." I turn and reach back into the cupboard. Oregano. Coriander. Sea salt. "I have too much going on in my head."

"So talk to me about it," he says, his voice rising. I can feel him. He's moved from his spot at the counter and I can feel the energy coursing off his body behind me.

Laying my hands palm down on the counter, I push my shoulders up around my ears and take a deep breath as he reaches out to touch my back.

"Steph, every time you feel like running away, every time you try to hide, I still come looking for you. That's what I do," he says, turning me around and gently pushing my chin up so he can see my eyes. "It's not just because I love you a little more than I should. It's not just because you're my brother's wife's little sister. It's because you're my friend, a really beautiful friend who I wouldn't mind making out with. A lot. Like, I would suck your face all day long if that would keep you happy and out of a bottle every night."

I can't help but laugh at him.

"You aren't mad at me?"

"Mad that you tried to devour my mouth upstairs and then ran away? How could I be angry about that? As much as it hurts knowing you don't want me and probably pretended I was Max, I still can't be mad. But you need to stop," he says pulling me in for a hug. "I can't be the guy you make out with all the time just because I'm safe. I know it's been hard, and we seem to take two steps forward and then leap backward, but we'll get through this. Whatever this is."

I feel his smile lift my hair as he rocks me back and forth. Wrapping my arms around his waist and breathing in the smell of his cotton T-shirt, I close my eyes.

"I'm sorry," I whisper against his chest as my silent tears slowly seep through the fabric clinging to his body.

"For what?"

"Everything."

"I haven't been around for everything. You don't owe me apologies," he says tightening his grip on me and resting his chin on my head. "The thing is, Steph, a lot of shit has happened to you but it isn't who you are. The things that have happened aren't what have made you into the person you are. It's how you've reacted that's turned you into ... you. Whatever happened, it's in the past. Can you move on from the past?"

Chapter Nineteen

Max

This is the first step in moving forward.

I turned down a double shift last night and came home. I slept at night like a normal person and actually stayed asleep for a solid six hours before waking in a cold sweat. Nightmares. Bad dreams. Call them what you will, they're terrifying all the same. Those are the only things I haven't figured out an escape from.

This one was different than the others, though, and I'm not sure I'll ever figure out what it was trying to tell me.

I was holding Steph's hand as we walked along the canal. Something was wrong. She was afraid of something I couldn't see. I felt like I was struggling to hold onto her as she was being ripped out of my grasp and when I woke up with the sheets wrapped around my legs, my hair soaked, and a tightness in my chest, I fell apart.

I carry a gun for a living. I don't wake up afraid of things. But this morning I did and instead of climbing down the stairs to the basement and beating the shit out of the heavy bag, I curled up on my side in my empty bed as I clutched my pillow and sobbed like a little kid.

And it felt good.

***

At noon I send her a text message. I've had her number for months; she's had mine just as long. This is the first time either of us has gone so far as to contact the other, though. That's not to say I haven't typed and deleted a hundred messages to her in the past, but this is the first time I've sent one without thinking twice before pressing "send."

Me: What time would you like to have dessert this evening? Am I picking you up or would you prefer to meet somewhere?

Simple and easy and I've effectively put the ball in her court where it needs to be. Then I wait. I pace back and forth before I give in to the urge to do something with my hands other than switch the phone from one to the other.

It feels like hours have gone by when my phone vibrates in the back pocket of my jeans. My head's under the hood of the Chevelle and when I feel the phone go off I stand too quickly, slamming my head into the metal.

Cussing, I grab a rag and wipe the grease and oil from my hands before reaching into my pants to see if it was Steph who texted. Glancing down at the phone and rubbing the back of my head, I hear it.

The softest sound.

"Is your head okay?"

With one hand still on my head, phone in the other, I lean to my right to see around the car and find a blonde-haired woman leaning against the open garage door. She's not familiar to me, and I grunt my response, irritated not only with smacking my head, but more because the text was from Brian instead of Steph.

"Yeah, I'm fine," I say pulling my hand from my head to check for blood. "Can I help you, ma'am?"

She's fidgeting and acting nervous, so I give her a minute to compose herself.

"I just moved into the split-level next door," she says, twisting her head to look over her shoulder at the house next door. I still haven't moved from my position at the back of the garage. "The movers got everything into the house for me, but I have a few rather large items I can't put where I want to because they're huge. I saw the open door and figured I'd come introduce myself to my new neighbor and beg for help."

I look at my watch and it's not even two in the afternoon yet. I breathe out a sigh, "Uh, yeah, I've got a little time."

Walking through the backyard, we do some awkward hand-shaking introductions. Sutton rambles nervously about being out on her own for the first time. The house she's moved into is a rental owned by her parents, but she had been living with a now ex-boyfriend closer to Rochester until recently. The breakup, which was something her parents wholly approved of since the boyfriend was a "douchebag" — her words — and freeloader, prompted her to move to Brockport where her business is and rent from her family.

"You're the bookstore owner?" I ask, holding the back door to the house open to let her enter.

 Chapter Twenty

Stephanie

I check my watch again, but I'm pretty certain I'm eating this box of cannoli by myself. He stood me up.

Pulling my shoulders back and standing up straight, I walk toward the water and plop myself down at the edge of the Erie Canal. Setting the box of treats next to me on the cement and placing my hands beside my legs, I cling to the wall and resolve that I will — barring any instance of complete sugar overload — eat the whole damn box myself. In one sitting.

I look at my watch. It's 7:05 p.m.

I check my phone. Not even a reply text to say 6 p.m. was going to work for him or that he was going to be late.

I shake my head, close my eyes, and lift my face to the sun slowly disappearing to my left before taking a deep breath and diving into the container of cannoli. I knew I should have gotten the bigger box.

Chapter Twenty-One

Max

So many modern conveniences and ways to charge electronics on the go, and yet I didn't realize until I walked back into my house at 6:45 that my phone hadn't made a single sound in hours. As soon as I saw what happened, I threw it on the charger and ran to the shower. In the five minutes I washed, dried, and found clean boxers, it had charged enough to turn on ... and that's when I saw it.

Steph: Meet me at 6 at the bakery on Water St. by the basin.

How do I tell her I was helping my neighbor and lost track of time? That my cell phone died while I was moving dressers and bookshelves around for another woman?

Then I see the one from Brian that I ignored while working on the car.

Bri: What's this I hear you're going on a date with my little sister?

I can't win — Brian's not going to be happy I lost track of time and Stella is likely going to threaten to harm me in some unimaginable way — but I can grovel. I'll beg Steph to let me attempt this again, and if I'm lucky she'll still be down by the basin. I trip over my feet pulling on clean jeans and knock a lamp off the top of my dresser as I'm tugging a polo shirt over my head. I look preppy, which is the last thing I am, but there's no time to worry about it. I pull socks on and shove my feet back into my boots, tying them as quickly as I can before grabbing my phone and rushing down the stairs and out to the bike.

My phone vibrates as I'm strapping my helmet on, but I don't take the time to check it. I have somewhere to be and I hope she waited for me.

***

I ease my way down Water Street looking for the bakery as I go. As soon as I see it, I pull into an empty spot on the street and shut the bike off. At almost quarter after seven, I'd be surprised if Steph waited for me near the bakery if she waited at all. But I'll take my chances.

The sweetshop door says "closed" and I cautiously follow the sidewalk around the building until I hear the gentle lapping of water against the canal basin. I stop short when I see a brunette sitting on the edge with her legs dangling over the side like she might jump in at any moment, a half empty container of dessert beside her, and wearing the heavy shoulders of a woman who was let down.

I pull my phone from my back pocket, turn the volume back on, ignore the new text from Brian and text her instead.

Me: I'm sorry I'm late. Did you save me any?

I hear the notification alarm and she reaches for the phone next to her. She reads it and I see her fingers moving deftly across the screen. A moment later my phone rings. I watch her back stiffen, knowing I'm close behind her, but she refuses to acknowledge me.

Steph: You don't deserve any dessert. These were for me to share with my date. He didn't show.
Me: He sounds like a real dick.
Steph: I hope not. I kind of like him.

She turns around and my heart skips, just a couple beats. Her hair falls softly down either side of her face, the sun shining to create a perfect halo that fits her like a crown. The moment would be perfect if I could remember how to breathe, but I can't catch my breath as I watch her lift her hand to carefully wipe the moisture from her cheek.

I'm the reason for those tears, I think. Slowly, I walk toward her and lower myself down beside her.

"Please, just give me a good excuse and I'll forgive you," she says quietly while staring at her hands, the skin picked at and nail polish chipped.

"I won't make up an excuse just for forgiveness. I'll tell you the truth," I reply just as quietly.

"The truth then, Max, because I was really looking forward to this." And she turns just enough for me to see up close the hurt in her eyes.

"The truth," I say and watch as her eyes widen while I tell her about the neighbor. She doesn't want to look at me, but makes sure to watch my eyes long enough for me to see the flash of anger that permeates her features and the jealousy raging below the surface. "My phone died before I got your text. When I got back home and saw it was almost seven and my phone wouldn't turn on, I rushed through a shower and came here. It charged just enough for me to know exactly where to go, but I was afraid you would have left."

Steph lays her head on my shoulder, letting out a ragged breath, and I soak up the moment as the sun dips lower on the horizon. To anyone else, we look like lovers taking in the sunset.

"I thought about leaving." She's staring across the canal, watching a couple walk hand-in-hand along the Heritage Trail on the other side as she speaks. "But then I decided maybe you were different than the others. You are different than the others. Most guys run away when they realize a girl has issues. You, though? You literally jumped on the swing next to me ... and then still showed up for dessert. Late, yes, but you showed up and there are extra points for just being here."

I smile into her hair, breathing in deeply the scent of her shampoo. It's something floral and calming, a smell I know but can't place. We watch the people coming and going on the opposite side of the water from us. It's comfortable, the silence and the closeness, and I have the odd sensation that this is what being whole again feels like.

Until both our phones start making noise simultaneously. She lifts her head from my shoulder and we look at one another before grabbing our phones.

Steph reads out loud the message on her screen as I silently read the same one on mine.

"Water broke. Contractions 3 min. apart. Meet us at hospital."

I stand up quickly and grab for her hand, pulling her to her feet as she reaches for the box of cannoli. Guiding her to the bike, I'm thankful I thought enough to grab the spare helmet before coming to find her tonight.

"Are you serious right now?" she asks in a huff. "I can't ride that thing."

"Yes. You can," I say grabbing the spare helmet and setting it on her head. "It's easy. I'll get on first and then you just swing your leg over and straddle ... just do what I do."

Her cheeks flush at the word "straddle" and her mouth falls slightly open. I can't help but feel like a teenager suddenly aware that everything I say can and will be turned into an innuendo.

"Dirty, dirty mind, Max."

I wonder if her lips taste like powdered sugar still or if she licked away all the evidence of her sweets bender.

"Me?" I scoff. "I saw your face. Just get on the bike so we can go." I climb on, placing the dessert she bought between my legs, and gesture to the space behind me. It feels like a thousand years pass too quickly as she places her hands on my shoulders, slips her legs over the seat, and grips the sides of my shirt. I reach behind me searching for her hands, pulling her arms around my ribs. It's more for safety than intimacy, but there's no denying there's a charge ignited when I hold her hands together at the base of my sternum. "Like this. It's easier for you to move with the bike if you move with me."

"It's my first time. Be gentle," she says quietly as I reach for the ignition.

"I'll always be gentle with you. I wouldn't have it any other way."

Chapter Twenty-Two

Stephanie

I'm on a motorcycle. What the fuck have I gotten myself into now? I could have just run the couple blocks back home to get my car, but no.

It was his eyes and the way they always convey safety, security. They pulled me into their mocha brown depths and held me captive. In April, I felt such desperation that I wanted to drown in those eyes. Today? I wanted to dive in and swim laps for all eternity when he looked at me while strapping on my helmet. All it took was one look, the quirk of his lips as he tried not to smile down at me over the play on words.

In less than an hour I went from sad and angry that I'd been stood up to wanting a second date, wishing he would hold my hand.

I want a kiss goodnight.

I've never wanted a kiss goodnight as much as I want one from Max Wyatt.

We can't talk to one another over the noise of the bike and the road beneath it, so I focus on feeling — the vibration of the motorcycle, the heat from his body, and an overwhelming emotion I haven't quite found a place for.

I've followed his instructions to hold him and allow the movement of the machine between our legs to dictate where my body should go and I find myself enjoying the ride. The air feels cool against my skin as evening nestles in across the community and we follow the signs to the hospital. It's not that far away, but it feels like time has slowed down as I cling to Max's chest, my heart racing against his back, as we close the distance between my sister and us.

Lifting my right arm carefully, I point him toward the non-emergency parking and he nods his head once in response as he angles the motorcycle toward the open lot.

Max finds a spot as close to the building as he can, turns the engine off and waits for me to climb off from behind him. My legs are shaky, though, and I try to catch my footing as I bring my right leg over the seat. But he catches me instead, grasping my left thigh high up near my ass with his left hand, as I set my right foot down and steady myself.

"Are you okay?" he asks, his voice raspy, like he's walked through an arid desert.

All I can do is nod, swallowing back that deceitful emotion I couldn't before place. It's want. I want him. I want him to touch me again, even if it's just to take my arm and lead me into the building.

His hand slides down my leg until he reaches my knee, pulling it closer to him, before he twists his body to face me. Moving his hands to my waist, those eyes drag me down as he says, "Are you sure? You didn't want to ride and I made you anyway. I overstepped. I'm sorry."

He reaches up to remove his helmet, glancing down at his hands as he pulls it away. Remorse. Is that what that look is? I use my fingertips to lift his eyes back to mine and shake my head. "If deep down I really didn't want to, I wouldn't have."

Like a magnetic force pulling me to him, I let my body reassure him that I'm okay. I take that final moment before jumping off the edge of reason to watch his eyes dance, merrily, as we both prepare ourselves for what I'm about to do. Without another thought, I lower my mouth to his and like a freight train speeding through the night I know all the metaphorical swimming I could do in his eyes will never compare to the instance of my lips finding his this first time. It's tender and rough; it's gentle and passionate.

It's the last almost year of hurting and healing and finding my way through the dark to this moment.

His hands are in my hair as he slowly assaults my lips, a slight nip to the bottom one that causes my breath to catch and I give him the password to my soul, to deepen the kiss. Pulling back he captures that same lip and holds me in place as he stands straddling the bike and maneuvers off to position himself before me as he quietly breaks our connection but holds my forehead to his.

"You're going to make me a weak man, Stephanie," he mumbles, but I catch a smile playing in his eyes before he closes them.

"I'm not trying to make you weak. I just feel stronger when you're near," I murmur and he kisses me once, twice, three more times in quick succession before wrapping my arm around his and pulling me toward the hospital.

"Come on, crazy girl, let's go see if you're getting a niece or nephew. Maybe our next date will be more normal," he says bumping his shoulder into mine.

I laugh loudly. After all, what's normal?

Chapter Twenty-Three

Max

This girl makes my heart race.

It's yet to slow down as we step off the elevator and onto the labor and delivery floor, and then speeds up even more when we're greeted by Tommy. His eyes zeroed in on Steph's arm draped over mine and I watched his jaw clench, but then the glint of jealousy is gone. It wasn't imagined, though.

"Glad you guys are here," Tommy says pulling Steph into a hug despite her arm still being entwined with mine. "I just talked to Brian and he said she's already at a six, but I have no idea what that means."

As if we'd practiced, Steph and I say simultaneously, "Centimeters." An amused look crosses her face as she looks at me.

"What?" I look down at her and grin. "I know lots of things."

Her smile brightens the room in spite of the flickering from the fluorescent lighting and she turns her attention back to Tommy. "It's how far she's dilated."

"How far does she have to be to get the baby out?"

"Ten centimeters. Basically, the diameter of a bagel." Stephanie barely finishes her sentence before Tommy's eyes widen and his face looks panicked.

"And she'll push a baby out of that? I ... I need some air. She's in the first room on the right once you go through those doors," he says and makes a quick escape down the stairs instead of waiting for the elevator.

Steph shakes her head and pushes through the doors to get into L&D. I'd never made it onto this floor back in Cleveland and a rush of emotion washes over me like a cold shower while Steph checks Stella's room number at the nurse's station. We head over to 201, but I can't make my feet move to enter the room.

She notices my hesitancy and rubs my arm. "Do you want to wait here? I'll go see if she's okay with extra company first?"

It must be the look in my eyes, the way I swallowed one too many times before answering, because she stands on her tiptoes and kisses the corner of my mouth like comforting me is the most natural thing for her to do. For her sake, I pull myself together and nod. "Please? I don't want to make Stella uncomfortable."

"Okay." And she disappears through the door, closing it softly behind her.

I don't hover, so I step away from the door and am drawn to a large whiteboard hanging on the wall. It's an organizational chart filled with patient names, doctor names, what interventions the mom has had, how dilated she is, and if the baby's been born already the sex, weight, length, and time of birth. I find Stella's name.

I wonder how it would have felt to have seen Adrienne's name up there and try to shake the thought from my brain.

A hand lands on my shoulder and I recognize Brian's wedding band.

"You okay, Max?" He's the one with a wife in labor and he's worried about me? "Steph said you were out here. Stell and I know this might be hard for you, but we want you here with us if you want to be here. We'll both understand if you need to leave. But ..." His voice trails off.

"But what?"

"Steph doesn't know about your past, does she?" I shake my head. "So, she might not understand you having an anxiety attack up here. Or she might. She may just think your behavior is because vaginas are scary and pushing babies out of them is superhuman and something you can't emotionally handle."

I pull in a deep breath and hold it before slowly letting it out. And again ... I try to remember my conversations with my mom about letting the past go and moving forward.

"Nah, I'm good," I say with as much conviction as I can muster. "At least I'm not puking in the stairwell like I'm pretty sure T was when he found out how big ten centimeters is."

Brian lets out a laugh as the door to Stella's room opens and his mother-in-law, Jenny, pokes her head out. I hear Stella cry out from inside the suite and Steph sternly say, "Pay attention to me. Focus on me."

"Bri, I think she needs you in here," Jenny says as we move toward the door. "The nurse just checked her and she's almost to nine. We might be having a baby before midnight at this rate."

We step into the room, with its dimmed lights and music coming from a small radio on a table, and if it weren't for Stella sitting on the edge of the bed groaning and breathing through back to back contractions I would never know I was standing in a hospital. When they told me a few weeks ago the hospital had birthing suites I assumed a deeper bathtub and no roommate. This? I could have fit most of my first apartment in here.

Trying to stay out of the way, I walk around the end of the bed to the side Steph's on. I feel out of place until Stella breaks her focus on Steph and looks up at me. "Max," she breathes out. "You came. Good. Fuck, this hurts."

"You weren't expecting this to be the easy part were you?" I laugh. Absentmindedly, I set my palm on Steph's lower back, rubbing in slow circles as she remains by her sister's side applying pressure to Stella's hips to relieve some of the pain.

I watch her face contort as the pain increases and she grabs for Brian's hand.

"Can I have an epidural? Some Tylenol? A shot of tequila?" she screams before tears begin coursing down her face. "Please, Steph, make the pain go away."

Steph stands up straight and places her palms on either side of her sister's face. "Stop it. We'll get through this. It's too late for drugs but I'll be sure you have a nice cold beer the day you bring this baby home. Look at me and breathe. You're almost done. You just have to work a little longer and then you can rest. Look at me, Stell."

I'm transported back to the emergency room downstairs and the night Steph was attacked, hearing Stella try to fix Steph's hurt, and coming back to stand outside the curtained cubicle to find Steph wrapped up in Stella's arms on the gurney.

These sisters will never cease to amaze me with the connection they have to one another.

"But there's so much pressure. I need to move." Stella's voice is pained, but at the word "pressure" her nurse calls for the doctor. She asks Stella to stay where she is long enough to check her progress and then helps her move her legs back up onto the bed while stammering through some "ums" while looking around the room before dropping an "oh shit."

Brian moves briefly toward the nurse and looks at Stella before dropping his eyes to the bed. "Is that ..."

"Yup," the nurse replies. "The doctor's on her way in from an emergency C-section, but if you ever played ball get ready to catch."

It's an out-of-body experience watching the sudden flurry of activity as the room goes from calm to chaotic. I step back and lean against the wall watching Steph and her mom on either side of Stella, massaging her lower back, breathing with her as her body works with each contraction to bring this little life into the world while Brian leans in front of her holding her hands in his. Two more nurses come in. One flips on the warmer while the other asks Stella if she's ready to have this baby, which results in an exhausted grunt.

"How are we doing in here?" an unfamiliar voice questions from the door a minute later.

"Just having a picnic is all," Brian says not taking his eyes off Stella. "You've missed most of the fun, Dr. Stace."

"Well, I figured you should be able to handle delivering your own baby, Brian. You work with bread; you know how to be gentle." She chuckles while pulling on a pair of gloves before addressing Stella quietly. She stands next to Jenny and takes Stella's hands, placing them on the crown of a little human head between her legs. "Lean back against your sister more and give me a big push with this next contraction. It's time to meet your baby, Stella."

It's at that moment Tommy reappears in the door, sees what he's been missing, and drops to the floor.

"Leave him. He'll be fine," Brian says as he watches wide-eyed as his wife pulls their newborn to her chest.

"Welcome to the world," Stella whispers into the sudden quiet of the room, and it breaks my resolve as I wait for the cries.

My body gives up and I slide down the wall until my butt meets the heels of my boots. I hang my head in my hands and I take the moment to pray. There hasn't been a cry yet, not even a whimper, as the room holds its breath. I'm not much of a religious man, but pray as I hear the sucking sound on the other side of the room.

I pray and I don't breathe.

And then it pierces my ears like the sweetest sound. My head lifts and my eyes meet Brian's, and neither one of us wipe away our tears as he gives me a thumbs up before leaning forward to kiss first his wife and then his new daughter.

Chapter Twenty-Four

Stephanie

At 11:03 p.m. on August 31, Emiliana Stephanie Stratford entered this world. At 11:05 p.m. I fell madly in love with Max Wyatt.

It wasn't difficult to do. Not when I saw Brian giving a thumbs up and I turned my head away from the sight before me to view the split open, bare display of emotions vibrating off his body as he openly wept in that hospital room. I can't explain it. I can't tell you which part of that moment took hold of my heart and squeezed it so tight I couldn't breathe.

I can't.

Because it was every part of it.

Since before Stella and Brian's wedding, something has drawn me to Max, and at first I thought it was because he was the officer to show up the night Darren tried to kill me. I'd built him up in my head as this glorious hero, put him on a pedestal, and offered him my thank you by sending him and the entire police department cookies.

Then the wedding happened and he was so ... genuine.

Max is more than a cop. He's more than that guy who came to my rescue. Watching him in the delivery room, crouched down like a scared little boy waiting to hear my niece scream her tiny heart out, I saw how much of him I had yet to be introduced to.

He's holding secrets, just like I am, and that's okay. The world is a scary place.

When my staring burns its way through the haze surrounding him, he quickly brushes the tears from his face and stands. I leave my sister to go lean on the wall beside him, waiting for the doctor and nurses to finish the jobs they need to do while Stella learns how to latch her daughter to her breast for the first time, and silently I slip my hand into Max's as we become spectators to this new life, this growing family.

"Are you okay?" I ask him like he asked me earlier in the evening.

"That's the second time someone's asked me that tonight," he says sheepishly. "The short answer? Yeah, I will be."

"What's the long answer?" I question cautiously.

Max looks down at our hands joined together between us and squeezes mine ever so slightly before looking up at me. Lifting his empty hand to my face, he pushes the loose hair behind my ear, pausing for a fraction to hold my face while searching my eyes.

"I'll tell you, just not right now. Are you alright with that, Stephanie?"

It's rare anyone calls me by my long name, it's always shortened to Steph, but hearing the entire thing fall from his lips makes me wish he'd say it again. And again. And again.

I hold my pinkie finger up in the air, waiting for him to catch on to the childish behavior I've long shared with my sister when he cocks one eyebrow at me.

"You promise?" I question, crooking my finger in his direction. "Pinkie swear?"

The words "I promise" tumble quietly from his mouth as he hooks his finger with mine.

Chapter Twenty-Five

Max

The box of cannoli was miraculously still on the seat of my motorcycle when Stephanie and I walked back to the parking lot, but after sitting out there for longer than either of us were comfortable with we tossed them in the closest garbage can. I don't know when we'll try another date, but I'll buy her a dozen of those things just to watch the sunset on the canal with her again.

She climbs on the bike and settles in behind me, but the chill in the early morning hours make her curl around my back to keep herself warm when we start moving.

When we left the hospital shortly after midnight, I knew I wasn't going to be able to sleep once I got home so I accepted her invitation in for a cup of coffee.

Stepping through the back door and into the kitchen feels strange, to say the least, since the last time I stood in this room Brian and Tommy eyed me suspiciously, my chief was trying to not give too much information about me away to them, and I wanted to throw up. I'd just told Steph I killed her boyfriend. It wasn't the easiest moment of my career.

I bend and rest my arms on the counter in the middle of the kitchen and watch Steph move around the room pulling coffee beans from one cupboard and a grinder from another. It's magical watching her make coffee. It's not like when I make it at home. She has it down to a science, doesn't spill the water, the beans are ground to perfection, and she's got it brewing in minutes.

I find myself wondering if it's always like this with her, if mornings are as smooth as evenings. If the coffee is always hot and the kisses always passionate. If the crazy is for show and the drinking just to chase the demons away.

I'm still imagining what a morning would be like with her when Steph faces me and leans on the opposite side of the counter.

"Those are some killer thoughts you're having, Super Max," she says catching me off guard and I smirk. "What's so funny?"

"My mom. She always called me Super Max. I hadn't heard her say it in years until I went home to see her last week," I confess. "I hadn't been home, not for a real visit anyway, in a long time. It was nice to have those moments with her."

"She sounds like a pretty special lady. She did a good job with you," she says then crosses her arms in front of her and lays her head on them with a yawn. "The coffee should be ready in a minute. I'm just going to rest my eyes for a second."

Her eyes drift shut as the last few words seep out of her and I smile knowing I've lost her to the Sandman. It doesn't take long before I hear her softly snoring. I take a deep breath before walking around the counter and lifting her against my chest. She sleepily wraps her arms around my neck and lets out the slightest sigh as she settles in my arms.

My heart lurches in my chest and I try to ignore it, but the staggering of beats is persistent as I hold her and begin my trek through the house. Walking through the downstairs, I contemplate laying her on the couch, but I know how long she spent on that couch after her leg was broken. I stand at the base of the stairs, counting the steps, and decide I've carried heavier backpacks longer distances; Steph is a feather by comparison. It's only ten or so steps and one hallway.

Slowly, methodically, I make my way to the top step as she falls deeper into sleep and gets heavier with each footfall. I look at the hallway before me and make my way toward the other end, glancing in the open doors along the way — bathroom, Tommy's space, a spare room still housing some of Britt's stuffed animals, and finally poke my head into the last room.

The scent of her perfume wraps around me like a warm hug as I step through the door. A small lamp sits on a desk near the window, its soft glow emitting enough light for me to see my way to the bed. It's the same light I see each night I drive past.

Keeping her cradled in my arms, I meander closer to the bed and gently lay her down. Kneeling down and making quick work of easing her sneakers off her feet, I raise my eyes ever so slightly and catch a glimpse of the article Stella ran in the newspaper about me joining the police department tacked to the corkboard above her bed. It wasn't a huge deal, basically a press release the chief and I sent out, but the newsprint is folded over so the black and white picture of me is the main focus and that's what makes me smile. The irony of watching over her every night isn't lost on me. It seems I'm there if I'm on duty or not. In any other situation, it would make me feel uncomfortable knowing my picture was hanging in some woman's bedroom, but this is Steph.

To Hold

She chose me to keep watch. Not some musician who will never know her or ex-boyfriend who disregarded her heart. Me.

Standing from my spot at her feet, I walk as quietly as I can with my boots still on to her desk in search of a piece of paper and pen. Quickly I scratch out a brief note asking what her plans are for dessert in the coming week and return to the side of her bed, slipping the corner of the note beneath the book on her nightstand.

For what may have been a beat too long, I watch her sleep before bending to place the whisper of a kiss on her forehead.

***

Stepping out of Steph's room, I pull the door shut behind me, holding the knob to keep the noise to a minimum.

I hear the low grumble of Tommy saying "What the fuck?" come from down the hall behind me and freeze. Turning to face him, I'm convinced he's trying to castrate me with his glare.

"Nothing happened, T," I curtly respond, narrowing my eyes. My defenses rise like the hairs on my arms and I feel the bitterness of anger in the back of my throat when he responds.

"Yeah, okay, nothing happened. That's a load of shit and you know it," he retorts.

"You know, man, not now. She's exhausted and I'm not going to have a verbal pissing match with you outside her bedroom door. Steph deserves more than that." I briskly walk down the hall and brush past him on my way back to the main floor of the house.

It's like he doesn't know better, and instead of going in and going to bed, Tommy follows me down the stairs and back to the kitchen.

"What are you doing, Tom? You act like you're looking for a fight. I'm not the guy you want to fight with," I spit out at him. "You have no claim on her. She's not something to claim! Stop acting like you're going to pee on her leg and mark her as your territory."

His face contorts as though I've bitch slapped him.

"I haven't done that," he counters defensively.

"Really? What was with the showy hug at the hospital when we stepped off the elevator?"

"I was relieved she was there. I was hugging my roommate, that's all."

"While her arm was still attached to mine. You didn't even give her a chance to let go of me. It was possessive," I say, bringing my voice back down to a normal volume. "Did she tell you we were supposed to go on a date tonight?"

His jaw clenches and I catch sight of him balling his fists.

"A date? No. She didn't mention that to me." Tommy reigns in his frustration, though I'm unsure whether it's frustration from Steph not telling him we were going out or from the fact she went out with me at all. Blowing out a breath, T changes gears. "You guys made coffee and then didn't drink it. I'm not one for wasting good beans."

He pours two mugs and sets one down on the island counter in front of me.

"Talk," he says.

"About what?" I reply.

"Do you care about her or are you doing this just for an ego boost?"

They're just words, Max. He's having a jealous moment. Don't let him get to you, I tell myself, giving me a moment to thoughtfully consider my response.

"If I were attempting to date Stephanie for an ego boost, I would have asked her out in April when I walked her home from the wedding. Tommy ... I've been avoiding her for months. You have no idea what I've put myself through trying to stay away from her," I confess to the coffee in my mug.

"Why in the world would you avoid her?" He sounds disgusted that I would admit such a thing. "She's kind of hard to ignore. She's actually pretty fucking persistent if you pay attention."

The laugh comes out of my throat without any warning.

"Yeah, she is. My mom warned me that stubborn girls like Steph won't be avoided forever." I smile more at the thought of sharing my feelings with my mom than the idea that she was right about Stephanie. "To be honest, I was afraid I was toxic to her. Pain seems to follow me. I don't want Steph to hurt more because of me."

It's true. I wanted her to be able to heal in my absence, but I think the only thing I accomplished was keeping the wound in my chest open longer than I had ever imagined. I toy with the handle on my coffee mug wondering how much longer I would have hurt if I didn't ask her out last weekend when I saw her standing at the end of my driveway. How much longer will she hurt now that mine is fading?

To Hold

Tommy's face softens and I see him mulling over what he wants to say to me, and I'm briefly left wondering if he's going to verbally assault me or if he's going to act like the friend I need.

"Did you ever think maybe she was starting to hurt more because you were trying to save her from you by avoiding her in the first place?"

I pull the words into my brain and let them roll around before giving a slight nod.

Taking a long, slow sip of my coffee, I admit to him that my mom essentially told me the same thing where my avoiding Steph was concerned. This is the beginning of the first real exchange we have had in months, and yet it's like he sat in on the conversation I had with Mom over salads.

"I care about her, T." The words come out so quietly. I clear my throat and try again. "I care about her and that's actually pretty difficult for me to admit because it's been a long time since I cared about anyone, including myself."

"Be careful with this one, Max. She's not like other girls." I get the impression he's not going to share more with me and I don't press the topic.

"I want to get to know her ... slowly. Not because of what happened. We can't change the past." I take the last swallow of coffee and walk the mug to the sink, rinsing it and leaving it in the basin. It's a clear move to end the excitement from the night before. "I just feel drawn to her. She's magnetic."

I think I hear him sigh. I know he's fighting back his own emotions about Steph, it's written all over his face and posture and in the way he bristled as soon as he saw me come out of her bedroom earlier.

"She's a force to be reckoned with, buddy," Tommy says as I make my way to the backdoor, but he grins at me. "You're good for her. I hope she's able to see that. Just know, if you mess it up or hurt her ... well, I'd threaten you but Steph's got a pretty mean right hook. She goes for the face, so tuck your chin."

I roll my eyes, say goodnight and walk out the door, but I can hear his laughter through the open windows as I make my way down the steps to the bike.

The streets are nearly vacant at this time of morning and I quietly pull into my driveway a few minutes after leaving Stephanie and Tommy's house.

If she had stayed awake, what would have happened? The question trips through my exhausted brain, but I can't shut down for the night. I can't possibly sleep when my body is charged up at the thought of her. Her lips on mine, her hands on me as we rode through town, her fingers wound together with mine fitting like they were made to sit side-by-side with mine.

Sleep simply isn't coming tonight. Not yet.

I plug in my once again dead phone and change into shorts, lose the socks and polo, and head to the basement to work out the adrenaline coursing through me. Maybe after a few rounds with the bag I'll be able to rest until sunrise, but it feels like the only thing that will calm my wild mind is her.

Chapter Twenty-Six

Stephanie

I wake with a start when the alarm on my phone goes off at six in the morning. It's my normal "get up and go running" time, but my body refuses to actually get out of bed. My legs are stiff from sleeping in my jeans all night.

I slept in my jeans? How did I get to my bed?

"Max!"

Sucking in a breath, I roll over searching for him, curious if he's stealthily sleeping beside me. When the other side of the bed turns up empty, I'm relieved and dumbfounded at once. It's the strangest sensation to wake up wishing someone was in your bed when for years all you've done is leave the beds you've fallen into. Not that there have been that many. I just wish this once there was another body lying next to me.

My alarm sounds again and it's then that I see the note from him. A man with nice penmanship? That's not something you find every day. It's the words that stick out more than the gently sloping script, though.

Stephanie,
If you're free this week, I'd like to try dessert again. The only taste I got was from your lips, though I'm not complaining. They were as sweet as I imagined they would be.

- Max

Subconsciously I lift my fingers to my mouth and can almost feel the pressure from his lips on mine. I kissed him. I never initiate the first kiss, but I did with Max.

My fingers are still on my lips when I hear the gentle knock on my door between the sound of a rushing waterfall and birds wailing. Tommy opens it enough to poke his head in.

"Can you shut your alarm off? Some of us wanted to sleep until seven."

I reach back to the nightstand and turn off the escalating nature sounds blasting from the tiny speaker, but the stunned expression never leaves my face.

"You can't sleep in. There's no way Bri is going to be there to open the coffeehouse and Greg can't handle a Saturday morning on his own," I ramble. He knows I'm right, he just refuses to admit it and instead embarks on uncharted territory, even for Tommy.

"What's up with you? You look like you woke up in a good mood. That doesn't just happen."

"How'd I get to my bed last night?" I blurt out.

His face pales slightly and he drops his head to study his bare feet, and then I'm certain but I need to hear him say it.

"Tommy?"

"Max carried you up." I know he can see the question on my face seeking more information, needing more detail. "And when I saw him coming out of your bedroom I might have confronted him."

"No," I say, but it comes out more like a long, low, slow moan of horror. "Please, please, Tommy, what did you say to him? Don't tell me you were an asshole? Please, tell me you didn't get all possessive and shit with Max over me." I'm talking as I'm crawling off the bed and pulling the door fully open, practically pushing him up against the wall on the opposite side of the hall. "You didn't, did you?"

"I may have started," he says. I pull my elbow up and back and almost — almost — punch him in his smug face until he holds his hand up in a stop motion and quickly adds, "but, he called me out on it. I couldn't keep up a tough guy act with Max, not when I saw his face when he talked about you."

His face.

"What about his face when he talked about me?"

I drop my arm, suddenly exhausted with emotion.

"He was defensive of you and got kind of dreamy-eyed, like Brian does when he talks about Stell. What I'm saying is, he seems to care about you, and, as much as I hate to say it out loud to you, I'm glad you've decided to chase after him." He smiles at me now that his face isn't in danger. "Can you tell me something, though? Why are you signed up for self-defense classes when you could basically pummel the shit out of me if you really wanted to?"

I scoff and turn back to my bedroom. "Because, T, not everyone backs down from me like you do. I'm going for a run. Be back in a few hours."

With that, I close my door, lean up against it, and swear I can hear my heart beating into the wood. I'm chasing him, that's what Tommy said, now I need to consider how long I'm willing to chase Max before I let him catch me.

Chapter Twenty-Seven

Max

Saturday morning came and went. I didn't hear from Stephanie, and I decided to give myself the day to let the night before sink in after a few hours of sleep.

That's a lie. I didn't sleep. My brain tried to shut off for a while when, really, I laid there staring at the ceiling wondering what it would feel like to wake up next to her even though it's way too soon to be imagining her in my bed. Too soon for whom, I'm unsure, but that's how I spent the hours between showering after working out and sunrise.

I get up when I can't get the memory of the smell of her hair, of her perfume, out of my mind. With autopilot in command, I pull shorts on over my boxer-briefs, throw myself into a clean T-shirt, grab socks, and find my running sneakers.

Flipping my ball cap off the hook I keep it on, I spin it around in my hand before placing it on my head backwards and pushing through the backdoor of the house.

All I need to clear my head is some fresh air, I tell myself, because pummeling the shit out of gear in the basement at two-thirty in the morning wasn't enough to do the job. Obviously. This run might not even get her off my mind, but I've got to try and get it together before work tomorrow. If I'm in a funk when I get to work I'm basically asking for someone to give me shit.

It already doesn't help that some of the guys think I'm the chief's Golden Boy. Self-defense classes start Monday evening, which means Chief had to redo my schedule, so the other guys on nights aren't taking it too well that the new guy gets a coveted days shift. I haven't worked days on a consistent basis in years and am a little afraid of what it will be like to see the sun for a whole eight-hour shift instead of just as I'm going to bed after a shift or waking up to go to work. I have days off, but I tend to give up those days for the guys with families who need them for their kids' school concerts and soccer games. I take the shift but rarely ask them to actually trade for one of mine.

There isn't anything pressing that would require me to have a night off anyway.

My new schedule plays through my mind as I hit my stride — I'll have a Monday through Friday schedule, working seven to three-thirty, and teach twice a week in the evening. It's not bad for only being here a year, but it's going to be an adjustment from my previous schedule, for sure.

Ticking off all the normal hours I might have to do things, like cookouts with my friends where I won't be showing up in uniform for a hamburger before heading to the station, pulls a smile from me.

The smile grows thinking about the first time I showed up dressed for work to an early Sunday dinner at Brian and Stella's. I tried not to notice, and she tried not to stare, but Stephanie watched me the entire time I was there. She stumbled through conversations with her mom and sister, but those hazel eyes barely left me.

I wonder where Stephanie would fit into all of this? Would she be willing to attempt dating like ordinary people or is that going to be too much? Is there anything ordinary about the two of us together? Not to mention it's been so long since I actually dated anyone that I'm not exactly sure how to do it. We tried last night, but that went in fifteen different directions before the "date" part took place.

I left the note. If she found it, she'll tell me when she's ready to try again.

Turning the last corner before reaching the coffeehouse, I slow my pace until I'm walking and then slow it more when I see Steph step out the door and turn in the direction of home. She didn't see me and I don't chase after her. I don't know why I let her walk away. All my reasons are unsound — ball in her court, she was probably in a hurry, I don't want to appear clingy, we aren't a couple, I don't have any claim on her — and they scamper through my head as I watch her slip away from me.

***

I texted Brian to ask how Stella and the baby were doing early Sunday morning, but refrained from going up to the hospital to visit during their stay. Knowing his parents would be arriving soon, I wanted to respect their time as a family of four before dropping in.

I did send flowers and a card to the house, though. Once in a while I am fully capable of sloughing off the façade, that rough and tough exterior, and revealing that beneath it all is a giant marshmallow. I am a giant marshmallow.

Maybe that's why it bothers me that I still haven't heard from Steph about a second date. I'm being too mushy when really I need to try not to overanalyze why she hasn't called.

My shift starts in a few hours and I just want one last calm night before getting used to a new routine, so I try to shove my thoughts of her into an empty corner of my mind. It's enough to pass the time, get laundry done, and go over the notes I've made for the first night of class tomorrow.

Walking from the house to the bike, a backpack slung from my shoulders, I hear my phone briefly ring inside the pack. I freeze hearing the sound, waiting for it to ring again. It doesn't though, and I drop the bag from my back to find my phone.

Steph: What's your schedule like this week? I'm busy Monday and Wednesday evening, but think I'm free other nights.

Finally. I bite the inside of my cheek to keep from smiling too broadly. Mulling over the schedule I had memorized just moments before, I recall that with my shift change I'm only working through Thursday. Crafting a reply to Steph takes longer than I anticipate, though, because I don't want to sound overeager despite the fact I'm fucking giddy right now. I finish reading what I've written and hit send when I see Sutton step around the end of the hedgerow between our yards.

"Someone sure does look happy today," she says smiling and crossing her arms across her chest. "Must be a girl."

Laughing at her comment I question how transparent I must really be. "It's that obvious?"

Holding her thumb and forefinger close together she rolls her eyes at me and lets out an exaggerated, "Heh, yeah, just a little bit, Max. Anyway, I didn't get a chance to thank you for helping me Friday, so I just wanted to stop over and tell you again that I appreciate you giving me a hand. You took off pretty quickly after leaving my place, though, so I hope I didn't get you in trouble with your girlfriend."

My girlfriend. It has a nice ring to it. Would Stephanie think so, too? I don't correct Sutton, mostly because I hope Steph will eventually consider herself part of my life and call us a couple.

I shake my head slightly and etch out a quick response without going into detail. Sutton looks like someone who likes details and I don't know her well enough, if at all, to know that she won't take my life and broadcast it to every customer to walk through the door of her shop in town.

"Nah, I was a little late but everything's fine now," I say, smiling down at my phone when I see her name light up the screen again. "I don't mean to cut this short, but I'm on my way out —"

"Another date, I assume?" she interrupts and her sudden presumptuousness makes me falter.

"Actually, no. I have to work tonight," I toss over my shoulder as I pull the backpack with my uniform and badge in it up my arms again and move to throw a leg over the bike seat. "My date tonight is with Brockport's bad guys and rowdy bar hoppers who don't have class until noon tomorrow."

The topic of what I do for a living never came up while I was moving her hutch and dining room table, so the look on her face is priceless. I'm highly amused she's got a business in this tiny town and yet doesn't know the local police officers. I don't mean to stereotype, but she seems like the type to know everything about everything.

"You're a cop, aren't you?" she questions like it's the most intriguing profession out there.

"Yes, ma'am, and my best friend owns the local coffeehouse. Irony at its best, isn't it?" I laugh, thankful I'm still able to surprise some people. I push the helmet onto my head and reach for the starter. Bringing the motorcycle to life and slowly easing it toward the sidewalk, I see Sutton take a slight step back like she's afraid of the machine. I yell above the roar of the Harley, "Anyway, thanks for stopping over. I was happy to help. If you need anything else, don't hesitate to ask."

I nod and smile at her once more, twist the throttle and take off out of the driveway with the hope I have a few minutes to read and respond to Steph's last message before my shift starts.

Chapter Twenty-Eight

Stephanie

He's busy on Monday and Wednesday, too, and I can't help but wonder if he said that because I've already got things going on those days, as though he's afraid I'd change my plans for him.

I wouldn't, but it bothers me a little that I even think he'd think that.

What should bother me — but oddly doesn't — is that I'm feeling like a damn teenager with a crush, when really I'm almost thirty years old and don't have time for the heart palpitations when my phone makes a noise or I hear his motorcycle take off a few blocks over. It's silly, but I know it's his bike. The sounds, smell, and sight of his Harley-Davidson are burned into all five of my senses.

Come tomorrow night, though, I'll have to clear some space in my head for all the ass-kicking knowledge I'm planning to acquire. I didn't tell him I was signed up for self-defense classes, and he doesn't need to know right now. Max doesn't have time to worry about how safe I feel or don't feel. The last thing I want to do is make him worry by telling him I'm going to go learn how to break someone's kneecaps from a stranger.

My ability to focus on anything for too long is gone and I find myself sitting at the dining room table trying to work on a press release for the bookstore but making no headway. I have a dateline on the page. That's it.

This man has destroyed my sense of duty to clients Tommy and I have worked so hard to find.

Audibly, I groan, staring at my phone again and waiting for Max to respond to the last message I sent. He said he has to work tonight, but his schedule is changing tomorrow and he'll be on days from now on. It's an adjustment for him, I'm sure, but the idea that he isn't going to be driving past most nights anymore is going to be just as much of an adjustment for me. Tonight will be the last night that happens.

I already miss the sound of the car slowly idling past before his shift ends.

Leaning back in the chair, I wrap my hands around my head and try to squeeze the life back into my brain cells.

"What am I doing?" I mouth the words to my computer like it just might answer me back. It doesn't. I save the three words on the page, pack the laptop into my shoulder bag, and head for the door. Too many things rush through my head and I need a break. Lugging the computer with me, I walk to the coffeehouse, grab my regular, check on Tommy and Greg, help for five minutes so I don't feel guilty for grabbing a box filled with muffins, and then leave again.

I need Stella. But, Stella just got home with a brand new baby a couple hours ago. The muffins, I convince myself, are for her and all her breastfeeding needs ... though the dark chocolate with chocolate chips are absolutely for me. This is by no means a peace offering for barging in on them right after they've been released to the wild blue yonder that is new parenthood.

Halfway to Brian and Stell's I send her a quick text message to let her know I'm on my way and bringing food. I get a message back with nothing but smiley faces and hearts. This baby has surely stolen her ability for adult conversation, but I can't wait to snuggle the itty bitty for five minutes while my sister eats.

More importantly, I need to sit with Britton, act like a six-year-old, and hear all he has to say about his new baby sister and his big brother adventures. I haven't seen my nephew since Emmy arrived, but Brian said Britt's been super protective and having a hard time being away from the baby for too long, so I'm hoping a little break to color and have some of his own attention will help the kid relax. School starts this week and I can just imagine the separation anxiety that'll happen while he's off learning for seven hours a day.

Walking up the driveway, I sneak in through the backdoor that leads into the kitchen and set the box of muffins on the counter before kicking off my sneakers. I walk through the doorway toward the front of the house, through the small dining room, and tiptoe toward the living room where I hear the soft sound of a blanket swishing back and forth with the motion of the chair as Stella rocks to and fro.

"Muffin. I need a muffin. Maybe a jug of coffee and some peanut butter, too," Stella whispers when she realizes I've come into the room. "She's sleeping and I don't want to put her down because then she's going to wake up, but if I don't ... Stephie, take her for me? I'm so tired. I don't think I've slept since a nap on Friday afternoon when I thought I was just having more Braxton Hicks contractions."

They've decided to shorten Emiliana to Emmy and we all assume it's for the purpose of using the longer name for when she reaches the troublemaker stage in a few years. If I didn't know better, I would think she was already working on a bit of that hard-headed, stubborn Barbieri-ness.

I toss my bag in the bay window and reach for the baby. The last time I held someone this small was never. Emmy, dressed in a little onesie with green hearts and wrapped lightly in a security blanket, feels lighter than a bag of flour, which is absurd because I know she weighs more than that. Even still, she's so tiny and delicate and ...

Stella sighs and catches my attention. "That looks good on you, Steph. Someday, okay? Someday it'll happen."

"All I need is the right guy for the job and then we can talk seriously about that." I drop my eyes back down to Emmy's face, memorizing her features, the way she smells, the slightest hint of a dimple in her chin. She has Stella's dark hair, but that could change. I pull her closer to my body and climb onto the couch to snuggle her for just a few more minutes. This will be gone in the blink of an eye and since we all missed this with Britt, I don't want to miss it with Emmy.

"You have the right guy, Steph. Give him a chance to show you." I look up as my sister stands from the rocking chair, her belly still swollen from being someone's home for the last nearly 41 weeks and her breasts looking like something out of Playboy, and she places her hand on my shoulder as she passes behind the couch. I open my mouth to respond, but she shushes me. "Max is a good man. He sent flowers. T didn't even do that."

And I laugh because in that moment all I can picture is Tommy's face right before he passed out when he walked into the delivery room.

"You're lucky Tommy's still talking to you guys after the show he got."

Stella chuckles as she makes her way to the kitchen. "Not my fault he got a front row seat to my birth canal. He should have knocked. Muffins. I need some muffins. Just keep doing what you're doing and ignore the starving woman in the kitchen."

Shaking my head and smiling, I'm suddenly fully aware of just how fortunate I am for the family I've been given, but it hits me right in the heart when Britt comes quietly through the front door. He sets a soccer ball next to his shoes, says nothing at all, and crawls up on the couch to rest his head on my shoulder.

The love and adoration he has for his baby sister is palpable. This little girl is going to have a really difficult time keeping a boyfriend once she's allowed to date. Between her brother, her father, and her uncle, I'm almost certain there will be threats of grounding her for life and bars on her bedroom windows just to keep gentleman callers away.

I free my left arm and wrap it around Britt, drawing him closer to me so I can smell the sunshine in his hair and kiss his topknot. The moment is complete when Whiskey saunters in and lays on the rug at my feet.

"Someday ..."

Chapter Twenty-Nine

Max

Four hours into our shift, Gill and I take a dinner break. I'm halfway through a turkey club sandwich at the diner across town when I realize I never sent a message back to Stephanie.

I finish the bite in my hand, wipe my fingers with a napkin, and grab my phone from my back pocket.

"This is your celebratory meal, Wyatt. What's so important it can't wait until we're done?" John says, a hint of sarcasm in his voice. He hates that I'm moving to days so much he's hardly spoken to me since getting in the car to go on patrol.

I stop chewing, my finger hovering over the digital keyboard, and just stare at him. Swallowing and clearing my throat, I set the phone down to give him my full attention.

"What's the matter, John? Are you having a hard time with me changing shifts?" I ask. I've gone through enough therapy in the past to know how to get someone to talk to me. "I'm not doing this to hurt you, you know."

"But why you? It's not fair. I always end up with shitty partners and then Davis puts me with you a year ago and it's been pretty awesome to work with someone close to my age for once," he whines.

"You're ten years my senior, John."

"No I'm not! I just act that way because I usually feel old. But, Max, I feel young when you're around," he exclaims, then goes back to pushing the pickle slices around his plate with a fork. "I know you're the best choice for teaching the self-defense class and I'm just worried you're going to focus too much on that and leave the department."

My eyebrow raises slightly in question. This is the first anyone has shown concern about my motives for accepting the teaching position.

"I'm not leaving the department. Why would anyone think that?"

"My wife goes to the community center almost every day to swim. She signed up for your class and overheard some of the people there talking about your credentials like they wanted to hire you as a full-time staffer," he admits. "You wouldn't do something like that, though. Would you? You're too good of a cop to give it up and work at the community center."

At some point while he was talking, my jaw dropped open slightly and I'm well aware of the look on my face when he finishes talking. Teach full-time? At the community center?

"No. Not even a thought that crossed my mind. Right now I've agreed to teach one session in line with their fall class schedule, and then we'll revise to see if I need to add a second section for the spring." End of subject. I pick my phone back up to send a message to Steph, but John interrupts me again.

"You're positive? Because my wife was going on about how the women on staff there were fawning over the idea of the local 'hot cop' teaching in a room that has windows so they can all stare at your ass."

"This is ridiculous. There's only one woman I want ogling my ass and you keep interrupting me from sending her a message I was supposed to send almost five hours ago." That shuts him up. "Besides, there's no way I'm leaving the department with the kind of pension package civil service comes with. I've wanted to be a cop since I was a toddler. This is my life," I say, my voice rising to exasperation.

"What girl?"

"Huh?"

His question and smile catch me off guard. I'm really starting to hate that feeling, the one where I don't have control over how my face reacts before I can get my emotions in check. I quietly mumble Steph's first name and look up from my phone just in time to watch his face widen with shock.

"Do you know what you're doing?"

"With Steph? I have an idea," I tell him, then finish out our meal by sharing with him what Friday night taught me about the girl so many men seem to think they can conquer but are too afraid to talk to.

"You, sir, are going to fall really hard for her," John says pointing at me as he slides from the booth. He stands and stops, looking me up and down. "I take that back. You already have."

"It's too soon to fall for her. We're just starting to know each other."

"Whatever you say, Wyatt. Just trust me when I say you have that look." He laughs, pulling a couple bills from his wallet to pay for our food — his treat because it's our last night working together — and I wonder what look he's talking about but don't voice the question before he says, "If you want to know what I'm talking about, watch the coffee guy's face when he talks about the newspaper girl. That should tell you everything."

***

I text her an apology for getting busy at work on our way back out to the squad car and let her know dinner after I'm done with work on Thursday sounds good to me. She replies with a picture of herself holding Emiliana and some text about getting her "snuggle time" in with the baby so Stella and Brian could rest.

My heart cracks open and heals in a matter of seconds seeing the image.

I want that, I think to myself. It's a shock because as much as I know I still want children, I didn't consider the enormity of the emotions that would rock me when I came to terms with it.

I hold onto the promise of Thursday evening throughout the rest of my last shift with John Gill. It's like a lighthouse beacon guiding me through treacherous waters. I know I'll get acclimated to the schedule changes quickly, I always have, and knowing I get to spend one more night getting to know Stephanie makes all those changes worth it.

She's worth it.

She's worth every single thing happening in my life.

I just didn't realize until now how big a role she was playing.

Chapter Thirty

Stephanie

Monday evening is here and I want to throw up. I haven't taken a fitness class of any sort since the physical education requirement in college. Now I'm sitting in my car at the community center wearing basketball shorts, an ugly T-shirt, and my running sneakers ... and a stranger is going to put his hands on me to teach me how to beat up bad guys.

An involuntary shudder runs the course of my body at the thought of someone touching me. Despite signing myself up for this, despite how athletic I was in high school or how toned I remain, I hadn't given much thought before now to how they were going to teach me to defend myself. Part of me thought it would be a lot of imitation, like watching workout videos in my living room. I never even asked if the instructor was a man, because I just assumed it was, or a woman or a team. I didn't ask for the name of the teacher. For once in my life I just jumped into a decision. This time, it was with my therapist's blessing, which may be why I didn't ask any of my usual twenty questions. She trusted my decision, therefore I trusted my gut and went for it.

"Stop overthinking it, Steph. You can do this," I mutter to my image in the rearview mirror. "It's no big deal. It's like starting a new class at the beginning of a new semester."

Making my way to the door of the center, I toss my keys from one hand to another. With my backpack slung over one shoulder like the cool kid in class and my Oakley's shielding me from the glare of the setting sun, no one I walk past can see the fear I'm feeling at trying something new.

This far exceeds my comfort level, and I realize just how far outside of it I am when I'm pointed to one of the yoga studios and the class is maxed out with women. Women who decided a self-defense class was a front for a fucking beauty contest. Leggings and crop tops galore. It's like 1987 exploded in here. My nervousness dissipates and I'm left feeling bad for the sucker teaching this thing, because every single woman in here is hoping to catch his — or her — eye.

I hear all the chatter. The comments about how hot the instructor is solidifies my assumption that it's a guy teaching. There are plenty of unsavory things said about his ass and abs and the things some of these women would do to them. I'm mortified that these people are so openly having conversations like this. It's like they can't help but share all their wildest fantasies. They have no shame chit-chatting about it in front of everyone, either. And these aren't all women in their late twenties like me. At least three of them are the moms of people I went to high school with.

Mortified.

Then he walks in and I get it. I'm standing in the back, though, so everyone is in my way and I can't get a good peek. I don't see anything but the definition in his legs and the backwards ball cap with sunglasses sitting on the brim. That alone makes me understand what all the fuss is about. It isn't until I hear him clap his hands together and start talking that my heart jumps to my throat and I can't breathe.

"Alright, ladies, let's get started," he says amid the giggling. "My name is Max Wyatt and I'm here to teach you how to defend yourself against a physical attack. For the last several years I've been a police officer, but prior to going to the Academy, I did this full-time. I've taught at community centers and women's shelters and make it a priority to know that those who take my classes can and will defend themselves against an unwanted attack. You will learn a variety of self-defense methods throughout the course of this class."

I don't think he's seen me yet, and if he has a class roster he never said anything to me about being in the class, so I stay hidden behind a woman who's taller than me. The chatter has died down a little, but by the end of his speech, I can hear the frustration in his voice.

"You've paid to be here ladies. If you don't intend to put forth your best effort, I can't teach you. This isn't coffee hour after church or your Tuesday night book club, so I'd appreciate it if everyone quieted down or I'll be refunding at least half of you."

That gets their attention, but I can't hold back my snickering and the woman I was hiding behind turns to look at me bent at the waist as I try to quiet myself. Then, probably in an act of self-preservation, she steps to the side and I see his sneakers directly beneath me.

"Is there a problem here?" he asks as I hold my right hand up trying to get him to not talk. It's pointless. He's Max and Max is apparently in teacher mode, which means he isn't going to shut up long enough for me to regain my composure. He even has the stance down pat with his feet set apart and his arms crossed in front of his chest. "If you'd like to step out to the hall until you can calm yourself down, you're more than welcome to, but please don't be disruptive."

To Hold

Sucking in a deep, cleansing breath to get the giggles under control, I prepare myself to face the storm. "You think I'm being disruptive?" I say incredulously as I stand and come eye-to-eye with him. His jaw goes slack as the grip on his biceps tightens enough to make his knuckles turn white, shock plays across his features followed by amusement in his eyes and I lower my voice. "You failed to mention you were moonlighting as a self-defense instructor, Officer Wyatt."

His smile warms me from my toes to the tips of my ears. My stomach dips as he momentarily loses his teacher tone then, squinting ever so slightly, huskily whispers, "Were you hiding from me?"

"Just a little. I heard how gorgeous the instructor was and didn't want to distract you from the others vying for your attention. Go easy on them. Some of these women are grandmas."

I wink. He chuckles. I watch as he lifts his arm to brush the hair off my forehead and set his hand on my shoulder. He has a habit of doing that, but when it's happened in the past we weren't standing in the midst of a mob of now bitter women. If he hears the sharp intakes of breath around the room, he ignores it.

"I have a feeling you're going to be my star pupil, Miss Barbieri."

"If by star you mean most hated, yeah, I'd say you're right." I bite my bottom lip and then let it go just as quickly when I notice his pupils grow wider and his nostrils flare. His involuntary reaction makes my heart beat faster and I mouth the words "not here" as I lift up on the tips of my toes to glance over his shoulder. He's in his own world. "Max, you have a class to teach. Stop looking at me like you're going to devour me whole."

"Right! Class. Let's get started," he says loudly, clapping his hands together and walking backward through the room until he gets to the middle of the group. He starts talking, but I'm not listening. All I can hear is my heart pounding in my ears.

Someone sidles up next to me and quietly says, "What was that all about?"

Looking up at the woman I had tried to hide behind, I give an innocent smile before answering. "He's friends with my sister and brother-in-law."

"Uh huh. Well, you two just made for a lot of jealous housewives with that show," she laughs.

"Trust me, it wasn't on purpose. I had no idea he was teaching this and he obviously didn't know I was signed up for the class," I say quietly as Max shoots a look in my direction. I make a zipping motion across my lips and settle in for what might be the most intense next six weeks of my life.

***

Sweat is pouring off me by the time Max is done for the evening. I'm pretty sure at least four women are dropping the class and several more are sticking with it simply because they can still walk. I didn't sign up to mentally undress the professor like it seems a lot of my classmates have, even though I am, so he's stuck with me no matter what.

My motives for joining the class run as deep as my scars. It doesn't matter that my attacker can't hurt me or anyone else anymore. It's the lessons that I've learned through the entire process of putting myself in those situations to begin with. I never want to be unprepared to defend myself again.

Through course of conversation at the end of class, I learn I'm not the only one here with scars. Jamie, the woman I hid behind, survived attacks for years from her now ex-husband. She suffered broken ribs and bruises at his hands because she was too afraid to leave it all and run away. She said it wasn't until they had a baby that she realized she was worth more, that her child didn't deserve the kind of abuse she would grow up knowing.

"So, I packed what I could of the baby's and ran. This is where I ended up. I got a job at the gas station and stayed at the shelter until I could afford rent. He found me when I filed for divorce. I answered the door holding a shotgun. After that, he gave me the divorce I wanted, said I was too much to control now with a kid. I haven't heard from him since. It doesn't mean I sleep any better at night, though." Her eyes are cast downward.

"But you survived, Jamie. And now you're here, learning how to fight back, learning your own strength. That takes a lot of courage." She doesn't ask me how I know, and my story is short compared to hers, so I don't share. All I do is encourage her to keep taking back the little pieces of herself that he stole over time.

We're saying our goodbyes while I grab a bottle of water from my backpack. A flash of blonde hair catches my eye as the door is closing, a melodic tinkle of her laugher echoing down the hall, and I would have thought nothing of a random woman flirting with some random guy at the gym if I didn't walk through that door myself and see it wasn't a random guy at all.

It was my guy.

No ... he's not mine. I don't have any hold on him.

It doesn't matter, though, because I saw him smile at her. His eyes lit up. I feel my jealousy flare and turn to walk the other way, leaving through a different entrance.

"Steph?" I hear him call after me, but I walk a little faster, pressing on and not looking back until I'm in the parking lot unlocking my car.

Pulling the door open, I toss my backpack in, and then I feel him everywhere. The hair on my arms rises up and the air around me crackles with the energy between us. He's thunder and lightning on a stormy night.

"Steph, wait." He places a hand on my forearm as I steady myself against the open door. "Please." The pleading in his voice stops me cold. It's an "I'm sorry" without apologizing. "That was my neighbor, Sutton. She didn't know I'm teaching here and I ran into her in the hall."

"The same neighbor who made you late last Friday?" Closing my eyes, I swallow over the lump in my throat waiting for him to answer, wondering why he left out the part about her being a blonde bombshell. The familiarity of her name is too much to be a coincidence, though. I only know of one Sutton in town and Tommy has handled all the face-to-face business with her.

I make a mental note to get my insecurities in check before I fuck this up.

The "yes" is spoken quietly before he goes on to explain that he was telling her he ran into me in class. "That's what we were laughing about. Chance meetings and irony, Stephanie. That's all."

I pull back the breath I just released when he says my name. He has no idea how it makes me feel when he says it. He tugs gently on my arm until I turn.

"I promise," he says as I look down at the pinkie finger held out between us. I hook mine around his and he pulls me toward him, enveloping me in his warmth, his strength, as I press my face against his chest and breathe him in. His chest rumbles slightly beneath me as he laughs. "I must smell horrible. I didn't shower after work before coming here."

"You smell like a man. I kind of like it." My voice is shy, even though in the past I've rarely been anything but confident. I feel the playfully wicked smile tug at the corners of my mouth and his fingers beneath my chin as he brings my eyes up to his. "I wouldn't kick you out of bed for smelling like this."

A groan catches in the back of his throat at the mention of a bed and he nonchalantly moves his arm between us to adjust himself.

"Those gym shorts leave little to the imagination, Max. I'd almost think you have a dirtier mind than me." Laughing, I press my face into his chest again to stifle the sound. He twists my body and places me against the back door of the car, leaning into me with his hands braced on either side of my head.

Brushing his lips against my ear, my eyelids lazily shut and my lashes flutter against the tops of my cheeks. Warm breath floats across my cheek as he presses his hips into me. "There's plenty of room left for imagination, Stephanie."

"I haven't wanted anyone like I want you in a long time, Max, if ever. It scares me a little bit," I tell him truthfully. Looking up at him through my lashes, I catch myself absentmindedly biting my lip. "Did you want to at least have dinner and hang out first? Take out and a movie at your place?"

He drops his mouth to mine and slowly pulls my bottom lip between his. He's soft and sensual, but the kiss ends before it even gains momentum. He won't let it get off the ground and take flight, and I'm left wanting more of him.

"We're still in the parking lot. Dinner and a movie. My place. I need to grab my bag from inside, so I'll meet you there?" His voice is husky, deep and demanding in the kindest way. "Figure out what you're hungry for and we'll order when I get home."

As he pushes off the car, I giggle. "You mean to tell me you expect I'll be hungry for something other than you?"

His hands are on my face, his lips hard against mine and searching for entrance as he kisses me like he never wants me to forget the way his mouth feels on mine. Like he's branding me, but in the best way. His fingers trail down either side of my neck until he's holding me like he would a stack of fine China. Like I'm delicate and worthy of admiration. I don't know what that feels like. "Stephanie, I promised I would always be gentle with you. Don't make me rush through the courting stage of all this. You have the power to break me," he whispers against my lips as the air rushes rapidly from my heaving chest. He places one more quick kiss to my lips before backing away. "I'll be home in ten minutes. Go home and shower if you want and meet me back there. I'll just surprise you with dinner."

He slowly backs away while I try to catch my breath.

I. Can't. Move. I feel like my body is liquefied, my legs are gelatin, my brain is mush. This boy is going to destroy me, and for the first time ever I can't wait to experience the destruction.

Chapter Thirty-One

Max

Sweat. I can still taste the salt from her lips on mine when I walk back through the door to grab my gear. My helmet in one hand and backpack in the other, I smile thinking about the reaction I had to her tonight as I turn off the lights and leave the room. That hasn't happened since I was a teenager experiencing hormones and porno for the first time.

All she has to do is flash a coy smile and think about being sassy, and my body wants to bury itself in her.

"Well, you're smiling. That's a good sign," I hear as I walk past the front desk. Debra, the fitness manager, has been my contact since I signed on to teach the class. She offers me a kind smile, but her eyes tell another story. "How'd the first night go? I think I saw some broken hearts and a few pulled muscles come out of that room earlier."

Laughing, I nod my head. "Yeah, I think they thought it was going to be nothing more than 'punch here,' 'kick him in the balls there,' instead of actual physical fitness worked into it. Not sure how many are coming back."

"A few dropped. I overheard a couple talking about you being taken and how depressing it was that your girlfriend is in the class." She cocks an eyebrow at me, questioning. Lowering her voice and leaning on the counter, making her cleavage even more visible in an already low-cut top, she asks conspiratorially, "So, who's the lucky girl?"

There's something about her that puts me on edge every time I have a conversation with her, like I'm talking to a mirage, and I know it's because she's attempted to pry into my private life more than once. This brings the total number of attempts to several. People are nosy and I understand that. It's part of the human condition. We all want to know the gossip, the dirt on our neighbors, and the sordid details about the couple fighting in the supermarket parking lot. I fidget. What do I say when it's really none of her business? It doesn't help matters that Steph and I haven't exactly pinned down what we're doing yet. Are we just getting to know each other still? Are we dating? Are we a couple?

I'm not saying anything until Stephanie and I are able to talk about it. That's the only way this will end well.

"Debra, I'm sure you'll hear about it through the grapevine. Isn't that how all small towns work?" Smiling to hide my annoyance, I step back from the counter as she frowns at me. "I'm sure she'll be here for class Wednesday, so feel free to get the bloodhounds out. Besides, if people drop because there's a woman in my life, they signed up for the wrong reasons. This isn't a dating service."

Her mouth pops open at the sternness in my voice, a tone I rarely use until something on the job dictates I use it, and she backs down. "No, I know. You're right. It's not my place to pry. See you Wednesday?"

I nod, confirming the next class and turn on my heel, lifting my hand in a wave. "Have a good night, Deb. I need to go hunt down some dinner."

Irritation rolls off my shoulders as I step out into what's left of the day. Checking my watch to see my ten minutes are already up, I pull my helmet down on my way to the bike then head to the grocery store for ice cream and Oreos.

***

Her car isn't in the driveway yet when I get home and I feel an absence all around me. Knowing she likely got caught up in a conversation with Tommy, I take advantage of the few minutes alone.

Notes are important to me — my mom used to send one in my lunch every day when I was a kid — and I've always enjoyed leaving them for others. I used to leave them occasionally for Adrienne, but she didn't appreciate them like I do. I always found even the most heartfelt ones in the trash. She never saved anything just because it held sentimental value.

The one for Steph tonight I left taped on the back door, inviting her in to make herself comfortable. I didn't want to take a chance she would leave if I didn't answer her knock.

Stripping down and stepping into the shower, the hot water rushes over me. The exhaustion of working eighteen of the last twenty-four hours crashes around me. I let the warmth billow around me, the steam building up, as I give myself five minutes to wonder what it would be like to come home to her every day.

I won't live in a fantasy. This isn't some cheesy romantic comedy on Netflix where problems are disproportionate to the people in the story or don't exist at all, but I get the feeling most days with Stephanie could be magical. She might have been broken, but she's mighty and strong and everything I love about her I also admire.

"Max?" I hear her call up the stairs. My entire body smiles at the sound of her calling my name.

The bathroom door was left ajar in case she got here before I was done. Yelling above the sound of the water I let her know I'll be out in a few minutes and shove my head back under the water to rinse away the rest of the day. The house is quiet as I step from the bathroom with a towel draped lazily around my hips and cross the hall to my bedroom. Reaching out, I gingerly touch the dog tags hanging on the bulletin board over my dresser and take a minute to feel thankful for the conversations I had with him about girls when I was a kid.

"Always treat a woman like a lady, Max. Open doors and offer your arm, but don't just act like a gentleman. Be a gentleman. Be kind, always," he'd tell me and then he would show me. He would hold doors open for women entering a store behind him, open the car door for Mom when they would leave the house together, hold her hand when they were out and about even if just walking into church.

I was given the best father, and the greatest example of how to be a good man, I could have. Someday it'll be my turn to set an example like that.

I'm lost in thought when I hear her cough downstairs and she brings me back to now. I dress quickly, skipping the socks, towel dry the hair that's gone too long without seeing a barber, and jump down the stairs in time to watch her carefully place a picture frame back on a shelf in the living room.

Shit. I feel the smile slip away from my face.

Slowing my movements, I feel like I'm treading choppy waters as I walk cautiously to stand behind her.

"You ... you have a family?" she questions not taking her eyes off the photo of me and a visibly pregnant Adrienne. It's one of the only photos of her I've kept out since moving to New York. The others I kept after dividing them with her parents and siblings are stored in my closet in a small memory box my mom gave me after the funeral. "Max?"

I take a chance and set my hands on her shoulders, steadying her or me I'm not sure which, and quietly say. "I did. At one time, I had a family."

The burden to tell her everything settles in my chest like a cancer that grows and grows and won't be killed. It's heavy and constricting.

And then she quietly asks "Did? What happened?" before turning to look at me and forcing my hands from her shoulders.

"Which version do you want? Long or short?" I ask, a humorless laugh climbing out of my throat as her eyes caress my face, the day old stubble, the exhaustion I feel again so suddenly under her penetrating gaze.

"I've got all night. Let's make coffee." And she touches my cheek, a touch so gentle I wonder how I've lived with myself knowing she was just a few blocks away, knowing I wouldn't let myself love her from the same room but only care for her from afar. Nodding my head, I reach up and hold her palm to my lips before pulling her into the rest of me and placing my forehead on hers.

"Okay," I whisper, and, taking her arm in mine, lead her to the kitchen and let her make coffee while I begin the longest road to my recovery.

Chapter Thirty-Two

Stephanie

I sit in stunned silence.

Listening. Learning. Hoping the urge to take flight doesn't take over.

"He murdered your family and then came here to start over." He nods. "And I started dating him, which led to some horrific bruises and you killing him." He nods. "And now, we're ... you're replacing your dead wife with me? Is that what's happening?"

"No!" he says emphatically. It's like he expected me to come to that conclusion after what we'd been through — together and separately — but hoped I wouldn't say it out loud. Max's hands reach across the table as if they have a mind of their own and he clings to my fingers as though they're his last hope, the thread that can sew his life back together. "Not at all. I can't replace Adrienne. I don't want to. She's my past, a past I'm trying to move forward from. I'm not going to forget her by any means, Steph, but you're not a replacement."

Staring into those deep, dark brown eyes, I know he's being honest. It radiates off of him. Part of me isn't convinced, though, and that might be what hurts the most right now.

I chew on the inside of my cheek. He came here to seek retribution, to avenge his wife's death, and there I was already being sized up by a murderer. A murderer he hadn't been able to catch.

"I could have been next. Why didn't you take him in before he came after me?"

His thumb and forefinger toy with the birthstone ring I wear on my right hand, twisting it slowly one way and then slowly back to center.

Quietly, I hear him say, "He wasn't my priority at the time. I came here because I knew he would come back to where it all started for them, but then I was also here to do my regular job. I'm not a homicide detective. Anytime I had a clue as to where he was or what he was up to, I called my contact at the state police."

"You weren't actively looking for him?" He came here on a whim hoping to catch a killer. What the fuck?

"My chief didn't know I asked to transfer here because of an open case back home."

"Davis doesn't even know?" I drop my eyes to my hand, watching as he continues to slowly turn my ring first one way, then the other, like he's searching for a combination to open my mind.

"He does now. After you were attacked, I told him everything I thought would be useful for him to understand, from Adrienne's relationship with Judson to the DNA evidence against him. I felt I needed to explain myself for why the Troopers were so suddenly involved in what would have been otherwise considered an assault. He'd flown under the radar for a long time, and when he went after you, we were finally able to track him down and end his reign of terror. It was a lot of action for a small town, Steph. You grew up here. How many times has there been a manhunt in your hometown?"

I snort out a laugh. "Rarely. The most excitement I recall from growing up was the night some guy climbed the water tower and spray painted 'OJ is innocent' on it."

"My point exactly."

We sit in silence, but I reach out with my left hand, holding his still so he'll focus on me instead of that one finger.

"Max? You swear you aren't trying to replace her with me? I can't do anything more than be your friend if you are. It would kill me to know you're looking at me and seeing her." God, I'm such a bitch. She was his wife and here I am practically begging him not to think about her when he's with me. "I'm not saying I don't want you to talk about her. I understand grief. It's just, if we're going to attempt a relationship, I need you here with me ... not somewhere else. Emotionally."

He pulls the corner of his bottom lip between his teeth, gnawing on it as he considers his words. His eyes shine with unshed tears and he wears his vulnerability like a sweater. He's a strong man, but even the strongest have a weak spot. I'm his.

Pulling in a ragged breath, he picks up both my hands from the table and brings them to his face to kiss each palm. "I don't want to be your friend, Stephanie."

***

"You pulled a Stella?"

I'm wearing one of Max's zippered hooded sweatshirts with a Cleveland Police emblem over the left breast. It was cold when he took me to my house on his way to work and I hadn't taken a hoodie of my own when I went over to his place last night. It's September, so I should have known better, but I also didn't expect to spend the night.

"Um, yeah, I guess so?" I ask as Brian stares at me. I stand, exhausted, in his kitchen waiting for an invitation to attack the coffee pot. I play with the zipper as I strategically make my way over to the cupboard with the big mugs. There is no messing around with normal size coffee cups this morning.

While Max might have taken me home, it doesn't mean I didn't have thirty different text messages throughout the night from Tommy, Brian, Stella, my mom, and Caryn, all wanting to know where I was ... obviously because they were concerned for my safety. At first. When I told them I was with Max it riled the masses and now I'm somehow supposed to explain in detail how nothing happened.

Nothing. Happened. Except my attacker murdered Max's wife and unborn child. I understand his protectiveness over me, his love for his job, his nightmares, his heartache. I don't understand why it's anyone else's business.

"A Stella? Is that what you call that?" Stell asks coming into the room. "Did you make Britt's lunch for today or is that on me this morning?" she questions Brian, who blanches and quickly starts throwing peanut butter and jelly on some bread.

"That answers that," I say, laughing and loving the dynamics of their relationship. "What is a Stella?"

They turn to look at one another and smile before Brian responds, pointing at me with a peanut butter covered knife. "A Stella is when you crash at a man's place with no intention of sleeping over and then wear his clothes home and never give them back. Case and point, *I* no longer own a Syracuse Orangemen hoodie. *Stella* owns it. It's belonged to her since the night her divorce from Keith was final. Do you plan on giving him back that sweatshirt?"

I suck a mouthful of coffee into my face and contemplate, really mull it over before answering. "Shit. I pulled a Stella."

"See. I told you," he says to Stella, while he finishes throwing Britt's lunch into the thermal bag that matches his backpack. Stella just smiles and nods.

"Bitch," I mouth to her and she sticks her tongue out at me.

"Okay, cowboy, get him out for the bus and then you go to the coffeehouse. I think I need to have a heart-to-heart with my baby sister."

I wander to the front of the house where Britt's putting his sneakers on to give them a few minutes together. I watch as my nephew intently loops and tugs until the laces are just right, remembering what it was like to learn those simple things that seemed so big when I was still so small. He finishes and stands to grab his bag before noticing me.

"Aunt Steph! You came to see me on the first day of school!" And that's all that matters.

"I sure did. I hope you have a great first day. Just remember to try your best," I say, the words slipping out of my mouth like my mother climbed into my brain and put them there.

"I will." He offers his closed fist and I bump it before setting my coffee down and pulling him into a tight hug and kissing the top of his head. "I love you, Steph. I love you, Mom," he calls toward the kitchen.

"Love you, too," my sister and I say in unison. Britt opens the door as Brian comes through with the lunch bag, gives me a hug, quietly tells me he wants details and will get them by any means possible, and then they're out the door, letting the latch fall silently so as not to wake the baby, because despite all the other noise the door would be the one thing to wake Emmy.

Stella clears her throat behind me and I turn to see my sister leaning in the kitchen doorway, a coffee mug cradled between her hands. "Speak. Now."

I nod and walk toward the kitchen, toward her. "But first, coffee."

***

"So, are you two dating now?" she asks when I've finished telling her all the things she never bothered to tell me she already knew. She felt it was Max's place to share with me about his past, which I don't disagree with, but she didn't even give me a heads up about him teaching the self-defense class. Not even a pep talk about how every man has a past. Instead she's done nothing but support and encourage the idea of Max and I ending up together.

And I can't be mad about that.

"We're going to try." I sigh, tapping my index finger on the rim of my coffee mug

"What the fuck does that mean, exactly?"

"It means we're together and exclusive but not defining it. We're trying a relationship. Taking into consideration his last one ended with murder and mine ended with me in the hospital —"

"And murder —"

"Max didn't murder him," I shout defensively. "He shot him in self-defense. But yeah, we both had horrible endings to our last relationships, so we're just going to take this slowly."

"Slowly. You spent the night at his house last night, Steph. That's not moving slowly."

"You spent the night here the day your divorce was final, Kettle."

"Point taken, Pot."

Emmy stirs in Stella's arms and sleepily pops off her breast.

"Are you supposed to be drinking this much coffee while you're breastfeeding? I thought the same rules applied to this as to pregnancy."

She drops her eyes before saying, "It's decaf."

I look down at my cup. No wonder it tasted off. Fucking decaf. Rolling my eyes at Stella, I walk to the sink and dump the remains down the drain and she has the balls to snicker at me.

"Sorry Steph. I thought you were going to be able to taste the difference. Brian makes one pot of caffeinated in the morning before he leaves and if I don't hoard an extra cup in a travel mug and hide it in the laundry room he takes it all with him."

Turning and leaning back against the counter, I see the new mom glow on her face. It's actually exhaustion, but after years doing the newspaper thing, these crazy baby hours are really no different for Stella. "He's being a coffee Nazi, and that's not fair, but I get it. And I probably didn't taste much difference because I hardly slept last night. By the time Max and I finished talking and fell asleep it felt like the alarm was already blaring in my ear. He let me go back to sleep while he got ready for work and told me I could sleep there, but after all the messages from you guys last night I figured my best bet was to get up and come explain myself in person. Tommy wasn't home to scold me, so I came here for my verbal lashing."

She watches me carefully. The questions are forming in her mind and I'm just waiting out the hurricane.

"How do you feel about the fact he was married before?"

"I'm not even sure what day it's supposed to be, how am I supposed to know how I feel about that?"

"It's simple. Today is Tuesday. Now, how do you feel about knowing about Adrienne."

"I feel like I should talk to my therapist about her." I'm speaking to my shoes, the toes of my sneakers, because they won't give me the look my sister is giving me. "Stell, Darren had a type. Do you know what that means?"

"It means you and Adrienne are both beautiful."

I shoot her a look. "It means Max has a type, too. What if ... what if, even though he says he's not trying to replace her with me, he actually is but doesn't realize it and it turns out I'm not good enough? What then? What if I'm not the perfect match for him?"

"And what if you are but you let fear drive you away from him?"

We're quiet for a beat, both considering the "what ifs."

"I'm in love with him, Stella. What if he decides he can't love me back because I remind him of her?"

"When did you realize you were in love with him?" Always the reporter digging for details.

A smile slips free.

"The first time? The night of your wedding when he walked me home. Then I hardly saw him, so I felt like I was obsessing over the unobtainable ... kind of like a middle school crush but with grown up feelings and fantasies." She laughs at me because she gets it.

"What about the next time you fell?"

"Friday night, right after Emmy was born. I don't think it was the heightened emotion in the room either. I don't give many extra chances when it comes to men. He was late for our first date that night and I gave him another chance. There was something in the way he came to find me even though he knew he was late. If I wasn't there, I think he would have come to the house to make things right. He didn't make excuses for why he was late; he looked me in the eyes and told me the truth. I didn't have a reason not to believe him. Then when Emmy started wailing after the longest moment in history, it was like I looked at him and just knew." I get the last word out as the first teardrop falls. "It's not even one thing in particular. It's the way he held my hand, the way he kissed me, the note he left me after he put me to bed. It's everything. He's everything. The only thing making me question my feelings is knowing about his past and it kills me that that knowledge could, under different circumstances, make me turn tail and run."

"You don't cry over boys, Steph." Her voice is soft and lacks accusation.

"I'm in love with this one, though." The words fall from me as she pulls me into an embrace only my sister could offer.

***

"You've missed a couple appointments. Is everything okay?"

I'm pacing her office, not that there's too much room to do that, but her question stops me in my tracks and I'm staring out the window overlooking Main Street again. It doesn't take much for me to spill everything. This woman has burrowed her way into my head and can tell if I'm bullshitting as quickly as my own mother can.

I give her all the details — our date, Emmy's birth, the self-defense class surprise, him opening up about his past.

"Did you tell him about your past?"

"My past ... no. I didn't tell him about Parker and all of that. It seemed unimportant at the time. I wanted to focus on him."

"But you slept with him?"

"No," I say quickly. "No. Yes. Yes, we slept together, snuggled up under the same blanket. No we didn't 'sleep' together." I make sure to use air quotes.

"You didn't have sex with him. That's good. You're taking things slowly, then?"

I take a deep breath and turn around to face her, leaning back against the wall lined with windows. "If by slow you mean he told me my ex-boyfriend-slash-attacker murdered his wife and baby and the only reason Max is living here is because he came to hunt his sorry ass down ... then yeah. Molasses, Doc."

The laughter that comes out of her makes me smile. I wasn't intentionally being funny. It's just frustrating that everything comes down to how quickly Max and I are moving forward with our relationship.

Fate. Sometimes I want to give her the middle finger and tell her to fuck herself. Today isn't one of those days. Instead, I want to crawl back under the covers with him so we can hold each other. My body has never fit against anyone else's like it does his. I've never felt safe with someone like I do with him.

"When do you see him next?"

"I have to work tonight at the library because someone called out sick, so tomorrow at class. I don't want to get too personal there, though," I express, running my hands through my hair. "Some of those women looked like they wanted to have me as a sparring partner eventually just so they could take a cheap shot. I'm not looking forward to those nights if they find out Max and I are actually seeing one another."

Not that I want our relationship to be a secret, but it would be better for us to get through this session without everyone in class knowing we're a couple.

"No, I understand. Work with him on having a regular date night, though, and keep professional interaction professional. If you're both off on Friday, let him plan a date. Give him a little control in this relationship, share the control. Relationships are partnerships. You don't have to run from Max, Stephanie."

"You speak like you've met him."

"I have. He's a police officer, I'm a psychiatrist. There have been different times I've helped Chief Franks with his officers, particularly after they're involved in a tragedy of some sort — a shooting, a fatal car accident, things of that nature — so, yes, I've met Max on a few occasions. Their work isn't easy, on the body or the mind," she explains. I guess it makes sense.

She must have talked to him about the shooting when he killed Darren. I ask. She can't tell me. Patient confidentiality, she expounds. She won't tell me if he's talked to her about me or Adrienne or details surrounding his job. Nothing. She can't tell me anything. I turn my head back to the window just as a police car pulls up to the curb across the street. It doesn't surprise me when Max steps from the cruiser and his demeanor is filled with authority and purpose.

"Doc, come here a minute." I'm not asking, but I'm not demanding either, and she stands to step up beside me. Together we watch silently as Max helps a young mother pull a stroller from her trunk and unfolds it for her. She'd been attempting the task one-handed with a baby in her arms while I watched from my perch above Main Street. "He's not from here, but he sure does fit in."

The woman's mouth lifts in a grateful smile as she pushes her hair behind her ear and shifts the baby on her hip. Her lips form the word "thanks" and Max nods at her as she turns to set the child into his seat. Max bends to pick a tiny hat up off the sidewalk and places it back on the infant's head. The gesture is sweet, but if I were down there looking in his eyes I'm sure I'd see a flash of pain.

"Is that one of your worries? That he'll leave now that he did the job he came to do?"

I shrug my shoulders, a quiet admission of my fears.

"Maybe."

"Someday, Stephanie, you're going to have to let someone love you. Don't push him away before he even has the chance."

Chapter Thirty-Three

Max

"You and me ... we need to talk," he says as soon as I walk through the door. I follow him through the kitchen to his office, like an obedient dog, because I know what's coming. "You're sleeping with Stella's sister?"

"He's doing what to Steph?" comes the cry of opposition as Tommy and Greg crowd the doorway behind me.

"She spent the night at his house last night. She showed up at our house this morning freshly showered and wearing his clothes." I never took Brian for the gossiping kind. It's like a high school locker room in here.

"Telling tales over the clothesline, that's all this is," I say to myself, muttering the words under my breath but feeling their eyes boring into me as they wait for me to say something.

"She's in my self-defense class, guys. After class she was going to come over for dinner and we ended up talking until after midnight. I had to work early and she had walked to my house, so she stayed the night and I drove her home this morning on my way in." Why do I even need to explain myself? I point at Brian and say, "And the sweatshirt? It was cold at six this morning. I don't want her to end up sick. You guys are dicks."

I turn around and push my way through the barricade Tommy and Greg have made.

"Dicks! The whole lot of you," I call back over my shoulder. "I bet neither of you gave Brian shit like this when he was chasing Stella." I direct the comment to T and Greg as I come through the café doors and round the counter, grabbing a to-go cup and pouring myself a fresh cup of coffee like I'm supposed to be on this side of the cash register.

"That was different. They already had a history," Tommy says sidling up next to me. "I know you care about her, but this is moving kind of fast, don't you think?"

"No, I don't. And history? I killed the man who attacked her, Tom. If that's not a little bit of history, I don't know what is." I push past him, dropping a couple bills on the register, as I take a sip of my coffee and head back toward the door to leave.

"She's working tonight. Got called in. Meet me at Brian's for a beer in the woodshop after we close. We'll talk."

"See ya then," I say over my shoulder and lift my cup as a thank you and goodbye all rolled into one.

Maybe I should offer to work a double tonight. Nothing good can come of a conversation with Tommy, Brian, and beer.

***

I walk purposefully up the driveway carrying a six-pack of Yuengling. The kitchen light is on in the back of the house and Stella sees me step up onto the porch. Opening the door with a smile, she pulls me into the room and hugs me into stunned silence.

"Not the reaction I was expecting, but I'll take it," I say and bark out a laugh as I hug her back. I nod a hello to Steph and Stella's mom sitting quietly with the baby at the breakfast nook and she gives me a knowing smile. Of course she knows. "Good evening, Mrs. Barbieri."

"The guys are already upstairs in the shop. Tommy is bound to act like an asshole because he's protective of her, but Brian and I talked after he got home," Stella says biting her lip. "I told him he acted out of turn and he feels horrible. Steph's an adult. She cares about you. Those two, and Greg, had no right to pull that nonsense this morning."

I nod, looking down at my jeans and boots, feeling like the kid who was bullied on the playground and then got scolded for not standing up for himself.

"Yeah, but I can see why they would react that way. I'm the new guy and Stephanie is like everyone's baby sister around here."

"But she's not. She's *my* baby sister and I'm telling you, you have my full support. Just be careful. She spooks easily and has trouble with letting herself be loved, Max. I don't know what happened when we were younger, but she's had a hard time letting anyone get close since she and her high school boyfriend broke up a decade ago," she says quietly, peeking out the kitchen window. "I think they saw you walk up the driveway. Brian's on his way to the house, so go on and have a few beers with the guys. Let me know if they get to be too much and I'll come out and put them in their places."

She gives me a big smile and shoos me out of the house before I can say anything else.

I come toe-to-toe with Brian on the back porch and he grabs my free hand, pulling me into a man-hug.

"I heard you got in trouble with your wife," I say, grinning at him.

"Someday you're going to be in this position again, too," he responds and the smile falls from my face. That hit close to home and he sees it as soon as the words leave his mouth but we leave that conversation on the deck to die. Grabbing a beer from the six-pack in my hand and popping the top off, he says, "Come on, maybe you can give Tommy some insight into how you're not just trying to get into Steph's pants."

"What kind of insight did you have in mind, Bri? You know I'm kind of a private person," I say gruffly as we make our way back across the driveway. I wouldn't have even told Stephanie about Ohio yet if she hadn't seen the photo of Adrienne and asked me about it.

He stops and looks at me. "Yeah, I know. The thing is, Tommy, as much as he might respect you for what you did when Steph was hurt, he's not going to understand you actually have a heart unless you let him see inside it."

Setting the beer on the ground, I grab a bottle and twist the cap off. Pointing the bottle in Brian's direction, I confront him. "You, of all people who know what happened in Ohio, want me to go upstairs and tell Tommy how my wife was murdered by her crazy ex-boyfriend? The same guy who dated Steph and then put her in the hospital? I've been working really hard to let the past remain in the past. Why can't we just do guy shit, like talk about baseball and scratch ourselves?"

Laughter howls from his lungs as he watches me pull a long sip from my bottle. "You are just as much of a softy as I am so don't give me this 'let's do man stuff' bullshit. Come, Max, let's go bond," he goads me, wrapping an arm around my shoulders and pulling me toward the barn.

"Fine, let's bond, just stop patronizing me," I grumble as I reach down for what's left of my six-pack.

***

"Okay, wait ...," Tommy says after my Reasons I'm A Good Guy speech.

Brian and I wait. And wait. And wait some more as I witness Tommy's genius brain in motion, mulling over all the information I just threw at him.

"You were married?" he asks incredulously and I wonder why I told him everything if that was the one part he was going to get hung up on. Brian and I stare at him dumbfounded before looking at one another.

"T, that's the only thing you heard out of all of that?" Brian asks.

"No, I heard all of it. Max just didn't seem like the marrying kind, I guess. I had no idea any of that had happened. You haven't talked about it in all these years?" I hear softness in his voice; he's my friend, not Steph's unruly roommate.

Sitting on an old onion crate, rolling an empty beer bottle between my hands, I contemplate how much more strength I have to continue the conversation. "I have, but it wasn't until recently. I didn't tell Brian and Stella until a month or so ago. I told Stephanie last night. That's why she stayed over. We talked about my past and it took a long time to get all of the words out. It wasn't my intention to tell her so soon, but she saw a picture of Adrienne on a shelf and asked me. The last thing I wanted to do was start a relationship with her based on lies, so I came clean about what happened."

"And here I kind of thought you were just trying to get with her because you did the hero thing. Even after we talked the other night at my house, part of me still didn't fully trust you were in it for anything more than a good time," Tommy says as Brian kicks him in the leg and whispers "you're an asshole, T."

Pulling the last beer from the box, I tell them honestly, "You think I didn't know you thought that about me, Tom? I can read you like a book, brother."

Looking at his watch, Tommy, stands up, "Yeah, I hear you. Mama's told me I don't hide my emotions very well."

"For real, Tommy? You're going to bring Mama into this?" Brian laughs at him. "By the way, they'll be here tomorrow and might need to crash at the other house, so make sure the spare room is picked up for them."

Tommy rolls his eyes. "Damn it. I've got a ton of business stuff in there that we haven't moved into the office space yet. Alright, I'm going home now then since I have to clean."

Handshaking and backslapping hugs are given and Brian and I are left staring at each other.

"You okay?" he questions. "I didn't think you were going to tell him all of that. It's a lot to keep rehashing."

Thinking carefully, I realize I am okay. "It doesn't hurt as much to talk about it now. I think the talking about it is what's helping the hurt subside."

He smiles at the thought. "That's kind of how that healing thing works, Max."

Chapter Thirty-Four

Stephanie

"Hey, Steph. I didn't know you were in the self-defense class. Did you sneak onto the roster after people dropped on Monday?"

Debra. I forgot that motor mouth gossipy wench worked here.

"Nope, I signed up a while ago. I'm surprised you didn't see me Monday. You might have been busy with other members, though," *or eye-fucking every guy walking from the fitness room to the locker room since you're too much of a whore to be casual about anything to do with the opposite sex.* I smile politely and continue walking past the counter.

"Oh, well, I heard from some of the women who dropped that the instructor's girlfriend is in the class. As though she'll be able to keep tabs on him in a room full of hormonal women," she stage whispers to me. "Once he starts with any hands on instruction, all bets are off as to who's going to be touching whom and where."

The heat creeps up my neck and I feel my jaw involuntarily clench, my molars grinding together in an attempt to undo all the orthodontic work done during my awkward pre-teen years. *He's a professional,* I remind myself, *and she's a fucking idiot.*

"Yeah, I know, right," are all the words I can muster before briskly walking away from the bloodbath that could occur if she kept talking.

He's the only one in the room when I walk almost silently through the door and it gives me a moment to take him in — the toned muscles, the tan that hasn't faded yet, the way he holds himself like he belongs everywhere.

As though he could feel my eyes on him, he turns and flashes me a smile before walking in my direction.

"You're a little early," he says once he's standing close enough I can feel the heat radiate from his body. Lowering his voice, I hear him ask, "Trying to impress your teacher?"

"Maybe just a little." I smile up at him and allow his lips to softly graze mine before I pull away. "Be careful. We don't want anyone to think I'm trying for brownie points here."

He pushes my hair back behind my ears and kisses me deeply. "Never. We'll keep it professional in class. Class hasn't started yet, though."

Pressing a hand against his hard chest, I tell him, "You can kiss me all you want later, but I just had a conversation with Debra that makes me think right now isn't the best time to be making out."

Max's eyes widen and his nostrils flare just a little as he clenches his jaw. One eyebrow raised, he says, "The gossiper out front? She likes to talk, doesn't she?"

I laugh. "That's putting it mildly. She was the queen of gossip in high school, and an absolute suck up to all the administrators. If someone was in trouble, chances are word got back to the main office because of Debra McCarthy." I laugh again when he rolls his eyes and says "fantastic" in the snobbiest voice he can fathom.

He's easy to be around and it makes me want to kiss him more.

But my opportunity to taste his lips again is cut short as Max takes two steps back, away from me, and I feel the warmth from his body leave my space. Curious, I look up at him, wishing he'd come closer, when he sorrowfully says, "It's time to be professional."

The door opens and a stream of my classmates walk through, a few taking notice of me. Jamie enters last and sees me still standing with my back against the wall beside the entryway. Kneeling down, I pull my water from my bag and take a quick sip before retreating to my spot beside her in the back of the class.

I've tried so hard to be nonchalant but then I get near enough for her to elbow me. "What's that about?"

"Talking with a friend before class, that's all."

She smiles but still hums out an accusatory "mmhmm" and I wonder if she's going to press the matter.

I'm saved by Max's booming voice — solid and strong, knee weakening — as he begins class.

Only being the second day, it's been more learning about personal strength and the fundamentals of thinking and reacting defensively than actual maneuvers and training. Tonight, though, after some complaining from a small sect of women, he decides to give us just a taste of the kind of moves he plans to spend the next several weeks teaching us.

We've promised to be professional while we're here, but he needs someone to demonstrate on and chooses me ... out of everyone here, he chooses the only girl with an invisible target on her back, and while it thrills me that he wants to use me for the demo, I know it's only going to feed the rumor mill. It's something we're going to have to deal with, I decide, and step forward to take my position beside Max as he explains how to move out of a hold when someone comes from behind.

He has me stand behind him and put him in a loose choke hold so he can still talk to the class as he shows them how to dip down and twist their body, reaching up to touch my face as though he's going to shove me away and I drop my arm. It's all in slow motion. It's all part of the lesson.

But tonight, it's a lesson that could change everything. It's one that will prove to him just how vulnerable I still am.

"Everybody see how that works?" Heads nod, there's some nail-biting in the front row, and a few of my classmates are chomping at the bit to give it a go. Class doesn't seem so boring anymore to those who prompted the quick lesson. "Steph, I want you to try it," Max says and I whip around to face him.

"Huh?"

"Change roles with me and show me what you learned," he asks more than says and gives me a questioning look before walking closer to me and lowering his voice. "If you're uncomfortable once you're in the hold, reach up and pinch my arm."

Swallowing back the emotion, I lift my chin and nod my head assertively. "Okay. I can do that." He's giving me an out. He knows he's offering it to me, but he doesn't understand how much it really means to me. Not yet. Not right now.

I hear him talking to the class, going over the steps again, telling them what I'm going to do and I think I'm ready for this.

My back is to him as he finishes talking. He asks me if I'm ready and I hear myself say that I am. He takes three big steps behind me to close the distance between us and grabs around my neck with his arm, his elbow beneath my chin.

I feel the panic start to creep up, but I can hear him talking to the class.

I know it's just Max. I know he wouldn't hurt me. But no matter how many times I tell myself "it's just Max," all I can feel is Darren. It's the night I broke up with him and, as though I'm still stuck in that alley, I can almost feel the brick against my face.

I feel the panic rise into my chest, my heart racing and my pulse rushing in my ears. Fear. And blackness.

And when the black stops clouding my vision I feel pain in the back of my head and see half the class staring wide-eyed at me with mouths gaping and the rest are huddled around Max.

Max, who's hunched over with his hands covering his face.

Max ... who's bleeding.

"Oh my God," I cry out, my hand going to my mouth. "What did I do?"

Jamie is the first to walk over to me and between the "are you okay?" and "what happened?" I find myself fighting back tears as I walk closer to Max. The distance between us is unfathomable. He must have stumbled backward to end up that far away after the back of my skull made contact with his face.

"I don't know what happened. He had me in the hold and then I blacked out." The words fall frantically from my mouth like shipwrecked victims clamoring to get on the last life raft aboard the vessel. Reaching out for him, I touch his jaw and he cautiously stands to his full height, pulls his shirt off, and holds it to his face in an attempt to stop the bleeding.

Those brown eyes, so full of worry, stare down at me. "I don't think you broke it," he says so only I can hear.

"So, class, that's not exactly how I showed to get out of that situation, but as you can see ... it works."

He's an optimist, that's for sure, I think to myself as a few of the women release nervous laughs. I'm glad when he dismisses class and no one chooses to stick around to mingle. The room empties quickly as Max and I continue facing one another. I'm waiting for him to say something to me, to get mad at me, to be furious at me for screwing up his lesson.

To be downright pissed off that I made him bleed.

But instead he tosses the bloody shirt over with his motorcycle helmet and steps into my body, enveloping me in his warmth. His lips are in my hair, kissing me there, and he's asking me if I'm back. It takes me a minute to realize he knew I was going to react, that I was going to do whatever I could to get away.

"When did he grab your neck?" his voice a harsh whisper, his arms tense but protective and tight.

Feeling my body relax against him, I carefully wrap my arms around his waist. My face nestled against the sparse and soft hair on his chest, the hard ridges of his pecs the perfect place to lay my head.

"The night I broke up with him, he came after me in an alley when I ditched him in a restaurant. It was almost a year ago. He never put me in that kind of hold, but it felt like it was happening again and then ... I don't know what happened," I breathe out against his skin. "I'm so sorry."

"Despite the blood and possible fracture to my face, I'll tell you what happened. You. Defended. Yourself." He releases the words slowly, making sure they sink in, before placing two fingers beneath my chin and tipping my eyes up to meet his. "That's what you did. And while I'm really proud of you for reacting so quickly, I'd rather you attack me with kisses than with the back of your head."

He's able to draw a laugh out of me as he leans his face closer and places a light kiss to my forehead.

"Resorting to sweet talk now, are we?" I feel flirty Steph take a step forward. She hasn't made a true appearance in so long I wonder if he'll like her. I wonder if I know how to be her again. I wonder if I buried her too far beneath the surface.

"Baby, I've been trying to sweet talk you for weeks now," and his breath whispers across my lips just before he makes contact for too brief a moment. "If you brought spare clothes, you can shower at my place. A movie and ice cream tonight, I promise. I haven't even opened the Oreos I bought the other night."

"Be still, my heart. You really are a gentleman," I smile up at him. "Thank you. For not thinking I'm a head case or, you know, dropping my ass and arresting me for assaulting an officer."

His eyes widen. There's something primal about the way he looks at me.

"See, now I can't help but think about you in handcuffs. I need to get you home," he growls at me, pulling my mouth hard against his.

Dating Max is going to be unlike anything I've ever experienced. He is an experience, and I can see how his wife was so drawn to him. While I try to keep the feeling of being a replacement at bay, I can still respect her enough to understand why she would fall in love with him. I get it because I'm a lost cause when it comes to loving him, too.

I feel him hard against my hip and I can't hold back the laughter as our mouths separate. "You and those damn shorts. By the time you're done teaching this course everyone is going to know how big your manhood is, you know."

He glances down and shrugs. "What can I say. You have a certain effect on me, Stephanie," he says, leaning forward to kiss me again and subtly adjust his shorts. "Shower. Ice cream. Oreos. Any John Hughes movie you want. Or John Cusack. Pick a John and I'll watch it with you."

"Oh, buddy, game on."

There's something familiar about watching him move across a room, as though I've watched him do it a thousand times but the feelings that grip me never dissipate no matter if it's the first or one-thousand-and-first. He carefully folds his soiled shirt before placing it into his bag and pulls on a clean one before throwing the bag on his back and grabbing his helmet. The bleeding stopped, but I question if he doesn't need to go to the hospital instead of home. He tells me he's a man and men can handle things like this with ice packs and, obviously, ice cream.

"Someone has a sweet tooth," I laugh at him again as I pull my backpack up my arms and adjust it on my shoulders.

His eyes turn serious as he reaches for my hand and pulls me toward him again. "I'm sweet on you, Steph. Let's go home."

A sigh escapes me as he places one more gentle kiss against my lips.

Home.

Something just feels right hearing those words from his mouth. I don't want to let my heart get too far ahead of my head, but it's racing to bypass logic. Logic has no place here. Emotion is busy taking up residence.

"Kiss me again," I say, and he does, leaving me breathless.

Chapter Thirty-Five

Max

As I took Stephanie's hand and we stepped toward the exit, I saw Debra scurrying away from the window in the door and I knew it was only a matter of time before my antics got back to people I know.

News spreads quickly in a small town. It took even less time than I anticipated, though. I was sure I had at least a day before anyone at work found out, but by the time we got home, I had a text message from Gill saying his wife heard from a friend who works at the community center that I was practically screwing one of my students against the wall in the yoga studio.

I'm not going to let it bother me that someone saw me kiss my girlfriend. After all, I'm a grown man. Class was over. I'm allowed to kiss her. But this message? It's the entire situation blown out of proportion. I'm not the dry hump each other in public kind of guy; I'm hand-holding and quick kisses.

Leaning against the kitchen counter, I rub my hands down my face and groan. Then I hand my phone to Steph and show her the message. Her response: near hysterical laughter.

"You really have to give her credit. She works fast. Do you mind?" she questions, pointing to the screen. "Because I just want to put this to rest. It's nobody's business but ours. This is still so new and now I'm going to be labeled the village whore."

Stepping into her space, I take her face in my hands and see the emotional turmoil brewing. The look in her eyes tells me she's been here before. "You're not a whore. She's done this to you before?"

"It was called high school. Other girls were busy planning for prom while I was trying to undo the rumors she started about me hooking up with my boyfriend's best friend in the locker room. Do you know how embarrassing it is to walk into the cafeteria and have all your friends whispering about something that never happened?" she says crestfallen. "I'm almost thirty years old, but she's apparently never grown up. Mean girls don't mature, they just find new targets."

I slide my phone out of her hand and place a kiss on her cheek. I can fix this. "I'll take care of it. Why don't you go grab a shower?"

Amusement lights up her features. "I didn't actually bring spare clothes, Max. You lured me here with *Pretty in Pink* and ice cream. Plus, Tommy and Brian's parents are in town and I wanted to give T time with them tonight."

"What I hear you saying is you're going to steal more of my clothes. Already. We've been officially dating for like three days and you already own half my wardrobe, woman," I joke, pulling her closer to me.

"What can I say, Max, you have a certain effect on me," she uses my words against me, but I like the way they sound coming from her full lips. I like the way she says my name and how she feels comfortable enough with me to share the bits and pieces that hurt. She pulls out of my arms and grabs her bag from the floor, turning toward the living room. I watch her walk away, reaching up to pull the band from her hair, letting it cascade down her back. My breath catches in my throat watching her do these simple tasks and I wonder how long I'll last before I fall too far. Drawn to her, I follow behind slowly to lean against the doorframe and watch as she comfortably makes her way through the room to the stairs, as if she's come home with me a hundred times and this is our routine. She says nothing as her feet find footing on each new step, as she strolls effortlessly into my life, and I catch the playful look in her eye as she slowly ascends until she's out of sight.

The phone clutched in my hand vibrates with an incoming message. I pinch the bridge of my nose as soon as I see it.

Gill: It's true isn't it? You're getting it on with one of the single ladies in your class.

The water turns on upstairs and I tell myself to take care of this before I let my thoughts wander to Stephanie ... a naked Stephanie in my shower. I haven't thought of a woman the way I've been allowing myself to think about Steph in years. It's like Adrienne's death killed my libido and shattered any drive to be intimate with anyone.

Until Steph.

Me: Not getting it on. Tell your wife she shouldn't have dropped my class and she would know the truth.
Gill: Burn. She's giving you the finger. Who's the girl though?
Me: My girlfriend.
Gill: o rly?

To Hold

Me: She signed up for the class without knowing I was teaching it. I never told her I was and she didn't mention she'd signed up for self-defense. It was a surprise to both of us. Tonight she almost broke my nose.

Gill: Good for her. Someone needs to keep you in line.

Hearing the water upstairs turn off, I let him have the last word and walk over to the toaster. Buffing the side with the hem of my shirt, I lift the contraption and hold it up so I can see my reflection. Putting pressure on the bridge of my nose makes me wince, but it's not bad enough to make me think it's broken.

I never hear her come down the stairs. She's like a ninja. "How bad is it really?" she questions quietly and I turn in time to see her nibbling on her bottom lip. I can't take it. Standing just inside the doorway, she's only dressed in a towel draped around her body, her damp hair pulled forward across one side of her neck and down over her collarbone.

"It'll heal," I say setting the toaster back on the counter and moving swiftly from the other side of the room to pull her to me. Her body fits perfectly against me. "You smell ... different."

Her laughter shines in her eyes as she looks up at me. "I smell like you. No shampoo or body wash in my bag."

"Yeah, but on you, the soap smells different. It's less Irish Spring and more ..." I bend my head to breathe her in, trailing my nose along the side of her neck. Her breathing comes out in ragged little pants. Her heart pounds against my chest. My eyelids flutter closed and I feel her head drop back to her shoulder as my lips finally make contact with the sweet flesh below her ear.

I hear her breathlessly mumble, "More."

And I give more. My heart gives more. My body gives more as her fingers trail up my arm to my neck, into my hair where she holds me gently against her as I trace my lips from her pulse to her ear to her jaw. My hands follow the path the towel makes along her back but I lack the bravery to tug it loose, I'm not ready for that. I'm not ready to move beyond nips and teases and getting to know her important features. I'm not ready to do more with her body than leave an imprint of myself on her heart.

"Lips," she says, and I oblige, delving into the minty flavor of her tongue, my lips parting hers to capture the fullness of her flesh. Our bodies move as one, only coming to a stop when we reach the wall. Her hands are in my hair as I drop my arm to the curve of her waist and feel her instinctively bend her knee, setting the sole of her foot against the wall, and my fingers follow the trajectory of her hip, her thigh, her knee until I can grasp behind it. Holding her closer as I fall gracefully against her body, pinning her softly against the wall of my kitchen. I feel her entire body sigh in contented silence.

My lips slip slowly away from her mouth as our foreheads come together, our breath mingling in the distance between us as we slow our panting to gentle exhalations, and I rest my nose alongside hers. Her hazel eyes sparkle and read my soul the moment I open mine. I feel her climb inside my chest and wrap around my heart with just one look.

"I'm going to have a lot of trouble not falling in love with you right away, Stephanie."

Closing my eyes again, she places against each of my eyelids kisses so soft they whisper like butterfly wings sharing secrets with the breeze.

"You're not the only one feeling the fall, Max."

Her unspoken words hide behind the emotion of the ones I heard — the ones where she asks if it's okay for me to fall in love again, if I'm okay with those feelings for someone else. Instead of talking about it, I place another kiss to her lips, pressing my hips into her more, feeling the urgency to further let Adrienne go and love Stephanie fully.

"You're here with me, Max. You don't have to prove that to me. Feel the fall," she breaks away from my mouth, her hands resting along my jaw, her fingers caressing the shadow forming there. "We don't have to get there overnight. I don't want to. I want to feel every moment with you and I've never wanted that with someone before."

With every word she speaks I feel it happening faster. How does she do that? How does she so completely shatter me and rebuild me like this?

"I want to feel," she whispers against my lips, leaving another chaste kiss in her wake as a tear spills free.

Pulling back, her body follows mine and I wrap her into my arms while silent sobs wrack her body with emotions I haven't yet had the chance to learn from her. For the second time in our short relationship, I carry Stephanie to bed with no intention of anything other than letting her sleep. We make it to the top of the stairs and into my bedroom where she watches me with wide, bloodshot eyes as I pull a T-shirt from my dresser and place it carefully over her head. She lifts her arms through and lets the fabric slide down her body over the towel. Kneeling before her, I carefully push a pair of grey sweatpants up her legs until I can go no further and she stands, her hips level with my eyes. I swallow the lump forming in my throat as I look up into her tear stricken face and push the waistband up her thighs, never breaking eye contact. When she removes the towel, she's fully clothed, and I've never seen my clothes look so good.

"I'll take care of this," she says quietly, holding the nearly dry towel in her hands. Before she can make an attempt to hide in the bathroom, I reach for it.

"I promised you *Pretty in Pink* and ice cream. I'll take care of this," I say, reaching out to wipe an errant tear from her cheek. "Give me five minutes to shower and then I'm all yours."

I step into her body and pull her tight against me, feeling her fingers twist the bottom of my shirt like she's searching for something to tether her to the present. "Five minutes," I repeat. "If you need me, I'm right across the hall."

She smiles against my chest and I kiss her hair. She nods her head.

"I'll be in here," she says placing her palm against my heart. "Promise."

I watch her walk to what is quickly becoming her side of the bed and pull the covers back. Turning toward the bathroom, I pull my shirt off with one hand and do my best to make good on that five minutes.

Five minutes, I think as I stroll back across the hall, my hair still damp

Time is relative, though. From the moment I walked out of the bedroom until I walked back in, Stephanie's exhaustion took over. I look down at her still frame beneath the covers as twilight filters in through the blinds, casting shadows across the comforter and walls. Curled up in the fetal position, her hand draped across my pillow and the blankets pulled up over her shoulder, she takes up such a small amount of space. She never turned the television on so we could watch a movie. She never snuck to the kitchen to get a bowl of ice cream.

Even though it's still early, I slip into a clean pair of boxer briefs and then into bed beside her.

Chapter Thirty-Six

Stephanie

He's chasing me. I'm running across campus. He won't stop.
Nothing will stop him.
Not until he's finished with me.

Crying out in my sleep, I wake and find my legs wrapped around Max's lower body. As I attempt to untangle our bodies I realize it might not have been my voice after all that disturbed my rest. It's his.

"Max," I whisper, unwinding my ankles from his body and sitting up. Sweat glistens on his forehead despite the chill in the room from having not yet turned the heat on for the winter. Cautiously touching his arm, I scoot myself up the bed to lean against the headboard and reach to touch his face as it contorts. A look of disgust mars his perfect features, his brows draw together, and he moans out a low, painful, "no."

And then again, louder.

And again, nearly shouting. "No. No!"

He shakes his head from side to side and I move closer to him, brushing the tiny hairs from his brow out of the sweat, and shushing him, lulling him back to a sleep I hope is dreamless. I continue to caress his temple as his arm snakes up around my thighs and he nestles his body against my legs.

I fall back to sleep sitting propped up against the headboard, my hand gingerly stroking his face, and wake up as daybreak leaks through the blinds. The sun isn't to blame. It's the boy tentatively kissing his way up my pant covered leg who causes my night to end again. Sleepily, I smile down at him as he crawls over me beneath the covers and drags me under with him.

"Did you sleep well?" he asks, tracing the line of my jaw with tip of his nose until he reaches my ear. His hands tenderly grasp my waist, left bare from being tugged back beneath the blankets as the shirt rode up around my ribs, and he softly trails his fingers along the underside of my ribcage. He makes no attempt to plunge his hands beneath the fabric, and despite making me want more, I'm content with just this for right now.

I sigh, a great big girly sigh, and he chuckles. It's a low throaty sound that makes my body tingle and respond, but respond and prepare for something I'm not ready for, not emotionally or psychologically. I don't want any of my firsts with Max to be hurried and rushed because one of us has to leave.

"I slept." My response isn't what he expected. He hears it in my voice and lifts his head to look into my eyes, searching for the answers to my restless night. I offer them freely. "Nightmare. Both of us had one, but yours woke me."

His brows come together in a wrinkle above his nose. "Was I talking?"

"Saying 'no' over and over. Whatever was happening was painful." I reach up to touch his face, massage away his worry, and close my eyes as his forehead kisses mine. "You were super sweaty."

"Seems I'm always super sweaty around you. We haven't even done anything fun to get sweaty."

I laugh, a genuine from my belly kind of laugh that causes him to pull away. A grin spreads across his face and those laughs fall away to flutters. The way he looks at me. The way he touches me. The way he makes me want to survive and feel things I stopped wanting to feel long ago rise up and creep along my spine.

"We will," I quietly promise him as his alarm clock begins beeping. I roll my eyes. "Just not right now, obviously."

His lips find mine, humor dancing in his eyes as he pulls away and says, "You're wearing my sweats home, right? I'd like to drive Tommy a little crazier."

My eyes widen, but I smile. "That's cruel, Max."

"Nope, what's cruel is that we're adults and I got scolded by him and Brian for sending you home in my hoodie since they thought we were up to no good." He kisses me again. "Stay for breakfast?"

"I've seen your fridge. I don't think we can make a feast on a box of baking soda, three beers, and what I assume is week old pizza."

"I hide all the good stuff in the cupboards?"

"Lies, beautiful boy, all lies. But I know a nice little coffee place that bakes fresh muffins around this time every morning."

"You're willing to take that chance? Walking into the coffeehouse in my clothes?"

"For you, and the love of chocolate muffins this early in the morning, yes. I would walk across fire," I say in all sincerity. He drops his mouth to mine again and kisses me like he means it. I never want it to end.

"Then breakfast at the Bean it is. Let me shower and shave and we'll head down."

***

To Hold

We drive separately because he needs to go to work after breakfast. I honestly never would have seen myself as the type to get out of bed at dawn to have breakfast with anyone, but Max is different. Max is special in a way I never imagined I could believe someone was.

I think that was evident the night we met.

He was doing a job, but then he went above that call. It feels like my heart has been making room for him since that night. My soul sings when he's around, and when he isn't it feels lost and like it's searching for the other half.

It wasn't until I pulled up in front of the coffeehouse that all those feeling could be put into words. I know I told my sister that I've fallen for Max, but it feels like that's a fraction of the truth.

I hear the door to my car open as I sit on Main Street contemplating all my emotions for this boy — this man — and hardly notice as he kneels beside me. He reaches out to pull my bottom lip from the hostage situation I have it trapped in between my teeth and I turn my head to catch the wistfulness in those mocha brown eyes of his.

"You're going to chew a hole right through it if you don't stop." His voice is thunder against the quiet of the late summer morning. As he pulls his thumb away from my mouth, I catch a glimpse of the blood on his finger and taste the metallic remnants on my tongue. "We left the house five minutes ago. What's got your mind working this hard already?"

I can't break away from his gaze. "You."

"And what about me?"

"You do things to me I never anticipated, things and emotions and thoughts no one has ever caused me to have."

He reaches across my lap, unbuckles the seatbelt, and pulls my legs until I sit facing him while he continues squatting next to the car.

"What sort of things have I caused that others haven't?" His face is blank, but his eyes are worried.

Tentatively, I list them off, starting with the early wake up calls for breakfast and ending with feeling lost when he's not close by.

"It's crazy. Right, Max? I'm crazy. I feel like my heart is going to rip in two every time one of us leaves to do normal things, like work or sleep," I say into my hands as I cover my face. Finally when I take a chance and look up at him, I see his smile. It touches his eyes and they sparkle.

"Then I'm crazy, too. I'm not going to push this, though, Stephanie," and I groan when he says my name because he doesn't understand what it does to me when he says it like that. His smile widens, if that's even remotely possible. "I want to take my time with you. I want to learn all of the things that make you tick. I want to know how you take your coffee."

"You know how I take my coffee. The rest of it, though, that could take decades."

"Then decades it is."

I sit in stunned silence as he picks my hands up from my lap and brings each palm to his mouth, placing a lingering kiss to one and then the other, before standing and kissing me back into the here and now.

"Decades, Stephanie. I want to know everything and I intend to take my time learning." My mouth is left hanging slightly ajar as I stare up at him. "First things first, though. I promised you fancy chocolate muffins."

He pulls me to standing, reaches in to grab my keys from the ignition, and reaches for me. We walk hand-in-hand, our fingers intertwined, and I realize I've never been this comfortable with a man.

Ever.

Together, we head around the back of the building to the kitchen entrance. The front door is still locked and the lights in the café haven't been turned on. The only visible light through the front windows are track lights above the counters that house the coffee makers. We silently make our way through the open back door and I giggle as I hear Brian scold Greg for licking batter from his fingers ... again.

"The health department is going to have a field day with you, Greg," Brian says before noticing Max and I propped against the open entryway. A smile splits his face when he says, "Hey there sunshine!" and walks over to give me a hug.

"Please tell me you guys have double chocolate muffins ready? I need them."

"They'll be out of the oven in three minutes," he says looking from me to Max. "What gives?"

He has his dad look on his face — it's concern dipped in authority — and I am never one to deny my brother-in-law information. If I do, Stella will call me before I have a chance to sit down and eat that muffin.

"I stayed at Max's."

"And his black eye?" Brian's level of observation at five in the morning is uncanny at best. I hadn't even noticed there was any bruising, yet.

"She almost broke my nose last night," Max points at me, obviously feeling the same need I do to spill all the details when Brian's in interrogation mode.

To Hold

Bri hums, a low sound in his throat. "Good. She teach you your lesson?"

"Me and my entire self-defense class," he mutters.

Brian holds his right hand up in the air and I instinctively high-five him. "Atta girl. Come on, you two can earn your keep. Scones need to be made still."

Max and I are led to one of the counters, handed a recipe, and left to fend for ourselves.

"Uh, Bri ... I'm not very fluent in baking. I can cook, but Stella and Mom are the ones who bake," I say turning around and facing him as Max walks to the sink to wash his hands.

He steps back toward me, looks me in the eyes and says, so only I can hear him, "Bake with him. It's one way to know for sure." I feel my eyebrow lift, my face telling him he's nuts. "Trust me, Steph. You want to know if he's the one? See how he handles that dough." His no-nonsense tone knocks me out of my element and I nod in response as he looks over my shoulder, an approving smile making its way across his face.

When I turn back to Max, he's already got most of the ingredients for a first batch in the bowl, his head bobbing slightly to the music climbing out of the stereo speakers on the shelf above us.

"You have secret weapons," I accuse.

He turns his head to smile at me. "I wouldn't call them weapons."

"Still, secrets nonetheless."

"Truth? My parents insisted I know how to cook and bake. I was probably Britt's age when I took a real interest to it," he says as he sinks his hands into the dough and begins to work it into the side of the bowl and then into a ball. I watch closely how he forms the dough, how his fingers damn near make love to it, and swallow against the lump forming in my throat and the heat rising up my neck. He stops and my eyes snap to his. "Are you okay, Steph?"

Like a fish, I open and close my mouth repeatedly before I can finally answer. All that comes out is "uh huh." His smile is even more of a turn on than watching him play with his food, and I'm afraid I might never be able to stop myself if I don't take a couple steps back from him.

Leaning against the counter, I watch him dust the butcher block countertop with flour and then neatly press the dough into a circle.

"After watching you manhandle that dough, I expect to never get turned down when I ask for a massage."

He doesn't even respond verbally, just leans to his right and places a kiss on my mouth that leaves me wanting more of everything.

From across the kitchen, I hear Brian call to me that the muffins are ready.

"Yeah, I bet her muffins are ready," Greg says a little louder than I think he intended. I smack him with a wooden spoon as I walk past to get my breakfast and smile to myself when I hear Brian and Max laughing at his expense.

Chapter Thirty-Seven

Max

"You deserved that," I call across the kitchen to Greg as soon as Steph slips through the café doors to the front of the coffeehouse.

"If she didn't stop watching you make those fucking scones she was going to have an orgasm right here," he counters.

"What can I say? I'm just that damn good."

"Enough!" Brian halts our bantering. "I don't disagree, but, guys, she's like my baby sister. I don't want to think about what you might do to her body with your hands, especially not when you're using those hands to make scones I plan to sell. I think I need to go call my wife or something and just not be in this room right now."

I shake my head, but smile to myself thinking about the look on Steph's face as I was working the dough. She walks back into the kitchen with two mugs of coffee and half a muffin stuffed in her mouth. It somehow makes this morning even more memorable than her flushed cheeks ever could.

I slice the dough into eight triangles, set them on a baking sheet for the oven, and start mixing a second batch.

"Can you make the peanut butter ones? With chocolate chips?" she asks as she holds out a piece of muffin for me. I pull the bread into my mouth, holding her hand still in order to lick the warm chocolate from her fingers, and wonder how I never actually tried these before. Maybe it's the company that makes them sweeter. She swallows hard, her eyes never leaving mine, as she finishes her thought. "They taste like Reese's."

"You really love your chocolate," I comment and reach for the baking chips.

She stops her arm midway to her mouth and stares at me as though she's contemplating whether she should share what's making the wheels turn or not.

"At least one week out of the month, yes, it's my favorite food group." Her lips clamp shut around what's left of the muffin after her admission.

I chuckle. "You must think PMS and biology scare me." The look on her face is priceless. I lower my voice and bring my lips dangerously close to hers again. "They don't. I aced biology in high school."

She closes the distance between us and I taste the sweetness left behind on her lips before she pulls away.

"Good. Because I'm not giving up chocolate for you," she says, her tone dead serious, as she watches me above the rim of her coffee mug. "My life depends on it ... and therefore so does yours, and Tommy's since he's the unfortunate one to live in the same house as me."

It's been nearly a week since Tommy and I had words about Steph in their kitchen. While I'm certain he's okay with our relationship now after sharing with him the details of my past, I'm not sure how he'll feel if I'm around the house.

"How's that going, by the way? Living with T?" I ask as I start working the second batch of dough. Maybe if I keep my hands busy I won't feel the jealousy reaching into the back of my brain.

She snorts, adorably, and I look up in time to see her roll her eyes. "It's ... going. Now that we've got the office space here we're able to spend a little more time apart. I've hardly seen him except for in passing since the weekend. If I'm not at the library, I'm with you or at Stella's. Why do you ask?"

Before I can come up with a response, she pokes me in the ribs to get my attention.

"Guys can get possessive. I don't want to step on his toes if you and I are over there, is all," I answer, hoping it's enough. It isn't.

"Jealous bone?"

"Maybe a little."

Her arms snake around my waist as I mold the dough into a circle and begin slicing it. Her breath is warm against my back where she trails kisses over my T-shirt along my spine. "Max, I'm yours. If you're going to be jealous of something, be jealous of someone else's car, not my living situation."

I move the last of the dough to the baking sheet and say in all seriousness, "I'm not going to be jealous of somebody's car. Have you seen my baby? She's pretty amazing. She makes grown men drool because *they're* jealous of *me*."

Her hands travel up my stomach to hold on to me tightly around my chest, the warmth of her palm radiating against my heart. Placing one more kiss against my back, she breathes out against me, "That sounds extremely cocky Officer Wyatt, but you just proved my point."

I turn in her arms, and despite the flour coating my fingers, they find their way to her cheeks and trace her jaw until I'm holding her face in my hands. My mouth connects with hers. I'm kissing her deeply, my tongue slowly caressing hers, and I'm stuck wondering why I waited to come for her. Why didn't I make her mine months ago?

The catcalls from across the room break through and, while her cheeks are flushed, I'm left grinning.

Her words from earlier resonate through my thoughts and I know. My soul feels a little more complete with her near, too. The heart I thought would never heal, is suddenly whole again. We're probably both certifiable at this point, but I'll take crazy every day of the week if it means Stephanie is by my side.

"Don't you have to work, Wyatt? Get your tongue out of my roommate's mouth and go serve and protect some little old ladies or pull kittens out of trees," Tommy calls from the doorway before closing the distance and staring down at my handiwork. "Since when do you bake?"

Steph pulls out of my grasp, leans in once more to place a chaste kiss to my lips, and grabs her mug to go refill it. I watch as she walks away, looking better in my clothes than I ever imagined any woman could.

"Since I was knee-high to a grasshopper. Isn't that what you southerners say?" I turn my head to smile at him. "How'd I do?"

"You made the special scones ..." he says, shaking his head. "You've got it bad for her."

"I told you I did," I respond as she pushes back through the café doors with a small paper bag and a to-go cup of coffee in her hand. She sets them next to my work station and points to the clock. Good thing it's a small town or I'd never make it to work on time. I wash the dust off my hands and reach for the bag and coffee, leaning into Steph to give her one more kiss before I quietly say, "It's Thursday. Dinner at my house? I promise to feed you more than baking soda and stale pizza." She smiles up at me and I feel the warmth emanate from her. "Come over around six?"

"I'm all yours," she whispers back so only I can hear her above the noise in the kitchen.

She's all mine.

I leave the coffeehouse feeling elated. It's not a feeling I usually associate with, but it's more than enough to carry me through a rough shift until I can have the other half of my heart back for the evening.

***

"Mom, what do you cook for a girl the first time you cook for her?" Silence meets me from the other end of the telephone line. "I'm asking for a friend."

I hear my mother's laughter loud and clear. "Max, you've never been a good liar and you know it. Is this for Stephanie? The girl you've been telling me about?"

"What do you mean I've never been a good liar? I'm so good at it. ... Yes, it's for Steph," I sigh out, my arms crossed over the shopping cart as I stroll through the grocery store. I look up from the still empty basket and catch the eye of a woman staring at me from around an endcap. "Ma, why do women stare at me like they're going to whack me over the head and drag me back to their cave?"

"You've never worried about that before. Are you just now noticing that women check you out?" She laughs again.

"Perhaps. Okay, so I wanted to get to the store quickly after my shift to get things for dinner so I tossed my street clothes into my backpack and wore my uniform. Is it the uniform? You work in emergency. How many of your nurses are checking out the guys I used to work with when they come in?"

"Sweetie, it's definitely the uniform. Let's get back to the important stuff, though. You're cooking for this woman. Is this the first time you're cooking for her and have you slept with her yet?" There's no playing around in her tone. I don't think I believe what I just heard.

"Excuse me?"

"You heard me. I'm your mother, not an idiot. Please don't make me repeat myself."

My legs begin moving and as I share with her one thing after another about Stephanie, she tells me what to put in my cart. I try not to answer her question about sleeping with Steph, but she asks again.

"Yes and no," I respond truthfully. "Nothing has gone past first base."

"Lord, I wish your father were still here to deal with this. Did you forget how to woo a woman, Max?"

"Are you condoning premarital sex?"

"I just want you to be happy."

"She makes me happy without that."

"Oh thank God, because you cannot build a relationship on sex alone." The relief in her voice is comical. "Did you pick up everything I told you to?"

When I tell her I did, she tells me to go back and get more ice cream.

"I bought some the other night."

"Go get more."

"What the hell, Mom. What am I even making?" I stare down into the now full basket. Three boxes of cereal, two dozen eggs, a bag of rice, four boxes of spaghetti, two giant tins of tomato puree, a slab of meat, soy sauce, and the list could literally go on and on. "I probably have two hundred dollars' worth of groceries."

"Did you think I was having you pick up things for just tonight? Max, I know you. The fridge is probably bare and the cupboards are just as bad. If you're going to be dating anyone, especially a woman who comes from an Italian family, you need to up your food game, buddy. I'm sending you a recipe for Mongolian beef. Make that tonight. The rest you can figure out what to do with."

I sigh deeply, thankful I called her but equally irritated she knows me well enough to know the kitchen is empty.

"I do have coffee and ice cream and Oreos, you know."

"That'll get her through one week a month."

"Does everyone know what her cycle is like?" I mutter under my breath and hear my mom let out another laugh. "When are you coming to visit? I think my kitchen needs an intervention. I can't call you every time I need to grocery shop."

"Super Max, you've got this. I'll be there in a few weeks. I was actually thinking about coming out for Thanksgiving, too."

It's been a long time since my mom had a holiday off. I find myself longing for a turkey dinner surrounded by family instead of inside a squad car.

"That sounds like a fantastic plan, Mom," and I'm nearly certain the smile in my voice is audible from one state to the other.

We hang up as I start unloading my groceries at the checkout. "Did you find everything today?" the cashier asks and I think I answer her. I know I nod my head, but there's something eating at the back of my brain the entire time she's scanning items. I swipe my card, sign, and load the rest of the bags into the cart. It doesn't register until I'm walking out of the store that I rode my motorcycle to work and have nowhere to put the groceries.

I stand staring at my bike for a few long minutes trying to figure out how I can get all the bags somehow hooked to it.

"That will never work," the low growl of a man's voice says behind me. "Nope."

I turn my head slightly. He's not a hulking figure of authority, but he's a respectable man nonetheless. Dressed in a Carhartt jacket and Dickie's work pants, I recall the last time I stood so close to him, sharing coffee in Stella's kitchen the morning after I put Steph's nightmare to rest. We exchanged glances then, but little more. I've tried since to give him a wide berth, afraid he'd think I was just a haughty young cop with an itchy trigger finger. I was surprised he wasn't at the hospital the night Emmy was born, but he'd stayed back to keep Britt occupied and have some one-on-one grandpa time.

"Sir," I say politely to acknowledge him. Then glance back at the bike. "I don't know. It could work if I put some stuff in my backpack and combine other bags into one, maybe balance them on the handles."

He barks out a laugh. "You sure you're not an engineer, son?" He smiles broadly and points his thumb over his shoulder. "Jenny had me pick up a list a mile long. Says she's making apple pies for the church bake sale. Toss your bags in and I'll follow you home so you don't tip that scooter over trying to get there in one piece."

He doesn't leave any room for discussion, just grabs a couple bags from my cart and walks to his truck, so I silently follow suit.

"Sir, I really appreciate this," I say as I load the rest of my groceries in the cab of the pickup. "I was in such a rush to get this stuff and get home to make dinner I hadn't even considered I rode the bike."

"It's no big deal. You're one of Davis' men, which means you might as well be family. What the hell are you making for dinner anyway? You bought enough to feed a family of seven." He looks at me quizzically and peeks into the bag closest to him. "Can't do much with a can of green beans and some corn starch."

I feel my face heat and I'm suddenly thankful he didn't look in the bag with the condoms and new razor. It's not that I bought them with the intention of doing anything tonight ... but eventually I think we'll end up in third base territory and I want to be prepared for a home run if it's going to happen.

"You'd be surprised what I can make given the right ingredients. I'm a real Boy Scout," I say as I close the back door on his truck. I walk back to the bike, fire it up, and head out of the parking lot with Stephanie's dad close behind.

We drive the two or so miles to my house and Mr. Barbieri pulls in the driveway right behind me. He's pulling bags from the truck when I approach. When he steps back I grab what's left and lead the way to the back door, entering through the kitchen, and set the bags on the counter. He does the same.

And then there's awkward silence I'm unsure how to fill. Do I mention I'm making dinner for Stephanie? Does he know we're seeing one another? He must. How could he not? He's a dad.

"So ..." I start. At the same time he mumbles, "Well, now ..."

We both stop talking and I turn to look at him, giving him the green light to say what he wanted to.

"You know she's my little girl, so I'm not going to give you all the dad warnings or threaten to dismember you if you break her heart." That answers that question, and his eyes tell me he'd make sure my body was never found.

I swallow my fear and close my mouth, taking a beat to think about what I want to say. "Thank you, sir, that's really reassuring to hear," I hear a quiver in my voice as I speak. In this moment it doesn't matter that I'm a trained police officer. To him, I'm just the guy dating his daughter. He doesn't have to respect me automatically because I wear a badge and gun to work. It's my job to earn it.

He taps his knuckles on the countertop as we stare at the cupboards in front of us. "I will say this, though. I never took the opportunity to thank you for what you did for my baby, but you can imagine how grateful I am you and Colton were there that night. I'm more grateful now that you're still in her life because it seems her best friend in the world has up and vanished from her social circle. You know better than anyone what she's been through," he chooses his words carefully, releasing each one slowly, before gripping the edge of the counter and turning his head to look me square in the eyes. He swallows once, but I see the sorrow mapping its way across his brow. "I've heard Stella and her mother talking, and I want to tell you how very sorry I am about your family. You've been through a lot for a young man."

His words catch me off guard. It's not often those who know my story talk about it, let alone give me the chance to feel like I haven't already lived a thousand lives.

"It hasn't been easy, but I'm learning to be stronger."

"You've got to be, Max. It's the only way to survive. Stephanie ... she's the same way. She's strong and resilient, and it's because she's been trying to survive. The thing is, she's been trying to do it alone."

I turn and lean my hip against the counter. "She doesn't have to. I hope she knows that. The other night she told me she wants to feel, and I think I understand, but maybe you can shed some light for me?"

He takes a deep breath, blowing it out slowly before looking at me again. "She's been doing what a lot of broken people do — trying to numb the pain. I talked to Tommy the other night, though, and he hasn't seen an empty wine or liquor bottle in a week. Something changed."

"Me." My brain doesn't even register the word until it's spoken, but it's me. It's been a little more than a week since I found her in the park. "It's me, isn't it?"

"That's the only thing Jenny and I can figure. She smiles again. Real smiles."

"She isn't the only one who smiles real smiles these days, sir," I say.

His eyes never leave my face. I feel like he's scrutinizing every facet of my life, of my mind, and it's a little uncomfortable after a few minutes. When he opens his mouth, he pulls in a breath and his eyes grow wide, "You're in love with her, aren't you?"

"I ... well, we just started seeing each other."

"Cut the bullshit, Max. I don't like being fed lines. Maybe you just started seeing each other, but the two of you have had a connection for almost a year now," he says, gently pushing his index finger into the center of my chest. "If you love her, you need to make sure she knows. My Steph isn't like other girls. She'll deny your feelings unless you tell her straight out exactly how you feel."

My face flushes and I'm sure he can see the sweat on my forehead. He's her dad. He's supposed to tell me to leave his daughter alone and shit like that. This ... I was not expecting this.

"But, it's been a week! You don't tell someone you're in love with them after a week," I squeal. I hear myself and I'm pretty sure I sound like a prepubescent boy.

"Again with the bullshit, son. I told Jenny I was in love with her at the end of our first date. If anything, you're behind the ball," he laughs and claps me on the shoulder. "Just ... don't wait too long. She needs to know she's loved by someone who is choosing to love her. All of her."

Staring at him, dumbfounded, I shake my head and mutter, "You're a very scary and confusing man, Mr. Barbieri."

"But you love my daughter, and she's all that matters," his voice serious as he turns to leave. "Get to making dinner. She'll be here soon, I'm sure. Have a good night, son, but not too good. I saw some of what's in those bags."

I hear his laughter start up again as he closes the door behind him and heads back down the driveway to his truck.

It takes a minute to process why his tone turned so serious and when it hits me, I grab the bag and run upstairs to shove of the box of condoms in my sock drawer like a nervous kid hiding contraband from his parents.

To Hold

***

I hear the door open just as I'm setting the last of the beef in the sauce. The rice is done. I considered pouring a glass of wine for each of us, but took into account what Mr. Barbieri said about the lack of bottles in the recycle bin over the last week. If she's trying to rid herself of her demons, the last thing I want is to offer her a glass filled with them.

I've been there, too. I don't want her to go back if she's come this far.

I push the meat through the sauce to make sure it's coated as her arms come around my waist.

"If I had known you could cook and bake, I would have stopped to take my shoes off in front of your house a long time ago," she says and places a soft kiss to the back of my neck. She's taller tonight — this morning her lips only reached the middle of my shoulder blades — so I look down, my eyes taking in the sight of knee-high high heel boots.

Setting the spoon down next to the stove, I turn to get a look at the rest of her. She left her hair long and free, and it cascades down the back of the blazer she's wearing over some strappy top. All business on top, but below her waist? She mixes professional with party and it looks ... too amazing. "That skirt is really short. I feel like I should give you another pair of sweats. Aren't you cold?"

She cocks an eyebrow at me and I know I sound like a lunatic because, really, what red blooded heterosexual male is going to suggest his girlfriend go put on more clothes? One who got caught by his girlfriend's father with a box of condoms, that's which one.

"We aren't sixteen, Max," she laughs at me. Placing her palm against my chest, I wonder if she can feel what she does to my heartbeat. "Can we eat before I change? It smells delicious and I'm kind of starving."

"I'm kind of in love with you," I blurt out.

"Took you long enough."

"Have you been talking to your father?" I question, pulling her face toward mine. I need to kiss her.

"Nope, but I take it you have," she lets sweet laughter carry through the space between our mouths. Lowering her voice, she says, "It's okay. I'm kind of in love with you, too."

Her lips fit perfectly to mine, like they were cast from the same mold and forced to find one another in the abyss. Her mouth opens slightly, and it's just enough for me to taste the mint on her breath from her gum as my tongue gently teases the inside of her bottom lip. I pull away and hear a disgruntled moan deep in her throat.

"You're starving. I'm going to feed you," I say, placing one more kiss at the corner of her mouth. "And then I'm going to clothe you, feed you ice cream, and we are going to watch a movie. No falling asleep."

"But we can make out during the movie, right?" she asks without skipping a beat. "I mean, if you want to."

The coy look in her eyes makes me laugh. "Nope. Why would I want to do that?" I say, but can't keep a straight face as I hand her a plate full of food.

"Because I have very kissable lips, that's why."

She yelps when I reach for her waist and pull her to me, her back resting against my front, once she's set her dinner on the table and her head instinctively drops back to my shoulder.

"They're the most kissable lips I've ever had the pleasure of tasting, Stephanie," I say, feeling her breath quicken. "So let's get through dinner so we can take our time enjoying dessert."

Chapter Thirty-Eight

Stephanie

We've been together for a little more than a month. We work like a well-oiled machine — when he's at work, I work or do research or work with Tommy. When we aren't working or at his self-defense class, we're doing normal couple things.

And I'm openly, madly, deeply in love with him.

It feels like things have moved so quickly, but at the same time it hasn't. Our relationship started almost a year ago, whether he or I want to ever admit it to one another. The night he came to my rescue, something changed in both of us.

He slowly began shedding his guilt about Adrienne's death. For me, after years of self-hatred and believing I was the poison in the bad relationships I'd had, I gave myself a chance to start healing.

In the midst of our pain, our hearts and souls took a vacation and shacked up ... it just took time for our minds and bodies to catch up.

The only thing that hasn't happened yet? Sex. There have been plenty of times when we've come close, but I always stop him.

"You should talk to him about it," Doc says as she watches me looking out the window of her office again.

It's the beginning of October and the leaves are changing. The green slowly disappearing and being taken over by fiery reds and raging oranges, and every once in a while on my runs these days they fall down around me like confetti. Like Mother Nature is throwing me a party for getting my shit together in less than a year.

"I'm going to. I don't see any way around it," I say to her reflection in the window.

Not once has he made me feel bad for stopping him from removing my underwear, or like I owe it to him to have sex, or that he's going to love me less because I haven't let us go that far.

Never has he tried to make me feel like he was worth more than what I was giving him physically. Max lets me take the lead and he doesn't even know how empowered I feel when he tells me it's okay to stop and then just holds me.

He hasn't asked me why we're "waiting," either, but he knows abused women so chances are he sees something in me he's seen in them, something more than the broken pieces Darren left behind in the wake of his fists and boots.

"He's got today off from work. We're going to the homecoming game at the high school and then home for a late dinner." Again, I'm talking to her reflection.

I'm afraid to look in her eyes. She knows this is difficult for me. Talking to her about my sexual past? No big deal. She's here to help me through all those shitty memories. But opening up to Max? He might be a tough guy, he might wear a badge and carry a gun, but to know about something that for so long I've blamed myself for ... I can't possibly know how he'll react to that.

Today might as well be the day to find out.

***

We find seats next to my parents and Britt. I know high school football is huge in the south, but I just don't get it. My dad never played, so I don't understand what his obsession is with it, either. He played baseball.

I grumpily sit down next to my mom, who stands up to hug Max. "You could have said hello to me, too, Mom. Guess I know who your favorite is," I say, laughing at the look on her face.

"He's a sweet boy and he lets you drag him to family dinners and functions. Yes, he's one of my favorites," she says leaning down to hug me. "And I love how sweet he is to you. That's what really makes me like him."

Britt pushes past my mom and climbs up onto my lap. Max finally sits, taking my gloved hand in his and rubbing the back of it gently before Britt scoots across my legs until he's sitting between me and Max. Our hands are clasped behind Britt and he reaches behind to hug each of us to him. I lean down and place a kiss to the crown of his head over his knitted cap. I couldn't care less about what's going on below us on the field if I tried. Something about this quiet moment in the midst of the crowded bleachers feels inexplicably right.

The spectators in front of us start standing up in a wave-like fashion, no doubt letting someone through to sit.

"Stephie? Holy shit. I never thought I'd see you at a football game." My head snaps up at the sound of his voice. It's one of the voices from nightmares that taunted me for years. It's a voice that makes it impossible to be intimate with anyone unless the anxiety is drowned in alcohol first.

"Parker."

He moves to step over the seat in front of me, attempting to give me a hug. My grip tightens on Max's hand where he's still got a hold on me behind Britt, grounding me without being aware. I don't let go and when I look over at Max, his jaw may as well be permanently clenched. His ears are red from the cold, but there's a flush of anger climbing the side of his neck as he holds my hand possessively.

"Damn, I haven't seen you since, what, sophomore year of college or something?"

I want to vomit. If he doesn't move I'm going to vomit on him. I swallow hard, not wanting to cause a scene in front of my family.

"Yeah, it's been a while." I won't give him more than an inch.

"Looks like you've been busy. A kid? Hey, man, I'm Parker. Steph and I went to school together," he says reaching his hand out to Max and neither of us correct him where Britt's concerned. He always did think he was smooth. I watch Max size him up before returning the gesture.

"Max." Looks like he's giving Parker even less than an inch.

"Right. I don't know you. You new here?" He looks Max up and down like I'd seen him do to guys in high school, always someone he thought he could pick a winning fight against.

"How is that any of your business Parker?"

"I'm just making conversation, sweets." The sharpness in his tone catches me off guard. The pet name has me wanting to crawl out of my skin. I jerk my hand, but Max pulls me back.

My mom continues to watch the entire exchange and finally elbows Dad to get his attention after the "sweets" endearment was dropped. I turn my head slightly and watch my dad's jaw clench and wonder if he taught Max that trick because the identical expression on both their faces is uncanny.

"Get a move on, Parker. We're trying to watch the game," Dad says, glancing at Parker out of the corner of his eye.

He turns on the charm, just like he always did when we were in high school. "Mr. Barbieri, I guess I didn't see you there. How are things? Mrs. B. you haven't aged a day."

Asshole.

My parents were told we had a difference in opinions as to where our relationship was going and that's why Parker and I broke up. They don't know the details. However, my relationship with my dad has always been unconventional. Unlike my friends and their dads, I grew up talking to him about boys and other matters of the heart. He knows Parker played the field. I think he probably knew before me, but didn't want to damage our father-daughter relationship by trying to force me to see it before it was time. The shadow clouding my dad's eyes as he stands to his full height, towering over my mother stuck between him and Parker, tells me he never let all that history go.

"Things are fine. They're better without you around. Go find your seat and leave my daughter alone," he growls. I don't think I've ever heard my dad growl, or talk to someone like that. Usually if he has something cruel to say he says it in the nicest way possible.

"Or what?" Parker snidely questions, a sneer marring a face I thought was beautiful a decade ago. He never grew out of the arrogant teenager phase. Such a god damn golden boy.

From the corner of my eye I see Max stand up, but he never lets my hand go.

"Mom," I whisper, leaning my shoulder into her. "What's happening?"

"Well, baby girl, this is what it's like to have a boy defend your honor." Then she snickers.

"Did Daddy do this a lot when you two were younger?"

"Not much ... maybe a few times. Ah, shit, now it's a pissing match." She lifts her arm and waves as Davis walks down the bleacher seats behind us. She catches me rolling my eyes and bumps her shoulder against mine. "Just watch. Davis will take care of the trouble maker. You know Parker never liked to upset the local authority."

"Seriously, did you and Dad never like him and just fail to tell me?" I whisper at her, exasperated. "It could have saved me some on my therapy if you guys had told me that fifteen years or so ago."

She shrugs. "You wouldn't have listened."

She's not wrong.

Chief Franks stands solidly behind me, arms crossed in front of his chest, and nods to Dad before addressing Max. "Officer Wyatt," the emphasis on "officer," "is there an issue here? I know you're off duty, but harassment is harassment, right?"

"Yup." And his jaw clenches again and he flexes the fingers on his free hand into a fist. The only times I've seen him do that is during a workout in his basement after a rough shift. "I guess it's up to Parker here if he wants to make a scene or not."

"A cop, Steph? And here I always thought you were into pretty boys," Parker says rubbing one hand down his clean shaven face as he reaches out and places his other hand on my shoulder, pressing his thumb into my neck.

I can't do this.

I can't sit here.

I won't let him touch me.

So I stand up, drop Max's hand, and swing.

My bare knuckles connect with his left eye and everything that follows is in slow motion.

"How dare you! How dare you think you have any right to talk down to me or about me," I spit the words down at him as he cowers covering his eye. I refuse to acknowledge the slight pang of pain coursing through my right arm. "You pansy-assed prick. You may have ruled my life as a teenager, you might think you're hot shit in this town, but you're not. No one cares who you were ten years ago, Parker. No one likes the person you were then or who you turned into. You use people for personal gain and abuse those who give their trust to you. Go to hell."

As I'm finishing my speech, I see Debra — mouth gaping, wide-eyed, shocked, small town celebrity gossiper Debra — approach and climb over the bleachers to get to Parker as she's fumbling through a litany of "oh my God" and calling me colorful names while demanding I be arrested.

It shouldn't surprise me she's his current lapdog. She followed him around like a puppy for years, so naturally the moment he steps foot in town she's going to be barking up his tree.

Flexing my fingers and wrist, I look over my shoulder at Davis and two other off duty officers who've joined our party and I realize I probably just ruined everyone's peaceful Friday night football game and beer fest.

"Are you going to arrest me, Davis?" I question because he hasn't moved. He stood there and watched me send a nice, polished right hook into my high school sweetheart's face and is acting like it's normal.

"Nope."

Debra's mouth starts, and she's screaming like she's the one who got hit. "What do you mean 'nope'? She assaulted him, Chief!"

Davis slowly rubs his chin as though he's thinking it over. "I stood right here and watched him touch her first. Looks to me like this is a case of self-defense."

Debra's mouth falls open and Parker stands up, his eyes burning a hole in my head as he glares at me. Despite my inability to seek help years ago and my fear that Parker would forever be the community's favorite son, Davis is still my dad's best friend and he just watched the whole thing go down.

"Of course, if Parker wants to press charges we can go down to the station, but considering there are four officers here as witnesses to him harassing her," Davis continues, pointing to Parker and me as he addresses Debra, "I'm going to bet no one's pressing charges tonight. What do you think, Debra? Or are you better versed in these scenarios than me?"

"I'm not pressing charges," Parker says shamefully as he turns and attempts to step back over the bleachers in front of us. Debra trails after him and I hear her demanding why he wouldn't have me arrested right before she questions his ability to act like a man.

Stomping up the stairs of the bleachers behind him, she says loudly, "What the hell is the matter with you? You let that prissy bitch hit you like you fucking deserved it."

Prissy bitch? That's one I haven't heard in a long time.

"I've got to get out of here. It's like a high school reunion, but none of my friends were invited," I say to no one in particular as I shake the pain from my bare hand, vaguely remembering I had gloves on. "Good thing you taught me how to hit someone, Max, or this could really hurt."

The adrenaline is still pumping through my system when I take a deep breath and look down into my nephew's face. Max has Britt's head pressed against his hip, covering the other ear so he can't clearly hear some of the things that were said. As he's released from Max's grasp, Britt stands up and buries his face in my jacket.

My guilt is overwhelming and I can't stop the tears as they begin to fall or my arms from shaking as I gently drape them over Britt. It's too much and I feel like I'm headed for a breakdown when I should feel on top of the world.

"Will you teach me how to do that?" his little voice slams into my ears above the sound of the blood pounding in my temples.

I couldn't have heard him right and look from his hopeful eyes to Max for help. Kneeling down he turns Britt around so they're eye-to-eye.

"I taught Steph. I'll teach you," he says as Britt's arms circle his neck and he looks up at me, handing me the glove that slipped from my hand when I wrenched my fingers from his grasp. "It's cold. Let's head back to your sister's and ice your hand."

To Hold

***

"I'm not going to teach him to fight. That's not what self-defense is, Brian. You're going to sign him up for karate, though. Karate will teach him control, self-defense will help teach him when he needs to exercise that control," I hear Max say to Brian. "The last thing I'm going to do is turn Britt into a street fighter. I promise."

The first thing Britt did was run into the house shouting that Aunt Steph beat up a guy at the football game. My sister may have been slightly upset and extremely concerned until I told her the entire story.

"He did what to you?" she screams. "Why didn't you ever tell me? Or Mom and Dad for that matter? Stephanie, we would have helped you."

The entire story. The one I need to tell Max still. The one I planned to tell him tonight anyway.

"You know how it was around here when we were kids. A boy pulls your hair, he must like you and all that nonsense," I stare up into her face but I feel like she doesn't understand because she didn't go through that. She had Brian when we were little, and then she had Keith. Stella has always demanded respect from men. She wasn't me. Stella always saw me as the female jock and her baby sister, not the girl who dressed like a pin-up model for Halloween parties once out of her parent's house for the night because her boyfriend said it was the only outfit he'd want to see her wear. "Parker was the boy who pulled my hair and slapped my ass, Stell. He's the boy you need to make sure Emmy never dates. He's the type of boy Britt will never become because you and Brian have taught him respect. Parker was the golden boy around here and you know it. Everyone loved Parker, and no one would have believed what happened the day we finally broke up. No one would have believed me."

Her eyes soften and her voice is meek, "I would have, Stephie. I would have believed you."

I bite my lip and lace my fingers together. "I know you would have tried, but I couldn't take the chance that you would look at me differently. I was so ashamed that I let it go that far. I swallowed it down and forced myself into studying after taking a few years off. I started dressing like an academic instead of a school girl."

"He's the reason for the rules?" she questions while sitting down next to me and wrapping her fingers around my clasped hands.

"You bet. I couldn't make myself that vulnerable again. But then again, look what happened anyway." Stella understands the reference. "I let my guard down."

"What about Max? You've let your guard down with him, too."

I chortle — she's right, I have let my guard down with Max and I try to find the right words to explain it all to her. My eyes drift away as I remember the night he stood outside the curtain in the emergency room, the night I heard him mumbling prayers and sniffling because something inside him was exposed during the course of my attack and rescue.

"The rules never applied to Max," I shake my head. "I knew the first night I was near him he was different than the rest, but it took me a long time to give in to that feeling, Stell, and it's still so new but feels like so much more. It's like we're tethered to one another. I think he feels it, too."

"Have you told him about Parker?"

"Not yet. I was planning to talk to him about it tonight even before I saw Parker at the game. I need to explain why I haven't let him slide into home yet."

I'm giving myself no choice but to tell him everything because if I don't, my actions make very little sense to anyone.

"You know," his voice comes from the kitchen doorway, his body a silhouette against the brightness of the other room, as he walks through the dining room and closer to where Stella and I are seated in the living room. He clears his throat before continuing, and my breathing falters. He only does that when he's nervous or upset and the rhythmic clenching and unclenching of his jaw tells me it's the latter. "You know, you're dating a cop. I'm sure there's an outstanding parking ticket or something we could arrest him for."

My mouth gapes open. He'd been so quiet until he spoke and grabbed my attention. "You heard everything I told her?"

"Most of it. Enough to know he's lucky to be breathing still. The thing I really want to know is ... how did it feel to hit him and why didn't you go for the groin?"

I mull it over, my gaze never wavering from his, before I say, "It felt fantastic, and I wanted people to see the damage I did. Going for the groin could have made him walk funny, but it's hard to cover up a bruise like he'll probably have."

"Come here," he says quietly and pulls me into his arms, smoothing my hair down my back. He doesn't say anything else, but the grip he has around me feels like he's trying to hold both of us together. I won't cry over what

Parker did to me when we were in college or what Darren did to me almost a year ago, but feeling Max's strength radiate from his body could be my undoing. "I love you, Stephanie. You're one of the strongest women I know."

"I don't feel strong," I sniffle.

"But you are. It's the strong ones who usually feel weak and the weak ones who want to take on the world without a second thought. You keep getting back up and fighting, though. There isn't a single thing about you that's weak."

"She's never been one to back down from a fight, Max," Stella says quietly behind me. "Love her gently."

Stella moves to walk past me but stops and kisses me on the cheek on her way through and whispers, "This one? He's a keeper. I'd start asking for a ring now. He's not going anywhere." She flashes a smile at Max before also kissing him on the cheek and making her way back to the kitchen.

Max's eyes follow her across the room and he clears his throat again as he turns his attention back to me. "Did she say ring?"

"She's Stella. She likes happy endings." The double-entendre smacks me in the face and I fumble through explaining her romantic-at-heart nature, but neither of us can keep a straight face.

"It's cool. I like happy endings, too," Max says, winking at me as he takes my left arm and winds it around his right. "I'm thinking, unless you want something big on your hand, we hit town hall for a license on Monday and figure the rest out after that."

My feet stop moving.

My palms get sweaty.

My heart starts racing.

I'm having a heart attack. That's what this is. This is what dying feels like.

I gasp for breath and watch the glimmer of hope in his eyes shine a little brighter.

"Officer Wyatt, that sounds like entrapment."

"Are you saying you wouldn't want to marry me, because, by definition, entrapment means you'd be doing something you otherwise wouldn't normally do? Would it be such a crime to become Mrs. Officer Wyatt?" he questions me, amused.

"Stella!" I call to my sister. "Stella, I need you!"

"What? What is it?" she asks, panic stricken, as she rushes into the dining room with her eyes darting from me to Max and back. When I don't answer, she asks again. "Steph?"

I smile at him as I say to my sister, "I need help picking out a white dress."

Chapter Thirty-Nine

Max

Stella looks from me to Stephanie as confusion creases her features. Then shock makes its way across her face. Her jaw drops open and it takes her a few seconds to realize she's just staring at her sister.

"A white dress. As in something requiring a veil?"

"I don't really care for the veil look. It's a little too Victorian for me." Steph turns her head to look at her sister. "Don't look so shocked ... you're the jackass who said something about a ring in front of him."

"Yeah, but I didn't think he heard me!" Stella cries out exasperated.

"Who's got the Vulcan ears now?" Brian pipes up from the kitchen doorway where he stands with Emmy cradled in his arms and Britt peeking around his side. "I get the feeling I missed a lot in the last twenty minutes, which is about par for the course lately. Someone care to bring me up to speed?"

"Max needs to talk to Dad," Stella says emphasizing the "needs to talk" part.

"No way."

"Yes way," the three of us say in unison.

I feel the color start to drain from my face. "Shit."

"Hadn't thought about that part yet, genius?" Brian says, laughing at me. "Just do what I did. Ask him out to lunch. He'll know why the minute you invite him. It's actually a play straight from Dale's own book."

I pull in a deep breath and look down into Steph's eyes. I don't think I can wait and invite him to lunch. Lifting my arm enough to see my watch, I say, "It's still early. Maybe I should talk to him over dessert instead."

Brian turns and walks back into the kitchen, returning a moment later with an apple pie in hand. "Here, take this. It's his mother's recipe," he says pushing the pie toward me. "He'll still know what you're up to, though. The man just knows things sometimes. It would be creepy if I wasn't married to his daughter and dealt with her doing the same thing all the time."

***

"You're sure?" she questions from the passenger seat. The pie sits precariously on her thighs as she picks at the outer seam of her jeans and watches me in the dashboard lights. The cooler weather has me driving the Chevelle most of the time these days, and usually at least once when we go somewhere I catch Stephanie running her hands over the leather seats. She's not one of those women who asks about a car because that's what the guy wants to talk about. No, she's genuinely interested. I love her inquisitiveness. The one thing I don't want her questioning, though, is if I really want her to be my wife. Of that, I'm absolutely positive. "We haven't even had sex yet, Max. How could you possibly know if you want me forever if we haven't made sure we're compatible in bed?"

I ease off the gas and gently press on the brake, gliding to a stop on the gravel shoulder of the road. Putting the car in park, I twist my body because I want to give her my undivided attention when I say what I'm going to say.

"I don't want to have sex with you, Stephanie," I reply, my voice gravelly. "What I want to do, is make love to you."

She won't look at me when she blurts out, "What if I can't do it?"

"You can say you'll marry me but you can't make love to me?" I question curiously.

"What if I can't ... sober?" she elaborates.

There it is. The fear in her words is unmistakable. As much as her reactions to various situations makes sense knowing now what that immature asshole did to her, I suspected there was more to why she was always apprehensive when we were in bed. I haven't pushed for answers because she's not a suspect; she's my girlfriend. I'm not going to interrogate her about why we haven't gotten fully naked together. I respect her enough to know she would tell me eventually. I love her enough to let her take her time.

I reach through the increasing darkness and turn her chin so I can see her eyes. "What do you mean?"

Her face bobs in my hand as she swallows and closes her eyes. Resting her cheek in my palm, Stephanie tells me quietly, "Ever since Parker ... If it was going to happen with someone, it was usually only if I'd had a few drinks. It's been a couple years since anyone has gotten that far with me, but when sex happened it was because I could be drunk and not think about what was happening."

"And with me? Do you think you need to have a drink?" I ask, the question sounding accusatory though it's not intended. I ask because I need to know, because if she says yes I know it's going to hurt but at least it's something we can work on together.

She opens her eyes and looks at me like she's reading the map to my heart despite already knowing the way. Subtly, I feel her head shake back and forth. "No. With you I want to feel everything."

Careful not to spill the pie from her lap, I unbuckle and slide closer to her, taking her face fully in my hands. "Stephanie, I will make our first time more special than you could ever imagine. I plan to worship every single inch of your body and give you back every piece anyone has ever attempted to steal away from you."

Her words pierce the night as they quietly fall from her beautiful mouth. "I believe you, Super Max."

My lips close over hers as I slowly kiss the life back into Stephanie, breathing her in and giving her breath at the same time. My teeth catch her bottom lip and on a sharp intake, she opens her mouth enough for me to slip my tongue between, melding us together as she whimpers. Resting my forehead against hers, I will my heart to slow down and my breathing to return to normal, when in reality my heart always beats a little faster when she's around.

She's always leaving me breathless.

Stephanie

"Are you pregnant? Did he get you pregnant?"

I yell "Dad!" at the same time Mom yells "Dale!" and the color drains from Max's face for the second time tonight. I take a deep breath and when my eyes make contact with my father's hard gaze, I lay it out there.

"You have to have sex to get pregnant, Dad. We haven't done that yet," I say in a low growl.

He lifts his right arm and points at Max. "But you bought condoms. I saw them that day I helped you get groceries home and we talked in your house."

If it was possible for his tan complexion to pale even further, Max would have been transparent. In fact, I think I saw his lips saying the Hail Mary as he was wishing he could be sucked into the floor of my parent's kitchen.

It's comical. The entire thing. Actually, the entire evening could be a Lifetime movie because it's just so fucking absurd.

"When was that?" I ask finally.

The room remains quiet, Dad refusing to look at me or Max and Mom busying herself with the pie we brought. We hadn't even had a chance to talk to them about getting married, no asking permission had happened. Dad saw the pie and blurted out his first thought, because while Brian asking to do lunch means he's proposing to Stella, an apple pie obviously means I'm knocked up.

I'm still waiting for an answer from one of the men in the room when Max gives up praying and says, "The night I made Mongolian beef. I went grocery shopping and only had the bike. Your dad saw me in the parking lot and helped me get stuff home."

"And he somehow magically saw a box of condoms in one of the bags?" I glare at my father. Max isn't careless enough to leave something like that sitting on the kitchen counter while chit-chatting with my dad.

Across the room, big, bad Dale Barbieri takes a deep breath, lifts his ball cap from his head and scratches the back of his neck.

"I might have peeked in his bags," he says, like a coward. No. He's not a coward. But he is a protective father. He lifts his eyes to meet mine again and opens his mouth. "I needed to know if he was trying anything funny. You've been through enough, Steph. I didn't want to see you get hurt again."

Mom pipes up from the counter. "So you went through the poor boy's groceries? Dale, what is the matter with you?"

"She's my baby, Jenny!"

"I've been hearing that for nearly twenty-nine years now. It's not a good enough excuse. Stephanie has been through enough, but so has Max," Mom says, then lifts her thumb to her mouth, sucking the juice off it from slicing and plating pie. She looks from Max to me, and finally her eyes land on Dad. "This pie. It's your mother's recipe."

"What's that supposed to mean?" he questions miserably.

"It means I think these two came here tonight for a reason and it's obviously not because we have another grandbaby on the way. Out with it, Max."

He reaches for my hand at the same time I reach for his. His palms are damp and his hands feel clammy. I don't know which one of us is shaking more and I don't know as though I was this worried about living up to my parent's expectations even when Davis brought me home in a cruiser after a party he broke up when I was in high school.

"I'd like to marry your daughter." Max's voice is strong as he squeezes my fingers carefully before looking at me and lifting my hand to his mouth and kissing my knuckles.

"I see." It's Mom who responds as though indifferent, but when I look at her all I see is love. "You two haven't been together all that long. How do you know she's the one?"

"How did Mr. Barbieri know he loved you after only one date?" My gaze volleys between Mom and Max and I see the wrinkles form at the edges of her eyes as she visibly softens. "He just knew. I've loved Stephanie for months, but I've known I need her in my life since last Thanksgiving. She told Stella earlier that she felt like we're tethered to one another, and I can't explain it, but I agree with her. I agree with him. Sometimes, you just know. I refuse to deny what I'm feeling for your daughter." He looks down at me before continuing. "I know why I came to this town, but it feels like there was a bigger plan at work. We were brought together for a reason. She's been a balm to my wounds."

The sound of my dad's boots walking away from us catch my attention and I turn to watch his retreating form. He comes to a stop by the back door where he pulls a cloth handkerchief from his back pocket and quietly blows his nose before wiping his eyes.

Without turning back to us, I hear him say to the wall as though it might talk back, "Who can say no to that?" He lifts his arm to wipe his face one more time before pivoting, his tearful eyes burrowing into my heart and squeezing the breath from my lungs. "Steph, you better not say no to that."

I smile at him, rejoicing in the knowledge that he's an emotional man who wears his feelings like a badge of honor. It's a strong possibility that I've found someone enough like my dad to truly survive in this world.

"I'm not. I sort of already said yes earlier, but we love you and wanted to make sure you were okay with this. Are you okay with this, Dad?"

He swallows hard and nods his head before giving me his confirmation, something I already knew we had. "You smile again."

"Good. Glad that's settled. Let's eat," Mom says, wiping her eyes with one hand as she reaches into a drawer for forks with the other. She hands Max a plate and leans in to hug him, placing a kiss to his cheek as she whispers just loudly enough for me to hear, "Welcome to the family, Max. We've been waiting for someone like you to save our girl."

"She's not the only one who was saved, Jenny," he says back to her, his eyes finding mine and holding me captive.

***

Driving back across town that night to the house I share with Tommy, I realize I don't truly remember the last time I slept in my own bed. I'm okay with that. I sleep better curled into the side of Max's body than the home I came home to after one of the scariest nights of my life.

Max feels like home.

"I just need to grab some clean clothes to get me through the next day or so," I say as we pull into the driveway, the headlights shining into the back yard.

Max parks the car and turns the engine off, but plays with the keys instead of opening his door. Pointing to the house he says nervously, "What do you think he's going to say about this?"

"About us getting married? I think he's Tommy. He's going to think we're moving too fast, he's going to say something stupid, and then we're all going to work past it. We're family and that's what family is supposed to do. Then tomorrow morning at the coffeehouse he'll bitch and complain to Greg and Brian and get the rest of it off his chest, because that's what Tommy does," I shrug when I finish my non-ranty rant. "It's not Tommy's decision who I marry or how long we date before that happens. He knows how you and I feel about one another and has been made well aware of those feelings countless times. Eventually Thomas Stratford will find the right girl for him and then we'll get to meddle in his love life. It'll be fun. You'll see."

I open the passenger door leaving Max speechless. A smile forms on his lips and he shakes his head back and forth in disbelief before climbing out his side. Coming around the front of the car and taking my hand, he laughs into the fall breeze before saying, "You never cease to amaze me."

"I know. I'm kind of awesome like that."

We silently push through the back door and into the kitchen, catching Tommy in the rare act of raiding his own fridge. Turning to Max, I hold my finger to my lips and then creep across the room until I'm right behind Tommy.

"If you didn't shop there isn't much in there." He jumps at the sound of my voice, slamming the back of his head into the freezer door, and starts cussing me out while rubbing his head. He glares at me. "Well, it's the truth. Have you been living off baked goods and coffee from the shop?"

The fridge is bare save for a stick of butter and a half gallon of milk. What is it with these men in my life not knowing how to shop? I'm pretty certain Brian is the only man in the family who lived without a woman and was self-sustainable. Then again, he had Britt to think about before marrying Stella, so he had to buy food on the regular.

"I've been meaning to make a list," he says rubbing the back of his head one last time before noticing Max still by the door. "Hey, man, what's up?"

"Nothin' much. Steph needed to stop for some clothes on our way back to our place," he responds. All three of us hear him refer to his house as "ours" at the same time. "My place. Because she's staying over tonight. Right. I'm just ..."

Max takes a deep breath and makes a beeline for the old servant's stairwell that leads almost directly to my room, reaching the bottom step as Tommy cries out, "You're moving out? What the fuck, Steph. When was this decided?"

"Calm yourself, Warden."

Anger flares in Tommy's eyes. "I'll calm down when you tell me what you're thinking. You've been dating him what? A few weeks? You can't possibly think this is a smart idea."

"Actually, I do think it's a smart idea ... particularly since I'll be marrying him," I say as I move around him to close the refrigerator door. "Before you say anything, you need to close your eyes, take a deep breath, and count to ten."

I wait as he rolls his slate blue eyes at me, huffs out an annoyed breath, and finally starts counting. "Ten," he says, though I wonder if he skipped a couple numerals in there because my ten-second count is a little longer than that. He opens his eyes and though I know he's trying to hide it, I see the hurt. "Explain."

And I try my best to do that.

"I think I fell for Max the night I was attacked. At the very least, it was two days later when he showed up here to tell me my worries were in the county morgue. But it wasn't because of what he did or the fact he stayed at the hospital with me. It honestly can't be explained, Tommy. I have felt a connection to him for a long time now," I say, watching his face to gauge his reaction. "Maybe us finally dating was a formality, and I know we haven't done the dating thing for long, but he's the only one I want to fall asleep next to. And while you're an amazing snuggle partner, I don't want to wake up next to anyone but Max."

"It's the uniform isn't it?" he says shoving his hands as deep as they'll go into his pockets. "I should have been a cop."

For a moment I fear he's serious, but he winks at me instead.

"Halloween is right around the corner. I'm sure you could play dress up and snag some hot chick," I tease. "In all seriousness, T, are you okay with this? Me moving out eventually, Max proposing, all of it?"

He takes two steps and closes the distance between us. Pulling his hands from his pockets and wrapping his arms around me is more reassurance than I could have asked for.

"Steph, there was definitely a moment when I hoped I could stop looking for a girl for me and just have you because you're fun and easy to be around. But you don't need a guy who wants to have fun. You deserve more than a roommate who forgets to buy groceries. You —" he extends his arms, holding me out in front of him "— you deserve nothing but happiness after all the shit that's been thrown at you. Max is happiness. He's your happiness. No matter what, I will always be here for you. I mean, you really can't get rid of me. You're my business partner. At least now I can stop worrying about putting the toilet seat down."

Shaking my head, I smile and look up at him through my lashes. "You're such a dick."

"But you wouldn't change me. Admit it, you love me the way I am."

I do. Out of everyone in my life, Tommy has become one of my best friends and it's a relief to be able to move beyond any hurt he might have felt about my future. I lean in and give him another hug.

"There's a fifty in the cookie jar on the top shelf of the coffee mug cupboard. Go buy groceries. I need clothes and sleep. It's been a very long Friday," I say against his chest as he breathes into my hair.

"You got it. Let me know what wedding planning things I can help with. I'm really good with fonts, you know."

"No comic sans or I'll murder you in your sleep."

"Aye aye, Captain," he says as he reaches into the cookie jar before backing away. He raises his hand in salute until he reaches the door, leaving Max and I alone in the house.

I take the stairs two at a time until I'm standing in my bedroom doorway quietly watching him at the window as he looks down on the serene street below. The glow of the streetlight climbs through the pane glass like a long lost lover come to take him away. He's deep in thought, but his breathing changes and I know he feels me close by.

The sleeves of his shirt are rolled up and the muscles in his forearms tighten as he flexes his hands deep in his jeans' pockets.

"I might have forgotten to mention my mom's coming into town tomorrow. I also may have promised her dinner out at a nice restaurant, so you might want to grab something nice to wear for tomorrow evening," he says not breaking his concentration from the window. "Where is Tommy going?"

"Grocery store. Your mom's coming? Tomorrow?"

I've obviously never met her. I've never spoken to her on the phone. I have no idea what she knows about me other than I'm dating her son. Dating. She probably has no clue we're making our little living situation legal. How would she know when Max and I haven't even had a chance to really talk about what we're doing other than to decide we're getting married? His proposal wasn't planned in the least, not that being unplanned makes it any less real.

It's definitely real.

I'm beginning to feel the tornado of emotions pick at my skin. My lungs start to burn a little and I feel the panic rise up my back as I think of all the ways I've already disappointed my future mother-in-law. The minute she walks in that house she'll know I've been sleeping there. I don't have enough time between right this second and when she arrives tomorrow to cleanse my presence from Max's home. How am I going to hide from his mom all the ways I've become part of him in that space? That would take days, maybe even weeks.

I don't even realize I'm practically hyperventilating until Max turns from the window and crosses the room to me, taking my face in his hand, massaging my temples slowly, reminding me to breathe slowly. "Steph, she's going to adore you." He speaks like he's talking to a scared child, and maybe deep down that's what I am in this instant. Then he chuckles. "I think she already does."

He leans in and softly peppers my forehead with kisses.

"I think the minute I started talking about you to her she knew I was a goner."

"When was that?" I question, curiosity getting the best of me as I lift my head to look into those deep brown pools. I search his face, a reflection of honesty and integrity, and wait for him to answer as a smile gently lifts the edges of his mouth.

"The weekend I went out to visit her, right before you showed up barefoot at the end of my driveway looking like the sweat-coated, caffeinated angel that you are," he humors me with the affection whispered in his words.

I won't say the obvious — that he talked about me, about us, to his mom before we even tried a first date — because it's not needed. We both know when that weekend was. He marks it with me at the end of his driveway; I'll remember it as the weekend before the last bender I went on. I feel myself smile at the thought of how clear things have been since then.

"What you're saying is I was gross and smelly that day, but what I'm going to choose to hear is 'Stephanie, you were glowing and beautiful', because it sounds nicer," I say sarcastically.

He lowers his mouth to mine and on the breath that kisses my lips before he makes contact, says, "Isn't that what I said?"

M.L. Pennock

Chapter Forty-One

Max

I'm getting married again.

This time, everything feels different. In no way would I ever want to disgrace Adrienne's memory or the short life we had together and the family we were growing, but there's something about my relationship with Stephanie that feels like it was meant to be. Adrienne and I, there were a lot of times when we felt forced — like our love was obligation and we were stuck trying to make it work. Maybe it was because I was the first to see the flicker of light still deep within her after the abuse she endured. I loved her, there's no doubt about that, but it wasn't the easy kind of love I've fallen into with Steph. It took more work than being in love with someone should have taken.

With Stephanie, the light was never just a flicker. It was a beam from a lighthouse searching for a ship lost at sea. I was that ship. Steph didn't need me to save her because she was the one doing most of the saving.

When she was ready, she wanted me there when she saved herself.

She doesn't need me to love her. She wants me to.

And that's where the difference between my two wives lies.

These thoughts keep me awake despite how physically and emotionally exhausted I should be. I should be drained between the confrontation Steph had with her ex-boyfriend and acting on my feelings for her instead of ruminating about them for weeks. Even when she asked me if I was sure I wanted to marry her, I didn't have to think about it. She's it.

She was asleep before I could show her how much she's it for me, but it doesn't even matter. I'm in love with her not because she can get me hard with one look, but because she softened my heart with another.

Lying in my bed next to her, her head on my practically numb arm, I feel full and complete ... but there's an itch that needs to be scratched and I won't sleep until I get rid of the adrenaline. I stealthily slide my arm out from beneath her still form wrapped in just a T-shirt and a pair of my boxers. Watching to be sure I didn't wake her, I slip through the door and down the stairs.

I reach the basement, first turning on the radio and then carefully wrapping my hands. Glancing at the clock on the wall, I feel like I've been cheating on what used to be a regular event made routine through insomnia with a real life. It's been a few weeks since I saw two in the morning and even longer since it saw me confronting my demons in the form of a heavy bag.

Starting out slow, I jab at the bag, as though I'm poking the bear still asleep deep inside me. My muscles warm to the motion until I feel the burn in my arms, my back.

I lose track of time as I release the anger I've held onto. Adrienne's death and Judson's life. New anger about Steph's high school boyfriend. The mounting sexual frustration. I get it out in the most constructive way I can until I feel devoid, until I feel like a clean slate, and the sweat runs down my bare back, collecting in the waistband of my boxer briefs. It pools at the creases in my elbows until it overflows and drips to the cement floor.

"Do you feel better?" she asks quietly from her perch on the third step down, a mug of coffee in her hands.

Consumed by everything I've buried, I never heard her come down from the bedroom. I wonder how long she's been sitting there when she answers like she's read my thoughts.

"You'd probably been at it about twenty minutes when I decided to get up," she says before gingerly taking a sip from the steaming cup in her hands, hands wrapped so delicately around the ceramic I forget for a moment how brutal they can be when she's beating her own demons into submission on this very bag. "It's been a long time since you did this in the middle of the night."

It has. I haven't left her alone in bed to battle it out on my own since maybe the second week she was sleeping over. Usually her presence is what calms me, but tonight it was her presence that proved to be too much.

Taking a deep cleansing breath, I lean the side of my sweat soaked head against the bag. Looking up at her I feel that calm come back to me, and tell her, "I feel a little better. Now that you're here."

Setting the cup beside her, she stands and cautiously makes her way to the bottom of the stairs before slowly walking to me as though she's approaching a wild animal. Her eyes never leave mine as she carefully begins unwrapping my hands, kissing the tip of each finger as she finishes pulling the fabric away, dropping it at my feet.

"I think I have something that can cure your frustrations, Super Max," she says, her voice taking on a velvety softness I haven't heard before. Taking my hand she pulls me along behind her — up the stairs to the kitchen, then up the stairs to the bathroom where she turns on the shower and slowly undresses us both.

Goosebumps crop up along her arms as she lifts the T-shirt from her body, pulling it carefully over her head until she's left standing in just the pair of my boxers she's claimed for sleeping. She holds my gaze as she slips her fingers beneath the waistband and gently pushes the fabric from her hips, down her thighs, until it's free to fall to the floor. I reach forward, my fingertips trailing along her jaw until I can lay the palm of my hand against her face and she closes her eyes. Swallowing and taking a shallow breath, I move half a step closer to her naked flesh as her hands caress my waist, her thumbs pressing beneath the fabric covering me. Closing my eyes, I drop my forehead to hers ... willing her to continue, wondering if she'll change her mind and stop.

She doesn't stop, freeing my growing erection from the confines of clothes, and steps into my body as I shift my feet to kick the clothes out of our way. Her lips trace against the stubble on my chin as she teases and nips at my jaw, but I leave my eyes closed, sinking into the moment her breasts fall against my chest and her pelvic bone presses into my groin, eliciting a low groan from deep in my throat.

I just want to feel her.

I want to feel her everywhere for the rest of my life.

Before her lips can nibble their way to mine, I whisper, "I love you."

"I love you, too, Max," she breathes against my mouth, finally bringing her lips to mine, and I feel like I'm home. Her mouth falls away and I feel lost. "Open your eyes, Max."

Taking my hand, she pulls me toward the shower, stepping in and making room for me before shutting the curtain. The warm water pulses down our bodies, baptizing us in its wake. Sweat and anger, frustration and hurt all are carried away as she lathers my torso in a layer of foam, her fingers nimbly tracing the outline of my hips before wrapping around me and tugging gently.

I say her name like I'm saying a prayer, closing my eyes and dropping my head back into the spray of the water.

"Max, look at me." And I do.

"I want you to be in control, I want you to take the lead, but I don't think I can keep my hands to myself," I growl as she moves her fingers deftly against my skin, cupping the heavy flesh beneath my shaft.

"This isn't about me having control," she says, leaning forward and grazing her teeth against my nipple. I breathe in sharply and she continues, "This is about mutual give and take. That's what love does. It's not about keeping score or control."

Reaching for her, I grasp the back of her neck and pull her closer to me. It's a moment of nothing but tongues and teeth, my hands in her wet hair and her nails gripping my back.

"I need you so much, Steph. Thank you for being my wife," I say against her ear before tucking her face under my chin and plunging us beneath the water to rinse away the bubbles.

"Monday. I want to be your wife on Monday," she asserts loudly before looking up at me curiously as though she fears I might say no, and I laugh lightheartedly. "I don't want to wait. I don't need a perfect moment or a perfect dress or the right weather. You make every moment perfect. That's all I need."

I lower my mouth back to hers, leaving a chaste kiss against her lips before making my way to her ear and lightly pressing my lips just beneath it. "Monday it is then."

"Maybe we should celebrate now since we didn't last night?" she questions, stretching her arm behind me to turn the water off.

"Maybe we should." I grab a towel from the rack beside the tub, wrapping it around her body before grabbing one for myself and stepping out of the bath.

Our mouths rarely separate from one another as we bump into doorframes and walls on our way from the bathroom to the bedroom. We leave the towels on the floor and the light on in the closet. The backs of her knees connect with the edge of the bed and we're falling against one another into the billowing softness beneath us.

Nestled between her legs, I crawl up Stephanie's body and watch a blush creep up her chest as I lower myself against her again, waiting for the apprehension wrinkling her forehead to dissipate. I kiss along her collarbone, tasting the hollow of her throat, nipping her shoulder, trailing my tongue along the edge of her breast ... until she lifts her hips against me, giving me permission, asking me without asking, positioning our bodies perfectly. A low moan reaches my ears as she slowly envelopes me and I watch pure ecstasy replace any fears she may have.

We make love slowly and recklessly, bringing each other to the brink and back until we give all we have as the sun begins to peek above the horizon.

To Hold

Steph curls up contentedly with her naked back against my chest. With one of my arms beneath her head and the other draped over her waist we fall asleep snuggled beneath the covers, hidden from the rest of the world.

M.L. Pennock

Chapter Forty-Two

Stephanie

I wake to Max's fingers clutching my hip. Not hard enough to hurt, but enough to wake me out of a sound sleep. A painful moan escapes his lips just before he tucks his head against my neck, nuzzling and seeking comfort.

Not again. Why today? Why after last night? I think. I roll over to face him and gently touch his chest, but he says her name in his sleep and I feel my heart crack open. It isn't like his normal nightmares, when he mumbles in his sleep and her name is barely audible, hardly enunciated, easily ignored. No, this time he's saying it and anyone would be able to discern who he's dreaming about.

Dawn was just beginning to break when we curled up against one another exhausted from hours of making love. I wish I knew it would be like this with Max; for the first time ever I felt like I was a participant in my own sex life. The fact he's dreaming about Adrienne now, though, is confusing. I know it's nothing he's purposely doing — it's a dream — but I can't just lay here while his subconscious is sucked deep into his past.

The sun high enough through the window that I make a guess that it's nearly mid-morning. To be honest, I feel more refreshed than if I'd slept a full night. Careful not to wake him, I crawl out of bed, pull on the cold weather running gear I stashed in the bottom of my bag, and tip toe out of the bedroom. Landing quietly at the bottom of the stairs, I pad through the living room and out to the kitchen where I grab my sneakers, phone from the charger, and car keys.

I hate feeling like I have to get out of here, but I need to move my body. My car is still new enough that the engine purrs to life but not loudly enough to wake the neighborhood. I pull the shifter to "reverse" and back down the driveway, headed only to a place my sister would think to look for me — Mount Albion Cemetery. The twenty-minute drive to Albion is just long enough for my brain to start working, and my guilt to start forming.

Max is no doubt going to wake up and think I've run away. He'll think I panicked after last night and this morning. This isn't about him though. It's about the things I cannot control. I can't stop his mind from dredging up memories and throwing them at him in his sleep.

Just like something bothered him last night enough for me to find him in the basement oblivious to me watching him for nearly an hour ... I need to run because this is bothering me.

I pull into the main entrance of the cemetery, parking my car in the lot by the chapel. Stepping out I'm greeted by nothing but the sound of the dead saying hello and the wind rustling the leaves that cling helplessly to trees lining each narrow road. I take the time to retie my sneakers before firing up the running playlist on my phone and starting out in a swift walk up the first hill to warm my limbs. Reaching a plateau, I pick up speed and let the beats pulsing through my ears carry me away down Veterans Companion, around the loop, and then I get lost — among the dead and among the thoughts racing through my brain.

Twice. I listened to my playlist twice and one-hundred-ninety-four minutes later my mind is finally at ease. Sitting at the base of the Soldiers and Sailors Monument, I'm taking a breather before heading back toward the car when an older woman approaches the hill. It isn't uncommon for people digging up local history to stop by cemeteries, but in all the times I've escaped and come here to run I've never seen someone as caffeine dependent as me and Stella wandering the grounds.

Carrying two large Styrofoam cups from Dunkin Donut and dressed in boots, jeans, and a hooded sweatshirt with the Ohio State University logo plastered across the front, I'm fairly certain this woman isn't here to research dead family members. Without a word, she walks over to the monument and sits down beside me. She doesn't look at me, but I'm staring at her as she passes me a cup and takes a sip from the one left in her hand. He looks so much like her.

"Where's Max? I would have expected him to come after me instead of his mom," I say, averting my eyes finally and looking north through the trees. I lift the cup to my mouth, pulling the coffee against my tongue, and when she doesn't answer, I shake my head and turn back to ask again when I see Stella poke her head around the corner of the monument. I wondered where she was hiding. "He must have been really worried if he called my sister. That part I understand, but why wouldn't he come with her?"

It's absolutely incredible that I mentally check out and, instead of my sister bringing my boyfriend to find me, she brings his mother. To someone somewhere that made sense.

"I wouldn't let him come with us. Honestly, I know my son. He could convince the Pope to buy Holy water. That said, I was afraid you'd run if he showed up. My understanding is you have a history of running away from good men."

I glare at my sister over Mrs. Wyatt's shoulder and mouth the word "snitch" at her. Jean catches me and laughs.

"No she's not. She was worried about you. That's why I'm here, too. Let me tell you a little bit about this boy we both love, especially since I have it on good authority that you're joining the family."

"The only truly good men I've kept in my life are my dad and my brother-in-law, and his brother, but that's mostly because they won't let me push them away," I look at her, speaking as honestly as I can. She reminds me of my psychiatrist, like I could slice open my soul and tell her everything and she wouldn't judge me for all the wrong I've committed.

"And for some reason you think Max will let you push him away? I think you need to see a therapist to help you with that, honey," she says, bumping her shoulder against mine.

I laugh humorlessly. "Too late. I'm already seeing a shrink. A lot has happened in the last twenty-four hours, so I haven't talked to her about it yet, but I'm sure she'll hear all about it. Fight or flight, you know?"

"I know all too well," she says, wrapping an arm around my shoulders. The closeness is comforting. "But the thing you need to understand about Max is it doesn't matter if you try to fly away. He's going to come after you no matter how far you go. If you stand and fight him, his affection, he'll give you every pro-con list he can think of for why fighting him will only make him love you more. He's insane like that. His father was, too. It's in his genes."

I take another long pull from my coffee, contemplating how much I want to say, when I decide she knows her son best. "He was dreaming about Adrienne," I say quietly. "I woke up and he was in the middle of a nightmare, saying her name in his sleep. I couldn't get him to wake up, not that I really tried all that hard, so I got out of bed and left. Usually I can handle it, but this time I just needed to clear my head."

"So you drive clear across to the next town over and run around a cemetery?" Jean shrugs her shoulders and presses her lips together, the motion alone telling me that on some level she gets it. "It makes perfect sense to me. The dead don't talk back. They don't stop you to chat as they're coming out their front door. They don't almost hit you with their cars when you cross the street."

"Mostly the 'don't talk back' part."

Stella comes around from her perch against the monument to sit next to me on the side opposite Jean, her arm automatically wrapping around my waist as she lays her head on my shoulder.

"Steph, why didn't you just come talk to me?"

Rolling my eyes, I try to suppress a laugh. She's serious?

"Let me count the reasons ... you have your own family, you have a newborn, it's Saturday and Brian was likely still home, I didn't want to cry. Oh, and, unlike the dead, you talk back. I was afraid you would sit there in your kitchen and tell me, 'Of course he's going to dream about her! She was the great love of his life. Get a grip, Steph.' I couldn't handle that today."

I swivel my head to look at my sister and then at Max's mom. Both have baffled expressions. Both attempt to speak at the same time.

"I don't think —" Jean begins.

"I never would have —" Stella starts.

I hold up my hands and stand, pacing back and forth pointing at my sister. "But you would have," I accuse loudly. "And if you didn't come right out and say it, it would have been implied. I mean, really, she was his wife! What do I expect? That he's just going to stop thinking about her because he has me now? I can't expect him to police his dreams and kick her out of those since she's not part of the rest of his daily life. For Christ's sake, I resemble her!"

I hold up a section of my hair to prove I must look identical to Adrienne because we have the same hair color. I sound hysterical. I know I do, but every time I hear him talk in his sleep I wonder if I'll be enough. If loving me will be enough for him. If someday having children with me will be enough.

Jean's whispered "oh, Stephanie" brings me back to the present and I look at her, noticing unshed tears glistening in her eyes. She takes a shuddering breath, clasping her hands together around her knees, and says, "My son loved that girl, yes, but as his mother I'm saying Adrienne wasn't the great love of his life. She was a wonderful young lady, but she had trouble drawing strength from within herself. There were a lot of times Max would show up at my house, emotionally exhausted, because he was always trying to fix things. Adrienne was the kind of woman who needed someone to love her in order to feel validated. She was pieces and parts when Max met her and I think she remained in segments up until her death."

None of that proves she wasn't his great love, and I say as much.

"No, I suppose it doesn't. You know how much Max loves his car?" I nod so she'll continue. "I hate saying this, but Adrienne was more like a project than a wife. He was trying to fine tune things and get all the parts working again, but each time he tinkered with one thing, three more would suddenly be broken. He hasn't once tried to tinker with you," she says looking straight into my eyes. "He hasn't because by the time he stopped avoiding you out of fear that you'd think he just wanted to save you, you'd practically fixed yourself. You're both filled with enough love and strength to buoy one another. That's what a great love is made of."

"But what if he doesn't realize that's what we are?"

"Have you ever known a man to throw all his chips in if it wasn't a sure thing?"

My sister and I both snicker. Brian. He gave up his entire life to move back to New York not knowing if Stella was still here and definitely didn't know if she was single regardless of his behind the scenes chats with our mom. He's the only person I know who would uproot himself without first checking to see if it was worth it. Good thing for him Stella was going through her divorce when he popped back into her life.

"I might know a guy, but he's an exception not the rule," I say, glancing at Stella. She's exhausted, but I've never seen my sister happier than she has been in the last year, since Bri came back home.

"All three of us know Max likes his rules. But, he wouldn't hand you his whole heart if he wasn't absolutely certain you were worth all of it, Stephanie."

***

On the drive back to Brockport, I put my earpiece in and call Max.

The phone has barely gotten through the first ring when I hear, "Are you okay? I woke up and you weren't here and your car was missing. Then you didn't answer your phone when I called you. You didn't respond to text messages. Where did you go? Are you okay?"

"You asked that already," I say quietly in the car. "I'm fine ... now. Stella knows where I run away to and they found me there."

Emmy wails in the background. Brian was probably at the coffeehouse by the time Max woke up and since Stella's with me, the baby and Britt are likely with my parents, which means Max must be there, too.

"Are you at home or Mom and Dad's?" I question to ease my curiosity.

"Home. Britt was hanging out with your dad, your mom wasn't home. After I called Stella she basically pulled in the driveway, handed me the baby and half her nursery, stole my mom, and took off saying she'd bring you home," he says, sounding exasperated. "Please come home. Tell me what I did wrong."

"I'll be there in about ten minutes. I'm just coming through Holley," I explain as I pull up to a stoplight in the middle of town. "Max, you didn't do anything wrong. I just needed to pause. I hope you can understand."

"A pause, eh?" he asks. "I might have to Google that, but I'm pretty sure I understand. That's not something I can hold against you. Sometimes we all need one of those. Get home. Drive safe. I love you, Steph."

I can hear the smile in his voice and it sounds like forever.

I'm going to marry that boy.

"I love you, too."

Chapter Forty-Three

Max

Stephanie steps through the door and wordlessly watches as I pick Emmy up out of the playpen. Stella damn near threw it at me as she was backing down the driveway and attempting to figure out how to set it up took Herculean efforts. I've decided that baby things are meant to make adults feel stupid.

Standing with a room between us, we consider each other before either of us speaks.

Just looking at her and knowing she's safe, I could die a happy man right now.

As I lift the baby and place her against my chest, I watch the hollow in Steph's throat dip as she swallows before the barely audible words leave her mouth.

"That's a good look on you."

I hide my smile and bury my face in Emmy's hair.

"What are you doing?" she questions, a smirk playing on her lips.

"Smell this," I say while nodding at the baby tucked into my arms.

"This? Come Monday she's going to be your niece, not a 'this,'" Steph chuckles as she takes a step in our direction and when she meets me in the center of the living room we're toe-to-toe with the baby between us. Her eyes flutter closed as she lightly presses her nose against the feathery softness covering Emmy's tiny head. She breathes her in.

"Do you smell it?" I ask her quietly, reaching up with my free hand to brush her hair behind her ear.

Her eyes still closed, Steph remarks, "She smells like a baby. What else is she supposed to smell like?"

"The future."

Her eyes slowly open and she breathes in deeply again, pulling Emmy's baby smell into her lungs before gently tugging the baby from my arms and cradling her to her chest so I can wrap my arms around them both.

"I want this kind of future with you. I want it like I've never wanted anything in my entire life, Stephanie. Monday, marriage. Next month, you present your Master's project and graduate in December. Next year ... maybe a baby? If you're ready for that."

"No rush, right?" she quips sarcastically.

I lift her chin so I can see her eyes. "Not at all. We have our entire lives, but what fun would it be to wait too long? We might as well get a jump start on forever."

***

"Chief, can I take a little longer lunch today?"

Davis looks up from his desk at me as I reach up and grasp the doorframe above my head and stretch my shoulders. He squints his eyes at me and cocks an eyebrow.

"Why?" he draws the word out and I'm sure an entire sentence is implied. Underneath that one word I hear "you never ask to take a long lunch" and "you're up to something, Wyatt."

"I sort of have this thing down at Town Hall and I'm not sure how long it's going to take. It shouldn't take more than an hour, but I just wanted to make sure it's okay with you if it takes a bit longer than that."

"Court isn't until tonight and you don't have to be there. What's going on at Town Hall this afternoon?" he asks, going back to shuffling papers on his desk.

"Nothing huge, really, just a small wedding I need to be at." He stops mid-shuffle.

"Wedding? You the witness?" he deadpans.

I know he's Dale's best friend so I wonder how long he'll put up this charade and act like he doesn't know what's happening today. I can't take the chance he's going to hold me up. I can't start my marriage the way I started my relationship with Stephanie — by showing up late.

"Sort of, sir. I'm the groom."

"You're what?"

"The groom, sir."

"Does Dale know about this?" Chief questions shifting his eyes to briefly look out his office window as though my soon-to-be father-in-law might be staring in through the glass. Here I figured Dale would have told him as soon as we left the house Friday night.

I just laugh. "Yes, sir. He gave us his blessing when we talked over the weekend. Did you want to come with me? He might need some moral support seeing how Steph's his little girl and we're moving kind of fast."

"No shit, Wyatt. I just found out you were dating her and now she's marrying you," he says standing from his desk. Grabbing his cap and jacket from the coat tree in the corner, he gestures for me to lead the way. "I never thought that girl would settle down. I've got to see this."

After Stephanie came back home Saturday afternoon, we made the decision to call the town clerk at home to see if she could pull a favor for us and let us apply for our marriage license that day instead of waiting.

Lucky for us, we live in a small town. Steph's aunt's daughter-in-law had no problem meeting us at the back door of Town Hall to fill out the paperwork on a weekend evening. I think she was actually kind of giddy about it and wouldn't stop hugging Steph.

Chief and I drive separately, which gives me five or so minutes to realize I'm not nervous and my palms aren't sweaty.

I'm not affected by what we're about to do until I'm standing in the justice's chambers with our families and Stephanie walks in wearing a tea length strapless white dress looking like she just wandered in out of a bridal magazine. Her hair is swept up and held in place with God only knows how many bobby pins I'll have to help her remove later and a tiara. She's channeled Audrey Hepburn for our wedding day — she's stunning and she's mine.

There's a small bouquet of white roses in her hands that shakes slightly as she steps further over the threshold. I watch her beautiful, ruby painted lips mouth the word "hi" to me from across the room and it's as if everyone else falls away to background noise.

"Hi," I whisper back, a grin slowly lifting the corners of my mouth. I catch the hint of pink as it rises in her cheeks as she spies me taking all of her in. "You look amazing. I like your shoes."

She smiles all the way to her eyes before looking at her feet, clad in maroon three-inch platform heels, and laughs, "I bet you do. You're not looking too bad yourself, Officer."

It's only a few long strides for me to reach her, for me to wrap her arm into mine, and I guide her further into the crowded office. "Are you ready for this?"

Her head swivels, a smile pasted in place, as she greets each of our guests — her parents, my mom, Brian, Stella, Britt, Emmy, Tommy, and Chief Franks — before her eyes trail back to mine. "I don't think I've been this ready for anything before in my life."

"Okay, then. Let's get this party started," the judge says from behind his desk as he claps his hands together. "Since there are so many of us and my office is relatively small, why don't we go out to the courtroom where we can be more comfortable and Stephanie can have a proper entrance?"

He leads us out of his office and when we get to the door of the courtroom, I'm surprised to see Greg, Caryn, and Sutton standing at a table near the back of the room — each has something placed in front of them. Coffee cups and a tray of pastries sit in front of Greg, a portable CD player and discs are in front of Sutton, and Caryn's checking the settings on her Nikon. I catch her taking a test shot of Greg while he acts like he doesn't notice the look of affection on her face.

Judge Filipowski directs me, Brian, and Tommy where to stand and Stella follows suit mirroring us on the opposite side of the judge. Jenny and my mom stand on their respective sides in the front row and Chief Franks looks slightly confused which side he's supposed to be on until he finally steps over and stands next to Jenny.

I hear the click of the CD player and then Cannon in D begins playing softly at the back of the room.

We turn to see Steph and her father begin walking the short distance to me and I feel like I lied to myself when I said she was stunning.

She's so much more.

This is what it was always meant to feel like. This moment when she's stolen my breath and made my heart beat out of rhythm.

She's practically vibrating with the love she has for me as she and Dale reach the front of the courtroom.

"You better be good to her, son. I know where you live," he says to me, just loud enough for me, Stephanie, and the judge to hear.

"Yes, sir," I smile and nod at him, knowing his bark is worse than his bite.

"Who gives this woman to be married to this man?" Judge Filipowski jumps right to the nuts and bolts of the ceremony and before long I hear myself reciting the traditional vows we'd agreed on.

"I, Max Edward Wyatt, take you, Stephanie, to be my lawful wedded wife to have and to hold ..."

She's beaming when I finish and I will the judge to hurry and get to the kissing part.

Finally, we hear those fated words, "By the authority vested in me by the laws of the state of New York, I now pronounce you husband and wife," but I'm pulling her to me before he can finish, savoring that first long kiss as

Stephanie's husband. Her lips are soft and she tastes like cinnamon, and I can't remember a time when I loved the taste of autumn as much as in this moment.

The catcalls and whistling from the guys reminds me we aren't alone and as I pull my mouth away from my wife's she follows me with hers, stealing one more kiss before we let the judge finish.

"Ladies and gentlemen, it is my honor to introduce Mr. and Mrs. Max Wyatt."

***

Chief gets called back to the station and grabs a pastry and coffee on his way out.

"This isn't half bad, Stratford. Maybe I should stop trying to make my own coffee and start giving you my business," he says to Brian.

"I've heard about your coffee, Davis. If you don't start coming into my shop, I'm just going to come confiscate your machine. No one needs that kind of negativity in their life."

"It's a deal. See you tomorrow morning," he says reaching to shake Brian's hand as he makes his way to the door before calling back to me, "Wyatt, when you're done mingling with your guests head back in to finish out your shift. You're off the rest of the week."

I take a sip of my coffee and eye him suspiciously. "Chief, I didn't request time off."

He places his cap on his head as he nods toward Stephanie and chuckles. "You might not have, but your bride wears the pants in the family now. Get used to it, kid." He turns and pushes past Tommy and Sutton who are in deep conversation and unfazed by Franks squeezing through the small opening they've left for him to get to the door.

"You took the rest of the week off for me?"

"I figured we could celebrate at home without obligations. I'm off from the library this week and Tommy and I are caught up on clients right now. I'm done with coursework and just finishing my paper," she says shyly. "Unless you'd rather spend this time catching bad guys in the rough and tumble village of Brockport, then I can go let the boys at the station know they don't have to repay all those favors you've done for them."

Words wouldn't do the moment justice, so I pull her into my arms and kiss her like I might not have the chance to kiss her ever again.

And I plan to kiss her like that every single day for as long as I can.

Chapter Forty-Four

Stephanie
Thanksgiving

Max's mom is in town again for the holiday and to help celebrate the one-year anniversary of my not getting murdered. My entire family hates how I refer to that night, but it's the truth. I have a huge reason to celebrate Thanksgiving and it's primarily because I didn't die.

Because I could have. That's a fact I have faced time and again through therapy, both with Doc and as I attempted to cope on my own before giving in to the idea of talking to her.

More importantly, Max didn't have to watch me die before he had a chance to love me.

I'm not intentionally being morbid. It's my sense of humor helping me get through this first year milestone, though. Max is having a much more difficult time getting through it than I am. It seems the less I'm reacting to the anniversary, the more he is. He asks how I'm feeling about it. I tell him I'm indifferent; he questions what I mean.

He's not thinking only of what I went through, but also what happened to Adrienne and the baby. He's stepping back in time and thinking about how almost a year ago he killed someone. I do understand. I can see where his head is at. What he's forgetting and failing to deal with, though, is he killed one man to protect himself and me and put Adrienne's ghost to rest. He's letting the trauma of our pasts survive when what he should be doing instead is reminding himself of how far we've come in the last year.

He's going to have to work harder on that, I think as I stare at the test in my hand. *This is the jump start on forever we were planning. It's just come a little sooner than expected.*

The knock on the bathroom door scares me and I feel myself jump from where I'm sitting on the edge of the tub.

"Steph, are you about ready to head to your parent's house? I told Tommy we'd stop to get him on our way and he's already called twice wondering when we're coming over," Max calls through the door. "Mom has already headed over."

I fumble with the box, shove the test inside, and then stick it in the cupboard between the bath towels. "Uh, yeah. I'll be right there." Once. We did it once without a condom. I look in the mirror, hoping I don't look like I've spent the last three days puking my guts out as soon as Max leaves for work, which is exactly how I've spent all of Thanksgiving week. "I just need to finish my ... hair."

I pull the limp strands out of my face, pinning them up and curling what I can to make myself presentable. Eyeliner, a touch of mascara, some shimmery lip gloss and I look almost like I don't want to hurl in the bathtub. Again.

Almost.

Taking a deep, steadying breath, I turn from the sink and open the door. The hallway is empty. I walk across to our bedroom and find Max standing at his dresser putting on cologne. He turns to me with a smile on his face, which almost as quickly evaporates.

"What's the matter?" he questions, looking at me in the reflection in the mirror. I feel my stomach turn as soon as I get a whiff of him and swallow in a vain attempt to keep it at bay.

I shake my head. "Nothing. I'm fine, I just wanted to grab a sweater before we go."

He's eerily quiet as I turn toward the closet and reach up to the shelf I put my sweaters and long sleeve T-shirts on when I officially moved in six weeks ago. My arms are hardly above my head when I realize just how vain an attempt it was.

"Steph!" he calls as I cross the hall as quickly as I can and make it just in time. I smell him again before he even enters the room to see me grasping the edges of the toilet and I try to wave him off. His parents, I sometimes think, did too well of a job raising a gentleman. He reaches over my shoulders and carefully pulls my hair back behind me, tying it into a loose knot at the back of my neck. "What can I get you?"

Spitting once more and blowing my nose, I finally look at him. "A shower. You need to take another shower. I can't stand how you smell."

The offended expression on his face would be amusing if I wasn't dead serious. He lifts the collar of his shirt and sniffs it. "I smell good, though. I thought you liked this cologne?"

Wiping the eyeliner from where it's run down my cheeks, I share the truth. "I love the way you smell ... apparently the baby doesn't, though. So, unless you want me puking all day, get in the shower," and I lay my head down on my arm, exhausted again.

The water turns on. Max strips and throws his clothes in the hallway, but he doesn't step into the shower. Kneeling down beside me, he touches my forehead, concern furrowing his brow while trepidation brews in his eyes. "Are you sure you want to go today? We could skip dinner and say you have the flu."

"If I say I have the flu, Mom and Stella will be over here with leftovers tonight and see I'm fine. I'll be okay in an hour. I just need some crackers and cold water," I whisper, closing my eyes.

"How long have you known?" he whispers back, but even blind I can hear the hope and excitement building in his voice.

"For sure? About twenty minutes," I smile before opening my eyes. With one eye open, I catch a glimpse of him, naked but for a pair of boxer briefs, as he hovers next to me. "But I've been getting sick in the morning for the last few days and then fine by early afternoon, so I was pretty sure before that second line showed up."

Making an effort to stand up, he wraps his arm around my waist to help me to my feet. His forehead kisses mine.

"Really?"

"Really really. The test is in the box between the towels if you need more visual proof than the contents of my stomach," I say, laughing quietly and then louder as he leaves me to rifle through the cabinet. I take advantage of his absence and brush my teeth again as his reflection pulls the box from between two bath towels, then the test from the box.

"It's really real. Should you take another one just to be certain?" he says, his concerned eyes meeting mine in the mirror above the sink.

I spit and rinse my mouth before turning to him. "With how quickly that one turned positive, I'm pretty sure we can trust the results. Hurry and get in the shower so we can go. I'm starving."

"You're so pregnant," he laughs as I walk back out of the bathroom. I hear him start humming to himself as I grab my sweater, unknot my hair, and head down the stairs to text Tommy that we'll be on our way as soon as possible.

***

"Just because you two are newlyweds doesn't mean you need to be doing it every chance you get and make us late for dinner. There are pies with my name on them and I'm pretty sure I'll stab my own brother if he touches the pecan pie before we get there," Tommy says as he climbs into the backseat of the Chevelle and buckles up.

I'm forever grateful I'm still standing outside the car when he mentions pie. I went from starving to nauseous again in the span of minutes and I'm not entirely sure how I'm going to keep this under wraps until after I see the doctor.

I don't think I'll last to the end of the day. With my family, I'll be lucky if I last until the end of the first hour.

"Steph, get your ass in the car. Pie is on the line," Tommy yells from the confines of the backseat.

And the mere mention of pie again has me wretching next to the back tire. So much for saltines and water.

"I'm going to be a dad," I hear Max say proudly.

"Congrats, man," Tommy says enthusiastically. I hear him slap Max on the shoulder and then say, "Congrats. Me too."

I wipe my mouth and stand up, thrusting my head into the car. "What did you just say?"

"Um, me too? I'm going to be a father," Tommy pales and says almost reluctantly.

"With who?" I scream at him. "Thomas, you don't date. You haven't had a steady girlfriend since you moved here. Actually, I take that back. You haven't had a single girlfriend since you moved here."

I climb into the front seat and stare at him incredulously. This is the biggest What The Fuck moment of the year.

"Bookstore girl. We did promo stuff for her ... she's kind of your neighbor now?"

"That doesn't explain how you exchanged bodily fluids and combined DNA with her." I reach into the backseat and smack him in the head. "I really wish I had my wooden spoon, I'd whack you so fucking hard. How did you end up getting Sutton pregnant?"

"Probably the same way he got you pregnant." Smack. "Okay! We were casually dating, until the condom broke and she failed to tell me she wasn't on the pill. And now I'm going to be a father. Please stop hitting me!" he blurts out, holding his arm in front of him to ward off another slap to the head. "I'm stressed and I really need some pie, Steph. Can we talk about this later? She's coming to dinner. I swear you can grill her in the bathroom or your girly childhood bedroom later, just please don't make a big deal out of it in front of everyone. Bri and Stella don't know. Neither do any of our parents. Oh my God, my mama is going to kill me."

"You're damn right your mama is going to kill you. Jesus, Tommy."

I sit quietly as Tommy drops his head into his hands. Max and I exchange glances. I can read his expression — we're in love, we're married, we were actually planning for this baby to happen sometime in the next year, and while all of that is true, it doesn't dismiss what Tommy is going through or how he's going to handle it. Me smacking him with a spoon certainly isn't going to solve anything.

"We're here for you and Sutton, T. Anything you guys need, we're all family," I quietly say as Max puts the car in reverse.

***

"You're both pregnant?" My sister's eyes grow just a tiny bit wider once she fully takes in the scene before her.

"Stella, seriously, keep your damn voice down."

Doing what Tommy suggested, I dragged Sutton off to my old bedroom between dinner and dessert. I told her I wanted to show her my collection of N*SYNC paraphernalia after a lively debate over who was the best boy band, which wasn't untrue, but once I got her alone I let her know I knew what she and Tommy were going through. The cat was already out of the bag for me and Max by the time the turkey was carved, so it took a lot of focus off Sutton's sunken features and pale complexion.

Stella found us huddled up together on my bed, Sutton weeping into my jeans, as I softly rubbed my hand in circles across her back and shoulders.

"I'm only twenty-five. I just got my life back together, my business isn't failing anymore, and we just started seeing each other," she says, sitting up and wiping her face with the palms of her hands. "Tommy and I hardly know each other, how the hell are we supposed to raise a baby together?"

Stella sits on the bed with Sutton between us, places her hand on the girl's knee, and says, "You figure it out as you go. You can buy all the books and how-to guides and read all the crap on the internet, but nothing — and I mean absolutely nothing — will prepare you. If I know Tommy, he'll talk to Brian about it and get some solid advice. Brian gets it."

I smile because I know the story, but Sutton shakes her head confused.

"Britt was the product of a one-night stand Brian had with a woman he met at a friend's wedding," Stell says nonchalantly. "They made it work while they could until Britton was born, but things didn't pan out."

"Britt isn't yours? He looks so much like you," Sutton stutters in quiet amazement.

"Nope. Not a drop of my genetic material went into that boy, but it doesn't mean I will ever love him any less than I love Emiliana," Stella says emphatically before turning the conversation back to Sutton and Tommy's surprise pregnancy. "Tommy is the kind of man who tries to always do what's right. Give him the chance to know you. Even if you don't last as a couple, you're now linked for life, Sutton. Allow yourself the opportunity to give this baby all the love you and Tommy could provide, together or separately."

Sutton lets her gaze fall on me. "You lived with him and you work with him. I feel like you'd know him best out of the three of us. You don't think he's going to run from this, do you?"

I bite my lip because how do you answer a question like that? It's so loaded.

"Tommy doesn't run, but he does get scared. And sometimes he gets clingy. He's a good man, though, and that's the God's honest truth. You guys need to take this one day at a time," I smile at her. "And remember, Max and I are literally going through this with you guys. If my math is correct we're due about a week apart. July is going to be amazing."

Stella and I slide off the bed, feeling like we've done our job. Turning back to Sutton, we each reach for one of her hands and pull her up off the mattress, wrapping our arms around her back so we're also holding onto each other. As we leave the room and come to the top of the stairs, Tommy's just starting to climb up them.

"Everything okay?" he questions, his eyes worried and never wavering from Sutton's blotchy face.

A small, nervous smile plays on her lips before she responds. "Yeah, I think it will be. Did you want to stay for dessert?"

"There's pie. He's not going anywhere yet," I whisper in her ear, eliciting a laugh from her for the first time all night. "Prepare yourself for the amount of baked goods about to come into your life."

"I just want one piece," Tommy says sincerely. "Which may or may not be equal to an entire nine-inch plate."

Stella and I let go of Sutton and walk the rest of the way down the stairs, but I stop briefly at the bottom when I come face-to-face with Tommy.

Quietly, I tell him, "She's just as fragile as you are, but be warned, she's strong enough to do this on her own if you can't do it with her. I love you like my own brother, but so help me God, I will beat you into a shallow grave with my wooden spoon if you think running is a better option than helping her take care of this baby."

Without a word, Tommy leans into me, hugging me tightly to his chest. "Thank you, Steph. Thank you." And he kisses me on the cheek before twisting his body to move past me. I turn as he reaches the top of the staircase and smile when I see him pull her face carefully to his, his full lips brushing against hers and punctuating the moment with the words, "It's okay."

***

"I can't believe Tommy is going to be a dad," I admit as I set my purse down on the kitchen counter.

"What are you talking about?" he chides, pulling me against his broad chest. He smells like my parent's house but feels like home. His mouth drops to mine and I get just a taste of his lips before he's pulling away, his eyes sparkling. "I can't believe we're going to be parents."

"Fair enough. We can't believe we're all having babies. The only thing that would make this entire day more bizarre is if Stella called me and said she was pregnant again already," I laugh.

"Don't say crazy things like that. I don't know if the men could handle all three of you having babies at the same time," he chuckles and then turns serious. "So you think Sutton's good for him? Him for her? I mean, we didn't even know they were seeing each other. She's sort of just been dropped into the family now, and we both know this family is very tight."

I consider him carefully, playing with the stubble starting on his jaw. "I think if they build the proper foundation, they can get through anything."

"Did we build a foundation first?" He cocks an eyebrow at me. It's sexy and combined with those dark eyes of his, it could be my undoing tonight, but I remain steadfast. I purse my lips together and think back over the last year.

"You saved my life, literally. You made sure he wouldn't hurt me or anyone else again. You avoided me like the plague. Oh, then you nearly suffered a broken nose because of my astoundingly thick skull," I say listing off the major points of our relationship to date. "Then you watched me punch some of my demons in the face and run away from you to clear my head because, holy shit, our relationship hasn't been normal."

I smile and pause to let that sink in. Despite the short amount of time we've actually been a couple, we've been through more than some couples who have known one another for years.

"I don't know about you, Super Max, but I would call that some major foundation building. All we have to do is raise some babies, be successful, and love each other unconditionally ... it's easy."

Pulling back a step from me, he smirks then shrugs. "It's easy," he repeats. "You're sure about that?"

"With you, anything is possible," I say, touching the pendant around my neck, the one Stella gave me the day she married Brian. "You fill my most miserable days with rainbows and butterflies."

Epilogue

Tommy

This isn't the way it was supposed to happen.

Those words have been on replay since Sutton called me on a Tuesday afternoon at the beginning of November. They were the first things she said when I answered. When I asked her what she meant, she burst into tears, called me a "stupid asshole" and hung up.

In my defense I really had no idea what I had done wrong. We had been seeing each other for just a few weeks. Casually seeing one another, I might add. We weren't calling us exclusive, I hadn't told Brian I was seeing anyone, Sutton hadn't asked to introduce me to her family. It was a case of taking things slow, like molasses in winter slow.

Then we went out one night for dinner, had a few too many drinks, enjoyed each other's company a little too fully.

It wasn't until I left the coffee house in the middle of everyone's mad dash for caffeine fixes to find her that I figured out why I was the asshole. Then? Then I wanted to burst into tears, too. I'm old enough to start a family, but I figured I would have done some traditional courting, planned a big fancy wedding, and then mapped out our entire lives first. I like things in order. Like my business. Everything has a place and a plan.

This wasn't part of the plan.

The plan ... is officially thrown out the window.

Now here we are, on the threshold of discovery, and tomorrow we're going to spend a late Thanksgiving with her family in Rochester. Her brother and his family live out of state so their parents pushed the traditional dinner back a day to include everyone, which means tomorrow I might very well take my final breaths gasping out an apology to people I've just met.

I don't regret that we created a life. I regret we won't have more time to learn about one another before we're creating a registry at Babies R Us.

But I don't want to think about regrets tonight.

I pull into her driveway, having driven her car back to the house because she was exhausted after what turned out to be an emotional day once Steph and Stella got their hands on her, and park near the front walkway. I'd rather she not have to walk so far tonight. Getting out of the driver's side, I'm quick to get to the other side and open her door, reaching in to take her hand and the leftover pie Jenny sent home with us.

Words don't come as she drops my hand and shuffles her tired feet toward the front of the house. At some point during the day, she pulled her blonde hair up into a ponytail. The line of her neck is inviting and tender, and when we reach the door I bend my head to kiss her there. She sighs like she's been holding her breath all day. Everything I don't know how to say is in that kiss.

"We'll figure it out, Tommy. That's what everyone does. No one goes into parenthood knowing how to do it," she whispers to me as we stand on her front porch. "I'm scared to death, but I'm in this a hundred percent. I need to know if you're going to be by my side or if I need to plan for a life of single parenting."

Placing the key in the lock, I turn it and twist the knob, opening us up to our future. Whether it's ready for us or not ... we're coming in.

The End

Acknowledgements

It took me eight months to write this book and almost as long to edit, format, and get it to you. A majority of it was written while I was shoving a sandwich in my mouth after dropping our second daughter off at school in the afternoon. I wish that was a joke. There were a lot of days I wanted to take a nap instead of talk to Max and Steph (mostly because I was growing the third daughter). There was never enough coffee.

Boy Wonder — I'm glad I could pop your romance novel cherry. I will never apologize for your tear duct malfunctions. Maybe someday you'll read the first one. There are a few copies on the bookshelf in the living room if you're ever interested.

Josephine, Charlotte, and Eleanor — Someday I hope you see how much you've influenced the characters in these stories. They may be figments of my imagination, but there are parts of you in Stephanie (and Stella, Britt, Tommy, and maybe a little Jenny). You're very powerful for such little girls and I want nothing more than to raise you to be strong women.

Jen Krider, Trista Ward, Liz Rodbourn, and Sandi Sullivan —Thank you for reading Max and Steph's story and guiding me through the editing process. I couldn't have asked for a better group of readers to take on my second book through first drafts, rewrites, and perhaps some ranting here and there.

Amanda Crans-Gentile — I can't thank you enough for jumping into this project with me, no questions asked. More than once I apologized for being a major pain in the ass as I asked if we could try something different with the covers, but you rolled with it and for that I am grateful beyond words. I owe you a margarita for your patience.

Mom and Dad — You get excited when I get animated about writing. When I get frustrated, you help solve the problem. You have never given up on me. These are some of the greatest gifts I could receive and you've given them to me.

You — You're reading this and I can't begin to thank you enough for giving me your time. I hope I made this story worth it.

M.L. Pennock

About the Author

Born and raised in Western New York, M.L. Pennock learned early on the benefits of growing up in the country — bare feet, lake swimming, bonfires, mud pies, and mastering the art of playing tag in the dark. As a young girl, she wrote stories, which evolved to writing crappy poetry on pieces of notebook paper during chemistry class in high school. Then there was some crappy poetry written on her bedroom walls. All this led to the decision to not be a veterinarian when she grew up, whenever that might be.

M.L. attended Alfred University, earning a Bachelor of Arts in English and communication studies, before going on to earn a Master of Arts in communications from SUNY College at Brockport.She's still barefoot most of the time and thinks playing in the dirt is the best thing for getting out of an emotional funk. There hasn't been a single crappy poem written in years.

M.L. and her husband live in the Syracuse area with their three daughters, geriatric black lab, and two betta fish everyone forgets to feed.

M.L. Pennock